T0015157

Sugar Plum Poisoned

Jenn McKinlay

BERKLEY PRIME CRIME
New York

BERKLEY PRIME CRIME
Published by Berkley
An imprint of Penguin Random House LLC
penguinrandomhouse.com

ISBN: 9780593549124

First Edition: October 2023

Printed in the United States of America
1 3 5 7 9 10 8 6 4 2

For Lynne Hansen Orf.
You're the best mother-in-law
a gal could ever have
and I so appreciate all of the times you've
been there for me—
for all of us—over the years.
You are one of the kindest
and most generous people I know
and I'm so very grateful
that I get to call you "Mom."

One

"Oh . . . wow," Angie Harper said. She was perched on a stool in the kitchen of the bakery Fairy Tale Cupcakes, which she owned with her husband, Tate Harper, and best friend Melanie DeLaura.

Mel blew the bangs of her short-cropped blond hair out of her eyes and glanced at her friend across the steel worktable. "What's up?"

"A VIP is coming to Scottsdale," Angie said. She wiggled on her chair, an indication of her excitement.

"And . . ." Mel twisted the end of the piping bag full of rum-flavored frosting before she lowered it to the top of an eggnog-flavored cupcake, which she decorated with a fat dollop of frosting. Angie didn't answer, so Mel glanced back up to find her friend staring at her with wide eyes.

Mel lowered the pastry bag. "Okay, you have my full attention. Or you will as soon as you garnish that cupcake."

"Oh, right!" Angie dusted a little bit of nutmeg onto the fresh frosting. She then turned her phone so that Mel could see the display.

It showed a picture of a woman wearing a sequined, hot pink, micromini dress and over-the-knee white leather stiletto boots, with a blond head of hair that was a mass of curls that reached her lower back. She was unmistakable. Shelby Vaughn.

"Oh," Mel said. She tried to say it without any inflection. She and Angie had a complicated history with Shelby in that Angie loved her and Mel not so much.

"She's in residence at the Hotel Grande for the entire holiday season," Angie said. "And, get this, she wants us, Fairy Tale Cupcakes, to cater her VIP events."

"Really." Again, Mel strove to keep her voice even, giving no indication of her feelings away. It didn't work.

"I know you don't like her," Angie said. She met Mel's gaze across the steel worktable. Angie's long brown curls were styled in a messy bun on top of her head. She was wearing her usual T-shirt and jeans under a bright pink apron with the bakery's logo on the front and her name embroidered across the bib.

"It's not that I don't like her. I don't know her," Mel protested. "She's from your life with Roach, in which Tate and I were not included."

Angie nodded. "I know, those were some crazy days, but I really like Shelby, and when you get to know her, I'm sure you will, too."

Mel stared at her friend. Before marrying their mutual childhood best friend, Tate Harper, Angie had dated a rock and roll drummer named Roach who played in a band called the Sewers. It had been a chaotic few months with Angie traveling back and forth from Los Angeles to Scottsdale and then going on tour with the band for brief stints. She had met a lot of famous people, one of which was Shelby Vaughn, who had been the opening act for the Sewers that summer and who'd had several hit singles since.

Mel had no idea how Tate was going to handle Angie's rock and roll days coming back into their life, and she wondered if she should point that out to Angie or let the married couple deal with it on their own. Being best friends ever since they'd all been in the sixth grade together with Tate Harper and Angie Harper née DeLaura made Mel's life a teeny bit complicated when things like this cropped up. Sort of like when Tate almost married Christie Stevens. During that drama fest, Mel had felt her best course of action was to keep her mouth shut. She suspected this was exactly what she should do right now. Consequently, she pressed her lips together to keep from saying anything.

"Um, Mel, we have a situation out here." Marty Zelaznik, their octogenarian counter help, poked his bald head around the swinging door from the front of the bakery.

Mel gently put her pastry bag down.

"What sort of situation?" Mel asked.

"A limousine has pulled up outside," Marty said. "A pink one."

"Ah!" Angie hopped off her stool. "That has to be Shelby."

She dashed towards the swinging door, barely giving

Marty enough time to jump back before she plowed into him.

Marty grabbed the still-swinging door and held it open. He glanced at Mel and asked, "Who is Shelby?"

"Trouble," Mel said. "I think she's a whole lot of trouble."

Marty's eyebrows rose as Mel walked past him into the main room of the bakery. The jukebox was playing Christmas carols in the corner, and the normally heavy-on-the-pink bakery interior was festooned with garlands of green and red and strings of white twinkling lights. Even the cupcakes in the display case were predominantly green and red, reinforcing the holiday season that was in full swing in Old Town Scottsdale, one of the most popular tourist destinations in Arizona.

Angie was kneeling in a vacant booth, staring out the front window, watching the limo in the street. Mel stayed behind the counter. She refused to act weird just because a celebrity might be stopping by their bakery. She'd seen celebrities before. This was so not a big deal.

"It's her!" Angie cried. She scrambled off the booth seat and ran for the door.

Before she could reach it, it was pulled open and in strode Shelby Vaughn. She didn't look like the picture Angie had just shown Mel. Instead, she was wearing jeans, cowboy boots, and a pink and purple flannel shirt over a plain white tank top. Her face was scrubbed free of makeup, and her hair was covered with a floppy brimmed straw hat. She looked like she had just come in from the cow pasture on a farm.

"Is that . . . ?" Oz, a former employee of the bakery, began to speak, but when Shelby turned at the sound of his voice and met his gaze, his words dried up and he blushed a deep shade of red.

Oz, whose full name was Oscar Ruiz, was now a chef in his own kitchen at the Sun Dial Resort but he lived in the apartment above the bakery and still popped in to help out or help himself to a cup of coffee and a quick visit at least once a day, sometimes twice depending upon what Mel was baking.

"Smooth, real smooth," Marty muttered out of the side of his mouth at Oz, who frowned.

"Shelby!" Angie cried. She grabbed the young woman in a hug and Shelby laughed, her whole face lighting up as she squeezed Angie in return. "I can't believe you're here."

"I know!" Shelby cried. She rocked Angie back and forth in an exuberant embrace. "A few weeks in one place. I'm so happy. Now where is this husband of yours and your baby girl? I'm dying to meet them both."

"Tate is off dealing with opening another franchise in Michigan but he'll be back tomorrow," Angie said. "And my daughter, Emari, is with my mother this morning while I work. She started walking a couple of months ago, so I can't bring her to the bakery anymore. That child gets into everything and she's quick like a cat."

"I can't wait to see her," Shelby said. "I'm sure she's as amazing as her mama."

"More," Angie confirmed. "But here, come meet Mel. She's been my best friend since sixth grade and she recently married my brother Joe."

Angie looped her arm through Shelby's and dragged her over to Mel.

"Hi." Mel waved but Shelby wasn't having it.

She opened her arms wide and pulled Mel into a big hug. "Any friend of Angie's is a friend of mine."

"Oh, okay," Mel said. She bent down to hug the petite woman. Being on the tall side, Mel always had to reach down to hug people, which she was used to, but Shelby was so tiny and delicate and perfectly formed that Mel felt like a giantess next to her, which was not something she'd felt in a very long time. It gave her a horrible flashback to her teen years when she'd been taller and wider than most of her classmates and incessantly teased about it.

Shelby's hug was mercifully short, and Mel straightened back up. She gestured to Marty and Oz. "This is Marty, our counter person, and Oz, a former employee who still helps out from time to time."

"Nice to meet you," Shelby said. She waved. Her fingers flashed pointy acrylic nails with gemstone-encrusted rings on every knuckle.

"Hey, I know you," Marty said. "You're the girl singer who does that . . ." He started to hum and did some wiggling pelvis and shimmy-shake thing. Mel feared he'd knock himself out but he didn't. She glanced at Shelby to see if she was offended but instead Shelby laughed in delight.

"That's right!" she cried. She moved to stand next to Marty and started singing and jiggling with him.

Oz stared at the duo incredulously. "Marty, how do you even know that?"

"I'm old not dead," Marty cried. He and Shelby finished the routine by dropping to the floor, her in a full split and him in a crouch with one leg kicked out.

Shelby popped back up but Marty stayed down until

Oz stepped forward, hooked him under the arms, and hauled him up to his feet.

"You may want to back off the split," Oz advised.

Mel noticed he flexed his pecs and his biceps a bit excessively, making the T-shirt he wore strain at the seams. She turned to exchange an eye roll with Angie but she was too busy beaming at her friend.

"Roger that," Marty agreed. He rubbed his hip and turned to Shelby. "What brings you to Old Town?"

"Angie!" Shelby said. She threw her arm around Angie's shoulders and pulled her into a half hug. "We go way back."

"Is a couple of years way back?" Mel asked. She knew she sounded snippy but, honestly, hanging out for a summer a few years ago was not a lifetime friendship.

"I suppose not." Shelby nodded. "But life on the road ages you. Right, sis?"

"Ha! I totally forgot you used to call me that." Angie laughed. She turned to the others to explain. "We started calling each other 'sis' because we're so much alike we're like 'sisters from different misters.'" They said it together and grinned at each other, and Angie added, "And you're right, I came off that summer tour five years older."

They both laughed and Mel felt as if she'd just eaten something sour. Why was this bugging her? She had friends outside of Angie from cooking school, and Angie still had friends from her teaching days. It wasn't as if this Shelby person was going to take Angie away. Why was Mel feeling so turfy and weird about Shelby Vaughn?

She glanced at Angie's face. Gone was the weariness that had been dogging Angie since Emari had been born just over a year ago. Instead, her eyes sparkled, and she looked as if she'd gotten a bit of herself back just by seeing Shelby. It was clear that Shelby was a blast from her pre-baby life, and maybe that was just what Angie needed right now.

Mel had a moment of self-doubt that perhaps she should have been helping Angie more with the baby, giving her more breaks or something, so that Angie didn't lose her sense of self in the feed-bathe-diaper-dress-rinse-repeat that was now her life. Mel promised herself she'd do better.

"Ms. Vaughn," Marty said as he gestured to the display case behind him. "May I offer you a cupcake?"

Shelby clasped her hands together. "I thought you'd never ask. Anything chocolate please, and call me Shelby."

"I'll get it!" Oz volunteered.

"Hey! I'm the one who offered," Marty protested.

"Well, I'm your backup during the holiday crush." Oz started to walk around the counter.

"You don't even work here anymore." Marty caught up to him. He gestured to the shop, empty except for Mel, Angie, and Shelby. "Does this look like a crowd to you?"

"Doesn't matter. I'm here now." Oz tried to block Marty. Marty wasn't having it. He hugged Oz around the middle and tried to drag him away from the display case. Oz was sixty years younger than Marty, well over six feet tall, and all muscle. It looked like Marty was trying to move a buffalo.

"I don't need your help right now," Marty huffed. He put his shoulder into moving Oz, who merely crossed his arms over his chest, waiting for Marty to tire himself out.

"Clearly, you do. You almost threw your back out with all the wiggling you were doing." Oz gestured to the area where Marty had been dancing. Marty took the opportunity to slip behind Oz. He was a wily one.

"Shelby, would you like some coffee with your cupcake?" Mel offered. She sensed the best way to deal with the situation was to give Oz a chore as well.

"Oh, that would be lovely."

"Oz, can you bring Shelby some coffee, please?" Mel raised her eyebrows at Oz, silently telling him to let it go.

Oz frowned at Marty and then turned back to the women. He met Shelby's gaze and turned bright red. "Coming right up." He disappeared into the kitchen.

"Can you stay for a while?" Angie asked. "I have so many questions about what's been happening with you. You're a star on the rise. It has to be amazing."

An expression of misery passed over Shelby's features so swiftly that Mel thought she might have imagined it. Shelby smiled big and bright and said, "Yeah, it's been pretty crazy. I never would have gotten my start if it wasn't for Roach and the Sewers. Do you ever talk to him?"

"No," Angie said. "Our lives went in very different directions after I got married. I get the occasional text from him but we don't talk."

Mel studied Angie's face. Did she seem sad about this? Was she carrying a torch for Roach? No, it couldn't be. Angie had loved Tate since middle school. Surely, a couple of years of marriage and a child couldn't change that. Still the uneasiness didn't dissipate.

"I have plenty of gossip for you," Shelby assured her.

"Excellent," Angie said. "This day just keeps getting better. Sit down, let's dish."

Shelby glanced at the limousine outside. Her forehead creased with concern. "I have to check in at the resort and start rehearsals but I can spare the time to eat a cupcake and talk business, I think. We can go over the VIP idea."

"Sounds good. We're all in." Angie gestured to a small café table with four chairs.

Mel wanted to say they were not all in until they knew what they were in for, but she bit her tongue. The holiday crush was already on top of them. She had no idea how they could take on one more event without it negatively affecting their current orders. She was going to head back to the kitchen and let Angie deliver the bad news but Angie pulled her into an available seat while Shelby took another.

"You got my text about the VIP opportunity?" Shelby asked.

"I did and we're very excited to participate," Angie said. "Did you have anything specific in mind?"

Mel turned to look at her friend with an expression that read, *Are you out of your mind?* but Angie wasn't looking at her.

"Holiday flavors," Shelby said. "We have to do a meet and greet with VIPs before and after every show, so I think it would be festive to have cupcakes on hand for the guests. After all, they're paying for the privilege."

Marty appeared, bearing a tray of perfectly plated cupcakes. He placed each of the five varieties of chocolate cupcake in front of Shelby, and she grinned at him with pure delight. Marty blinked, looking like he was about to pass out.

"I really do love your music, Shelby," Marty said. "Especially the ballads."

"Thank you so much." She grinned at him.

Not to be outdone, Oz appeared with a coffee tray with three different kinds of sugar, milk, cream, and a nondairy creamer, too.

"Well, I love more than your ballads," he said. "You've got such a great set of pipes. You can really deliver the songs that rock."

"You're too kind," Shelby demurred.

Angie leaned close to Mel and said, "'They don't even know what it is to be a fan. Y'know? To truly love some silly little piece of music, or some band, so much that it hurts.'"

Mel grinned. Angie was hitting her with a movie quote, which was a long-running game of theirs, and she quickly identified it. *"Almost Famous.* Well done."

"I thought so." Angie buffed her nails on her apron bib.

"Who's almost famous?" Shelby asked.

"We were talking about the movie," Angie explained. Marty and Oz were hovering and she made a shooing gesture with her hands. "Go away now. Let the woman enjoy her cupcakes and coffee in peace."

Shelby smiled up at Oz and Marty. "Thank you very much."

"Of course," Marty said.

"Absolutely," Oz chimed in. "And if you need anything else—"

"I'll be happy to get it for you," Marty interrupted. The two men gave each other stink eye.

"Oz, will you finish frosting the cupcakes in the kitchen for me?" Mel asked.

"Of course, happy to help out a fellow chef," Oz said. He drew himself up and said, "But I can't stay too late in case I have to be on television tomorrow."

Marty squinched up his face and silently mimicked Oz behind his back. Angie and Mel tried not to laugh. Shelby missed the whole thing as her attention was on the cupcakes.

"These look amazing," she said.

"That one is our Peppermint Bark cupcake, a chocolate cupcake with peppermint bark icing," Angie said. She pointed to the one nearest to Shelby. "Another of Mel's brilliant creations, which would be great for the holiday theme of the VIP room."

"Thanks, Ange." Mel felt a flush of pleasure at the high praise. She was particularly fond of this cupcake, as the decadently rich chocolate paired so well with the peppermint buttercream with chunks of peppermint bark mixed into the icing.

Shelby tucked into the cake with her fork and popped a well-proportioned cake-to-frosting bite into her mouth. She closed her eyes, savoring the morsel. She looked like she was lost in the flavors, and Mel felt like this was the greatest compliment a baker could get. She felt herself warming up to the singer, when a shadow fell over their table. A man in a suit loomed over them, and Mel felt a flash of foreboding and had to curb the sudden urge to hop up from her seat and flee.

"What's this, Miss Vaughn?" the man demanded.

Shelby started in her seat and swallowed the bite. Mel could see it went down hard. Angie pushed her coffee mug towards her, and Shelby sent her a grateful glance. She took a quick sip and dabbed her mouth with her napkin.

"Nothing to fret about, Doc. I'm just sampling a bite of the product for the VIP guests," Shelby said.

"Hmm, I suppose a bite won't ruin your waistline, but no more," the man called Doc said. He was frowning at the table as he took in the array of cupcakes.

Mel felt a flash of hostility for the man. She knew it was likely her own issues but she hated it when men voiced their opinions about a woman's looks, weight, diet, brains, or anything else, for that matter. She took a deep breath and studied him. He had short-cropped silver hair and a goatee, and wore a shiny dark blue suit with a narrow tie. His face was thin, his features sharp, and the glint in his eye was proprietary. Surely, Shelby wasn't dating this man. He had to be thirty years older than her.

"Angie, Mel, this is my manager, Doc Howard."

With one eyebrow arched, Angie stared up at the man. "Must be handy to have a doctor as your manager."

"Oh, he's not a medical doctor," Shelby said. "He has a doctorate in management."

"Really?" Angie asked. "Where did you go to sch—"

"Delightful to meet you both, but Shelby needs to check in at the resort," Doc said. "We can leave some tickets for you at the box office if you'd like. It's going to be a great show. Shelby?"

The tone of his voice didn't allow for discussion. Shelby rose from her seat, took another quick sip of her coffee, and smiled at them. There was a melancholy in her eyes that Mel was certain she wasn't imagining.

"I'll talk to you later, sis," Shelby said.

"Much later. You have a very full schedule," Doc said. "There'll be time to visit with your friend when we have the show ready to go."

"Right." Shelby nodded. She leaned down and gave Angie a quick hug. "I guess I'll see you when I see you."

"Oh, yeah, you will," Angie said. She hugged her tight and said, "I'll come to the hotel tomorrow to discuss the cupcakes you want for the VIP room."

"You can call me—" Doc began, but Angie hopped to her feet and crossed her arms over her chest.

"Not necessary since I'll be visiting Shelby . . . a lot."

Doc pursed his lips as if considering whether to engage. He wisely chose not to and gave Angie a curt nod.

Shelby's smile was tremulous, and she hugged Angie one more time. "I can't wait to hang out. I've missed you."

"I've missed you, too," Angie said.

Doc cleared his throat and Shelby stepped back. "All right, so I'll see you—"

"Tomorrow," Angie said.

"Tomorrow," Shelby echoed. She looked like a little girl who had just been granted her wish for a sleepover.

Doc led the way to the door, and Shelby waved at them before she slipped outside. Doc stared at them for a moment, and Mel felt her heart thump hard in her chest. This was not a man who liked to be countermanded. Mel didn't like his vibe, not one little bit. He glanced around the bakery, taking in Marty and Oz, the display case, the jukebox playing Christmas carols. His body practically vibrated with disapproval. He gave them a very slow nod and let the door slam shut after him.

Mel rose from her seat and stood beside Angie. "Something is weird there."

"Oh, yeah, it is," Angie agreed. "That Doc person was not her manager when she was on tour with the Sewers. I'm going to do some digging and find out what happened, I want to know the background on whoever this guy Doc is and whether Shelby is okay."

"Do you think you should?" Mel asked. "I mean . . ."

"It could be awkward?" Angie asked.

"Yeah."

"I don't care," Angie said. "I need to know that Shelby is all right, and I'm going to butt in and keep butting in until I am assured of that fact."

Mel nodded. The feeling of foreboding slipped over her again, so she reached for one of the extra cupcakes Marty had brought over on the tray and took a huge bite. The swift shot of chocolate to the taste buds immediately calmed her. Everything would be fine. Angie was just looking out for her friend. What could possibly go wrong?

Two

"Melanie, I hate to ask this of you but I feel I have no choice," Joyce, Mel's mother, said.

They were standing in the kitchen of Mel's bakery while Mel prepared the batter for her popular Orange Dreamsicle cupcakes. A luscious orange cake topped with vanilla buttercream, it was one of their most popular flavors and she was making a special batch for a retirement party.

"Mom, you know you can ask me anything," Mel said.

"Thank you, dear, I appreciate that, but this impacts dear Joe, too," Joyce said.

Mel ducked her head to hide her smile. Her mother had been calling her husband Joe "dear Joe" since they had started dating several years ago. Sometimes Mel wondered if she and Joe got into an argument, whose side her mother would choose. She suspected it would be Joe's, so it was probably for the best that she didn't know for certain.

Mel glanced at her mother. Average height and slender, Joyce styled her hair, silver with blond highlights, in a neat bob. Her makeup was understated but accentuated her blue-green eyes, so much like Mel's own, and her clothes were always perfectly suited for every occasion. Today Joyce was running errands so it was beige capri pants and a long-sleeved aqua and purple floral top. Joyce was the most put-together person Mel had ever known, and it wasn't as if Joyce's life had been an easy one. Widowed in her early fifties, she had been there for her twenty-something children all by herself and Mel knew it hadn't been easy.

With the holidays coming, Mel felt the familiar pang of missing her father Charlie Cooper a bit more sharply, and the reality of her dad being gone to the great fishing hole in the beyond punched her right in the chest. She had come to realize a while ago that there would never be a day that she didn't miss her dad, his terrible jokes, and his big bear hugs.

"I'm sure 'dear Joe' will be just fine," Mel said. She checked the consistency of the batter in her Hobart mixer, not too thick and not too runny, and then turned back to her mother. "What's up?"

"It's a small thing, really," Joyce said. Mel heard the alarm bells clang in her head. If the past was any indication, her mother's idea of a small thing and Mel's were vastly different.

"Okay."

"I was just hoping that you could host Christmas

dinner this year since I'm having the kitchen remodeled and apparently they won't be finished until after the New Year."

Mel stared at her mother. Christmas was Joyce's day. She loved everything about it from the decorations to the gift giving to the prime rib for dinner. The woman put up a Christmas tree in every room of her house and even tiny ones in the bathrooms. She had china with Christmas trees on it that was just for the holiday, as well as linen sets, bedspreads, and towels. And Mel couldn't even think about the tchotchkes around the house of snowmen and Santas and glitter-crusted pine cones.

While the rest of the world recovered from overindulgence, watched football, or shopped, Joyce's Black Friday was always spent turning her house into a Christmas wonderland. How was Mel supposed to uphold that sort of over-the-top holiday enthusiasm? Panic began to thrum in her chest just below her ribs, or maybe she was having a heart attack, she couldn't be sure.

"Well?" Joyce asked. "What do you say?"

"Of course I'll do it," Mel said. There really was no other acceptable answer.

"Wonderful!" Joyce said. "Thank you, my dear, you're the best. Charlie and Nancy and the boys will be down from Flagstaff, of course, and then there's you and Joe and your uncle Stan and me. A perfect group of eight. I'll drop off the Christmas china at your house this week."

"Oh, you don't have to—" Mel began but her mother interrupted.

"Of course I do, it's tradition. It won't be Christmas without the holiday china and whatnot," Joyce said. Mel was too afraid to ask what the whatnot was. Joyce stepped forward and gave Mel a smacking kiss on the cheek. "Talk to you later. Love you."

In a swirl of Chanel No. 5 and a flash of her pristine white tennies, Joyce was gone. Mel sat down on one of the stools in the kitchen. Dinner for eight on Christmas, during the peak busy season for the bakery, wouldn't be so bad. She was a professional. She'd graduated at the top of her class at culinary school. She could do this—totally—not a problem.

She reached for a Vanilla Beaned cupcake, a batch of which she had just finished. She took a bite and let the cake and frosting chase the anxiety demons away. Everything would be fine, completely fine.

"Are you sure she's expecting us?" Mel asked.

"I texted her," Angie said.

"Did she answer?" Mel persisted. She checked the time on her phone. It was one o'clock in the afternoon and they were waiting in a room in the backstage area of the auditorium of the Hotel Grande. The person wearing the headset who'd shown them into the room had seemed harried and not prone to conversation. With an abrupt "wait here," they'd shut the door and disappeared.

Mel took in the size of the VIP lounge. It wasn't a bad space. There were several couches and chairs and a bar set up in the corner. Two round tables with ten chairs each filled the rest of the space.

"Did we find out how many people are VIP every night?" Mel asked.

"I haven't been able to talk to her about specifics. I

don't even know what flavors she wants exactly," Angie said. She held up the bakery box. "I hope these work for her."

"So, not even an inkling as to how many cupcakes to provide," Mel said.

"Yes . . . I mean no . . . ugh," Angie groaned.

"There will be approximately fifty VIP guests for every performance." A man's voice spoke from behind them. Mel and Angie whirled around to face the door.

Doc Howard was standing there in another shiny suit and pointy-toed shoes. His hair was slicked back and Mel realized he was trying to cover a bald spot on the crown of his head. He'd be better off just shaving his head but she wisely didn't offer her unsolicited opinion.

"Fifty?" Angie asked. "Is that what Shelby told you to tell us?"

"Shelby can't be bothered with these pesky details," Doc said. "That's my job."

"Your job?" Angie repeated as if considering his words. "What happened to Diana Martin?"

Doc raised an eyebrow. "You knew Diana?"

"Of course."

"Then I'm afraid I have bad news for you. Diana died tragically in a house fire," Doc said. He watched Angie's face closely as if trying to determine how upset she was by the news.

"Oh, no, that's awful," Angie said. "When?"

"Last year," Doc said. "For being such a close friend of Shelby's, I'm surprised you didn't know about it."

He didn't directly accuse Angie of being a bad friend but the insinuation was there. Mel could feel it salting every word he spoke. In his unspoken opinion, Angie was just another hanger-on from Shelby's past who only cared about the singer for what Shelby could do for her. Mel would have protested but she doubted Doc Howard was the type of man to listen to anyone but himself.

"Friendships are like rubber bands," Angie said. "They stretch over time and miles but the real ones don't break."

"And you think you are a real friend to Shelby?" he asked. His tone left no doubt as to what he thought about that.

"I'm here, aren't I?" she asked.

"Looking to plug your business," he countered.

"I don't need to plug—" Angie began but Mel interrupted.

"If you could just let Shelby know we're here, that'd be great."

Doc Howard looked her up and down. "You're a very well-respected chef."

Mel glanced from side to side. This abrupt change in the conversation was unexpected and she wasn't sure what his point was. "I like to think so."

"It's important to Shelby to have you involved with her show while she's here," he said. "I have read up on your background, your training in Paris, and how you've managed to franchise your little bakery into shops all over the country."

"You did your homework," Angie said.

"If you like," Doc agreed. "I will allow you to provide the cupcakes for the VIP guests, but since you are a long-time friend of Shelby's I will, of course, expect a discount."

Mel raised her eyebrows. She hadn't really thought

about what they'd be charging Shelby for their catering. She'd assumed it would be their standard fee. One look at Angie's face and she knew her friend was about to volunteer to do it for free. No. Nope. Nuh-uh.

They already had a ton of holiday parties and private events to bake for. She was not doing two weeks of discount cupcakes for this man she was disliking more with every second she spent in his company.

"Don't be ridiculous, Doc," Shelby said. She swept into the room wearing a red sequined minidress paired with green thigh-high boots. Her hair was teased up high and her makeup was so thick she looked like a Barbie doll. "Of course we'll pay their regular price. Angie and Mel are doing us a huge favor on such short notice."

"It wouldn't be short notice if you'd let the hotel provide the refreshments as we'd discussed," Doc said. He sounded annoyed.

Shelby wrinkled her nose. "That's not very VIP though, is it? Our guests need to feel special and important. Isn't that what you said?"

Doc stared at her. His look was hard and assessing as if he didn't like being contradicted. "Whatever you say," he said. He didn't sound like he meant it. He made an exaggerated shrug. "You're the boss. After all, it's your show. I'm just the manager."

Shelby looked surprised by his acquiescence and said, "I'm glad we're in agreement, Doc. We ladies won't keep you another second as I know how busy you are. Angie, Mel, come and check out my dressing room or, as I call it, home for the next two weeks."

They had to walk past Doc Howard to get to the door. Mel half expected him to yell at them on the way out but he didn't. He smiled, a cold one that didn't reach his eyes, and watched them leave. Mel didn't take a full breath until they shut the door behind them.

Shelby led them down a corridor. There was a lot of bustle and another man, this one with long hair and wearing a Metallica T-shirt, said, "Sound check in thirty minutes, Ms. Vaughn."

"I'll be there," Shelby said. "And call me Shelby."

The man grinned and waved and took off in the direction of the auditorium. Shelby opened the door to her dressing room. A woman wearing a purple smock with big pockets and sporting a thick coating of matching purple eye shadow was seated on a couch, reading a lifestyle magazine. Her short fiery red hair was brushed back from her face in thick waves, and her acrylic nails were long and pointy, sporting lime green tips.

"Cheryl, meet Angie and Mel, they're friends of mine," Shelby said. "This is Cheryl, my stylist."

Cheryl tossed the magazine onto the leather seat beside her and stood. She was short and sturdy and not what Mel would have pictured as a stylist. She had a very maternal air about her, and looked as if she'd be more at home offering them milk and cookies than choosing outfits and hairstyles.

"*Stylist.* So fancy," Cheryl said with a chuckle. "I'm just a hairdresser from Tennessee, hon."

"Same difference." Shelby shrugged.

"Not to your manager it isn't," Cheryl said. She made an annoyed face when she said it. She glanced at them and added, "Angie, you look familiar."

"I used to date Roach from the Sewers," Angie said. She flashed a peace sign and Cheryl nodded.

23

"That's it," Cheryl said. "I remember the hair. You have an amazing head of hair."

Angie tossed a long curl over her shoulder. "This old rat's nest?"

Cheryl grinned. "I know people who would snatch that mane right off your head if they could."

Angie clutched her long hair with a comically alarmed look and they shared a laugh. Cheryl turned to Mel and gave her a quick glance. Mel was sure the woman found her to be too boring to notice. Medium height, medium weight, average features, she expected to be dismissed as no one of importance.

"You have fantastic bone structure," Cheryl said. "Nice cheekbones, strong chin, model worthy."

Mel's eyebrows shot up. She looked at Shelby and asked, "Can we keep her? My ego needs to have her around."

Shelby chuckled and shook her head. "No." She threw her arm around Cheryl's shoulders and gave her a half hug. "She's the only one who's still with me since I started out. I'll never give her up."

Cheryl gave her side-eye. "Even if Doc orders you to?"

"Even then," Shelby said. "It's you and me, forever."

Mel saw Cheryl's shoulders drop in relief. She wondered if Doc Howard was trying to replace the longtime stylist with someone else. She supposed it was none of her business but it seemed to her that Shelby should be the one to hire and fire her stylist, not her manager.

"Hair and makeup run-through after your sound check?" Cheryl asked. "We need to know how much time to allow for touch-ups during your performance."

"Absolutely," Shelby said. "I'll be here."

"I'm going to get myself something to eat then,"

Cheryl said. "The full rehearsal is tonight, and it looks like it's going to be a long one. Can I get you anything?"

"I'm good," Shelby said. "But thank you."

They watched as Cheryl shut the door behind her. It was then that Mel took in the very large space. There were racks of clothes at the back, all glittery and sparkling, mostly red and green with some gold as well.

A vanity with lights going all the way around it and every hair implement Mel had ever seen and some she hadn't. Makeup and hair products were on a rolling cart beside the mirrored dressing room table, and an adjustable barber's chair with a bright pink hairdresser's gown was draped over it.

On the other side of the room was a sitting area, with the leather couch Cheryl had been sitting on as well as several armchairs and a coffee table in between them. Shelby took a seat on the couch and gestured for them to join her. Mel wondered if she ever worried about sitting in sequins. What if they all fell off?

Angie sat beside her while Mel took one of the chairs. Angie opened the pink paper bag she'd been carrying and took out a box of cupcakes. She set it on the coffee table and said, "These were the holiday flavors we were thinking of supplying the VIP room with, and we can make them gluten- or dairy- or nut-free upon request."

Shelby let out a small squeal of joy and reached for the box, then paused. She glanced at Mel and said, "Would you mind locking the door?"

"No, not at all," Mel said. She hurried over and turned the lock on the door handle.

"Thanks," Shelby said. "I just don't want to get interrupted."

"Enjoying a cupcake is a moment," Angie said. "But now you have a problem."

"I do?" Shelby frowned. A tiny line appeared between her brows. Her hair rippled down her back in a mass of curls that sparkled with some sort of glitter spray. Despite the gobs of makeup, she was still very pretty with dewy skin and her big brown eyes. It was hard to believe this glamour girl was the same makeup-free, cowboy hat–wearing woman Mel had met the other day. As she studied the singer, Mel realized that the woman sparkled beneath the surface. Despite the fancy attire, Shelby looked like she could be a regular woman who jogged in the park, went out for sushi with friends, and had a regular order known by her barista at her local coffee shop. Mel wondered if that was a part of Shelby Vaughn's appeal. She was an everywoman, in other words, relatable.

"I'm not following," Shelby said. "What's my problem, other than stuffing a whole cupcake into my mouth so it only counts as one bite?"

"You have to choose—the Sugar Plum cupcake, the Eggnog, the Peppermint Bark, or the Gingerbread Man."

Angie gestured to the box and Shelby flipped open the lid. She gasped, actually gasped, which Mel took as high praise.

"These look like little bits of heaven," Shelby said. Then she looked at Angie and asked, "Why can't I have all four?"

"I thought you weren't allowed," Angie said. "Won't Mr. One Bite have a fit?"

Mel glanced at her friend. Angie's face gave nothing away but Mel knew her too well not to know that she was digging for information. She wanted to get a sense of how Shelby felt about her situation.

"Are you freaking out because Doc only let me have a bite yesterday?" Shelby asked. She smiled at Angie.

"Partly," Angie admitted. "And maybe it's the Italian mama in me, but you look thin, and I don't mean that in a bad way, just . . . you know, you should eat more."

Shelby laughed and said, "Does Emari have any idea how lucky she is to have you for a mom?"

"Not yet, but I plan on telling her repeatedly as she gets older," Angie said. "But seriously, are you okay?"

"I'm fine," Shelby said. "You heard about Diana?"

"Yeah, I'm really sorry," Angie said. "I remember how kind she was to me, a total shark with everyone else, but really nice to me. What a horrible way to die."

Shelby sniffed and glanced up as if willing the tears that had sprung to her eyes to slide back into her eyeballs.

"I sank into a deep depression after that," Shelby said. "I couldn't eat or sleep or sing. I refused to leave my house. My boyfriend left me because all I did was cry. Diana was more than a manager to me. She was like a second mom."

Angie reached across the couch and took Shelby's hand in hers. "I'm sorry I wasn't there for you."

Shelby shook her head. "Don't be. I didn't reach out, either. I was just consumed by my loss and I couldn't function. Finally, Doc showed up at my apartment and told me I had to get it together for Diana's legacy. He said that he and Diana had been friends and he couldn't stand to watch all of the groundwork Diana had done to get my career launched go to waste."

"That was good of him," Angie said. She didn't mention the obvious benefit to Doc if he got Shelby to let him represent her.

"Yes, it was," Shelby said. "And performing helped me to channel my grief."

Mel felt that the obvious gain for Doc needed to be acknowledged, so she asked, "When did you sign with Doc officially?"

"He brought me on tour with Miranda Carter," Shelby said. "We did a three-month swing of the southern states and then at the end of it, he asked if I'd like to sign with him. I didn't know . . ."

Her voice trailed off and she looked uncomfortable.

"That he was going to release Miranda and represent just you?" Angie asked.

"Yeah, and it was particularly awkward because I signed with Doc mostly because I wanted to tour with Miranda. She was like a big sister to me," Shelby said. "But then they split up, and Doc was representing just me. Given that my career had stalled out when Diana died and I needed to send money back home to my family, I had to go along with it."

Mel wanted to ask more questions but a horrible crash sounded followed by a woman screaming.

The three of them started and Shelby hopped to her feet. "Oh, no. Please don't let it be—"

She dashed out the door, leaving Mel and Angie to follow.

Three

"Who does she think it is?" Mel asked as she jogged alongside Angie.

"No idea," Angie said. "I mean I've barely had a chance to catch up with her. I have no idea what's going on in her life."

They raced down the hallway towards the auditorium, where the shouting could be heard over the hustle and bustle of the stagehands setting up for the dress rehearsal.

"You had no right!" a woman yelled. She was a tall, voluptuous redhead, wearing a low-cut, tight top and skinny jeans with high-heeled sandals.

"Miranda, you need to calm down," Doc Howard said.

It did not seem like a leap of logic to deduce that this was Miranda Carter. Mel glanced at Shelby to see her reaction. Her lips were pressed into a thin line but Mel didn't know her well enough to determine whether her expression was one of anger or anxiety.

"Don't you tell me to calm down," Miranda snapped.

"Yeah, that's a bad play," Angie said. "Never in the history of a man telling a woman to calm down has that ever worked."

"It doesn't work on them, either," Shelby said. "Have you ever told a man to calm down? It's like throwing gasoline on a fire."

"Agreed," Mel said. She'd never done that but she could imagine the men in her life, namely the brothers, would not be terribly receptive to being condescended to any more than she would.

"How dare you leave me for her and then set her up with a two-week standing Christmas gig!" Miranda shouted. "This should be mine!" She gestured wide, encompassing the entire auditorium.

"Now, honey, don't get overly emotional. We talked about this. It's just business," Doc said. His voice was cajoling and he tried to take her arm.

"Don't you honey me." She yanked her elbow out of his grasp.

Doc wasn't to be thwarted however and he stepped closer, looming over her, bent down, and whispered something in her ear. She glanced around the room as if suddenly aware of the scene she was making and allowed him to escort her off to the far side of the auditorium. With their drama subdued, the stagehands and set crew milling around the auditorium resumed their bustle to get ready for the show.

"So, that's Miranda?" Mel asked.

"Yup," Shelby said.

"You said they split up. Was she just a client, because I'm getting some real personal emotional baggage here?" Angie asked.

"No, not just a client," Shelby said. "Miranda was his number one client and his *wife*."

Both Mel and Angie turned to look at her, and Shelby asked, "What? Why are you staring at me?"

"You're not . . . I mean . . . that is to say . . ." Angie's voice trailed off as if she just couldn't find the words.

"Not what?" Shelby asked. She tipped her head to the side as if trying to figure out what Angie was getting at.

"What Angie's trying to ask is whether or not you're involved with Doc in a more personal way," Mel said. "You know, *intimately* involved."

"Oh. Ohhhh." Shelby's eyes went round and she shook her head. "No, never, nope, no way."

Angie let out a relieved sigh and Mel was right there with her. She didn't get a good feeling off Doc and it would be much harder to talk to Shelby about him if they were involved.

"You guys didn't seriously think that did you?" she asked. "He's old enough to be my grandfather."

"Sugar daddies come in all shapes and sizes," Angie said. "Usually, with thinning hair, a spare tire, and oodles of discretionary income."

Shelby made an appalled face. "My folks did not raise me to be that sort of girl."

Mel heard the twang in Shelby's voice get thicker as she spoke of her family. Angie had told her that Shelby was from Memphis, Tennessee, and now Mel could hear it in her voice.

"Are your parents coming to Arizona to see your show?" Mel asked.

"No, they can't make it." Shelby sounded disappointed but resigned. "They own a car-crushing business that doesn't give them a lot of downtime and my little brothers have a lot going on in school and all. This will be the first Christmas I haven't spent with my family."

She looked so achingly sad about it that Mel felt her heartstrings tie themselves in a knot of sympathy and she said, "You can spend it with us."

Shelby glanced at her in surprise. "But you don't even know me."

"Any friend of Angie's is a friend of mine," Mel said. "We're having my family at our house, so it'll be quiet but homey."

"Plus, I'm betting there will be cupcakes," Angie said.

"I'm supposed to have a show that night," Shelby said.

"On Christmas?" Angie asked, sounding outraged.

"Doc said people on vacation want to go to a show," Shelby explained.

"We'll eat early so you can get back here in plenty of time," Mel said.

Shelby put her hand to her throat and swallowed, clearly choked up. "That's really nice of you. Cheryl and I were thinking we'd just order room service and hunker down and watch old movies. I'd love to come to your house. Oh, but Cheryl . . ."

"She's welcome, too," Mel said. Truly, at this point, what was one more?

"Come on, let's go—" Angie began but was interrupted by the sound of a slap.

As one, they turned to look at Doc and Miranda. Her

eyes were wide and she was breathing heavily. Doc's face bore the mark of a bright red handprint. He waved to a man in the corner, and Mel recognized his uniform as that of hotel security.

"Escort Ms. Carter to her room," Doc said. His voice was tight as if he was barely keeping his temper in check. "She needs some time to herself."

The security guard went to take her arm and Miranda sidestepped him. "Don't touch me." She turned back to Doc and said, "This isn't over. You think you can just toss me aside like trash, well, I won't stand for it." She turned to stalk away but then paused as she caught sight of Shelby. She sauntered in their direction.

"Uh-oh," Shelby said. "This can't be good."

"Miranda, don't you do it," Doc called after her.

She sent him a rude hand gesture and kept on walking. The security guard followed her, clearly baffled by what he was supposed to do with a woman who refused to leave when she'd been instructed to do so.

Miranda stopped right in front of Shelby. Her gaze swept over the girl with searing disdain. "You think you're something special, don't you?"

"No, ma'am," Shelby said. She sounded as if she'd say anything to make the other woman go away. Mel understood that. She was a conflict avoider, too.

"You're nothing," Miranda said, drawing out the word. "You're less than nothing."

"Hey!" Angie snapped. "Just because you're a shriveled-up old has-been—"

"Oh, no," Shelby said. "We're not . . . I'm sorry, Miranda . . . she didn't mean . . ."

"Who do you think you are?" Miranda asked Angie.

Angie threw back her shoulders and stared up at the older woman. "I'm Angie Harper."

"Well, I've never heard of you, so as far as I'm concerned, you're a nobody, too," Miranda said. She waved a dismissive hand at Shelby. "Just like this one. A flavor of the month with a pretty voice and the dewy sparkle of youth. It fades fast in this line of work, pumpkin. Why, I bet you're all washed up by the end of the year."

Shelby narrowed her gaze and stared at Miranda. Mel could tell by the look in her eyes she'd had about all she was willing to take. "Listen, Miranda, I get that you're upset. I didn't like the way things went down between us, either, but I didn't know—"

Miranda threw back her head and laughed. "Oh, sweetie, do you really think I believe that? You're not nearly a good enough actress to pull off the innocent act. Save it for someone who's buying it. I'm not."

"Fine," Shelby snapped. "Say whatever you want about me then, but leave my friends alone."

"Friends?" Miranda scoffed. She stepped right into Shelby's personal space. "There's no friends in show business. There are hangers-on, people using you to promote themselves, wannabes, and performers who couldn't cut it but try to pretend they're somebody because they're in your circle, and then there are the users." She glanced over her shoulder where Doc stood, whispering furiously to the hotel security guard. "Those are the ones who will toss you aside as soon as something shinier comes along. Make no mistake, there are no friends in this line of work."

Shelby stared at the other woman and then shook her

head. "You're wrong. I have friends, good friends, and I trust them."

"You're a fool," Miranda said. "Especially if you think that man is your friend. He's only interested in how much money you can make him. The minute the money starts to dry up, he'll vanish on the wind, taking everything you earned with him."

"Doc was there for me when everything fell apart," Shelby said. "I'm sorry things didn't work out with you two but it's not the same for me. I feel sorry for you."

Miranda tossed her hair over her shoulder and leaned in. "It's exactly the same. Don't waste your pity on me. You're going to need it for yourself."

"Ma'am, you have to leave the auditorium now," the security guard said.

"Don't worry, I'm going," she said. She glanced past him at Doc and yelled, "This isn't over. I'll see you in hell if I have to drag you down there myself."

Every person in the room watched as she was escorted out. Shelby glanced at Doc and he shook his head. He crossed the room towards them, adjusted the lapels on his suit, and said, "Don't give her another thought. She is very bitter about the divorce and looking for someone to blame besides her relationship with the bottle."

Shelby nodded and Mel suspected they'd had this conversation before. Having Miranda crash the rehearsal hadn't rattled Shelby, so it seemed Miranda popping up wasn't a one-off occurrence.

"Shelby, you need to start prepping for the show," Doc said. "I'm sure your friends will leave you to that."

His tone didn't invite any debate. Mel and Angie

exchanged a glance. "I need to pick up Emari from my mother-in-law's house, so I'll call you later."

"Shelby will be very busy," Doc said. It was as if he just couldn't help himself.

Mel felt as if he was trying to put some distance between Angie and Shelby. Why? What was he worried about? That Angie might express opinions about Shelby's life? Of course she would. She was her friend.

"I'll look forward to it," Shelby said. She hugged Angie and then Mel. "Thanks for coming by. I think the flavors you picked for the VIP guests are amazing. They're going to be an absolute smash. They'll probably even upstage me."

Angie laughed. "As if they could. You bring out your hit singles and the guests won't even know what they're eating."

Shelby flashed a smile and then said, "Well, it's a Christmas show so I won't be doing many originals."

"Why not?" Angie cried. "That's why people come to see you."

Mel saw Doc's eyes narrow. Yup, Angie had just crossed the line he was trying so hard to hold. He obviously did not want anyone advising Shelby except for him.

"Let's leave the show to the artist," he said. "Shelby has chosen to sing Christmas songs so let's encourage her. We don't want to do or say anything that might shake her confidence, am I right?"

Angie opened her mouth and Mel gave her a quick nudge with her elbow. She suspected if they didn't say what Doc wanted to hear, he would cut off their access to Shelby, and given how lonely the singer appeared to be, Mel did not want to let that happen.

Angie glanced quickly at Mel, who said, "Of course not. Shelby could sing Wikipedia entries from her phone and the crowd would be enraptured."

Doc smiled at her. It might have been the first one she ever saw reach his eyes. He pointed at Mel and said, "That's right. That's the attitude to have."

"Well, of course, I think you can sing anything, Shelby, you know that," Angie said.

"Thank you, all," Shelby said. She hugged both Mel and Angie. "I feel very fortunate to have you in my corner."

Cheryl appeared in the entrance to the hallway that led to the dressing rooms. "I'm ready for you, Shel."

"Be right there," Shelby said. She turned back and squeezed Angie's and Mel's hands. "Thanks again. We'll talk later."

With a wave she followed Cheryl down the hallway. Mel and Angie turned to go but Doc moved to stand in their way.

Mel was taller than average but felt as if this man was looming over her, and given that Angie was shorter, she knew Angie had to feel it, too.

"Shelby had a very hard time after her former manager died," Doc said. "I do not want to see her upset in any way."

"What makes you think we're upsetting her?" Angie asked. "Seems to me, it's your past that's the problem."

The way she said *your past* made it clear that she was unhappy with what she'd seen, and if Doc was a smart man, and Mel suspected that he was, then he knew she was going to be looking into his relationship with his previous client.

"Don't you worry about my past—" Doc said but Angie interrupted.

"I'm not worried about it at all," Angie said. "I'm sure in her grief over losing her original manager that Shelby did her due diligence before she hired you." She took out her phone and scrolled through her contacts. "In fact, I'm going to get in touch with my old friend Roach from the Sewers and tell him this amazing news about our friend Shelby."

Doc's eyebrows lowered, forming a solid line across his brow.

"You did know that she's friends with Roach, didn't you?" Angie asked. "She opened for them during their summer tour because the Sewers have that unique country-rock quality that her country music blends so well with. Won't Roach be surprised when he hears you have her wearing sparkly outfits and singing covers instead of originals?"

"Miss—" Doc began but Angie shook her head.

"It's Mrs. Tate Harper to you," she said. "My husband is a financial genius and you can bet he'll be looking into the financials surrounding Shelby. If there is anything sketchy, we'll be calling you out."

Mel felt her shoulders bunch up around her ears. This was not good. So not good. If Doc wanted to cut off their access to Shelby, Angie was giving him the perfect excuse.

"Why, Mrs. Harper," Doc said. He looked her up and down like a used car salesman, trying to find the best angle. "You truly are proving yourself to be a devoted friend to Shelby. Please forgive me if I have been less than welcoming. I am just very protective of her, given that she's out here all on her own and all."

Angie's eyes narrowed with suspicion. Mel knew she wasn't about to fall for this one-eighty-degree turn, so Mel smiled, made her eyes wide and stepped forward. If Doc needed to think he had an ally among them, then she supposed it was going to have to be her.

"How good of you to be watching out for her so carefully, Doc," Mel said. She felt Angie's hot stare on the side of her face but she couldn't exactly explain her plan right now. "There is something about Shelby that brings out the protectiveness in all those who care for her. I'm so glad she has both you and Angie making her best interests a priority." She reached out and patted his arm. "I'm so glad we're all on the same team. Aren't you, Angie?"

Angie was silent, staring at Doc as if she could bore holes through him and see the inner workings.

Mel cleared her throat. "Right, Ange?"

"Right," she ground out.

"Excellent," Doc Howard said. "Now that we understand each other, I'll look forward to seeing you again soon."

He dipped his head and then stepped around them, heading down the hallway towards Shelby's dressing room.

"What was that?" Angie asked.

"That was me, selling my soul so that we don't have our access to Shelby cut off," Mel said. "You're welcome."

Angie closed her eyes for a moment. She sighed and then nodded, opening her eyes and looking at Mel with an expression of chagrin. "You're right. That was a good way to play it. Thank you for being so levelheaded."

"You're welcome. What do you suppose Doc's deal is?" Mel asked.

"I don't know, but I'm going to find out," Angie said. She stared down the hallway where Doc had disappeared. "Something doesn't add up with this guy. I bet he doesn't even have a doctorate. He looks like the type of snake oil salesman who just makes up titles to suit his grift. He'd better hope I don't find any problems, because if I do, I'm telling Shelby everything."

Four

"What do you think this Doc person is up to?" Joe asked. He was monitoring the pasta while Mel made her favorite chopped salad. This was definitely her favorite part of marriage, sharing the cooking, because while she loved baking, the day-to-day drudgery of what's for dinner was simply not her thing.

"I don't know," Mel said. "Angie is convinced he's a con man."

"Oh, boy," Joe said. "Angie's instincts are pretty good about these things."

"I know, and I have to admit that I get the same sketchy vibe off him," Mel said. "Plus, I get the feeling he's trying to isolate Shelby. Something her stylist said about Shelby keeping her on even if Doc wanted her fired made me think that he's trying to cut out the people in her life and potentially make her utterly dependent upon him. It would explain why he booked a Christmas tour when she always spends Christmas with her family."

"Yeah, that's a classic manipulator's move," Joe said. "Cut off ties with others, break down the person's self-esteem, make them dependent upon you. If there was a handbook, it sounds like he studied it."

"That's what I thought," Mel said. "Anyway, long story short, I invited Shelby to Christmas dinner and she accepted."

"Nice, very in the spirit of the season, cupcake," Joe said.

"Thank you." Mel smiled at the nickname, then she frowned. She didn't want him to think he had no say in their holiday dinner. "Are you sure you don't mind?"

"Not at all," he said. He stirred the pasta with a big wooden spoon and then set it across the top of the pot to keep it from boiling over. "In fact, I had an interesting call from my mother today."

"Oh?"

"She was thinking that since we're hosting your family that we'd potentially like to host my family, too, and make it one big party, because Dad has his hip procedure the week before the holiday and Mom isn't sure she can host the entire DeLaura clan and take care of him."

"So, we'll host your parents, the brothers, and all of their families?" Mel asked. She carefully put her knife down on the cutting board.

"Not exactly . . . um . . . well . . . wait, yeah actually," Joe said. He grimaced. "It's a lot of DeLauras, I'm afraid."

"So with my family and Shelby and her stylist, which makes ten, we're adding how many people?" she asked. Her voice came out high and tight and she cleared her throat, trying to free her Zen as if it was stuck in her windpipe.

"Well, Angie, Tate, and the baby," Joe said. He knew this was the selling point and lingered over the names. Then his prosecutor voice picked up speed and he said, "Dom and his wife and kids; Sal and his family; Ray and his girlfriend, Detective Martinez; Tony, Al, and Paulie, who are all single at the moment, I think."

"So, ballpark would be about twenty-two more people," Mel said.

"Yeah, something like that," he said. "Of course, Dom's kids are older and might invite their current partners, too, so I'll need to clarify."

"Okay," Mel said. She was pleased that she sounded so calm. "I'm just going to go step outside for a second."

She crossed the kitchen and opened the door to the back patio. The citrus trees at the edge of the yard were fully loaded and she knew she needed to get on that. She took in a deep breath, held it for several seconds, and then let it out until she was completely out of oxygen. Then she did it again.

Joe poked his head out the door. "Are you all right?"

Mel held up a finger. "Not a good time."

"Got it," he said. "Did I tell you how pretty you look today, cupcake?"

Mel almost laughed. Almost. She heard the door shut and then gave herself a stern talking-to. She was a Le Cordon Bleu–trained chef. This was a simple holiday dinner for thirtyish people. Surely, she could do this without making a big deal out of it. She'd just have to plan on spiking the eggnog so if the food was terrible, no one would notice.

With her calm restored, she turned and went back into the house. Joe had finished the salad, prepped the pasta and the sauce, and was just setting their plates on the small table in the eat-in kitchen.

"About Christmas dinner," Mel said. "I know I started to freak out a little."

Joe glanced up from the table with a cautious look in his eye as if he wasn't sure which way this conversation was going to go.

"Okay, more than a little," Mel said. "But of course, we'll host given your dad's surgery and all, it's just . . ."

"Just?" he asked.

"My mother and her Christmas china and tchotchkes and your mother being an amazing cook with very specific recipes like her handmade gorgonzola ravioli, the seafood salad, and the porchetta!" Mel sucked in a breath.

"Breathe, Mel, you're starting to hyperventilate," Joe said. He gently pulled her into his arms. "It's going to be all right. We are an amazing team and we have loads of backup."

"I know," Mel said. She rested her head on his shoulder. "I mean I have you and Angie and Tate. It'll be okay."

"Exactly," Joe said. "We've got you."

"Promise?" Mel asked. "I've worked very hard on my reputation and I can't have it destroyed by one Christmas dinner." She was only partly kidding.

"Absolutely," he said. "It'll be great. We'll deck the heck out of the halls and make it a Christmas to be remembered."

The doorbell rang and Joe released Mel. "Why does somebody always appear when dinner is ready? Do they smell it from the street?"

"If it's Ray, then I'd say yes, he does," she said.

Joe flashed her a grin, obviously relieved to see her humor back, and strode back through the house to answer the door. Mel glanced under the table to see their rescue dog, Peanut, in her spot. There was no sign of their cat, Captain Jack, also a rescue, but she knew he was probably doing that second-dimension thing that cats did. She'd search high and low for him and then she'd turn around and there he'd be, licking his chest as if he'd been there the entire time.

"Hey, Mel!" Angie appeared in the door with Emari in her arms. "Sorry to barge in but I have some news."

"Have you eaten?" Mel asked.

"We have not," Tate said. He followed his wife into the kitchen carrying an empty car seat and a diaper bag.

"I'll get more plates," Joe said.

"We don't want to be a bother," Angie protested. She looked chagrined. "Sorry, I should have just called you but I was picking up Tate at the airport, and Ray called—"

"Hold up," Mel said. She raised her hand in a stop gesture.

Joe appeared at her side, holding her wineglass. Mel took it and said, "Thanks." She turned back to Angie. "Continue."

"Okay, so Ray was at Turf Paradise yesterday," Angie

45

said. Joe heaved a long-suffering sigh at the mention of their brother at the local horse racing track, which she ignored. "And he got to talking with the guy next to him. He said the guy was in an expensive-looking suit, which was why Ray noticed him. Well, that and he was laying down heavy bets even though he was clearly losing gobs of money."

Tired of being held, Emari let out a wail, redirecting her mom's attention to her. Mel knew Angie would get to the point of the story eventually so she put down her glass and helped Angie spread the baby blanket on the floor with an array of toys for Emari to throw, shake, and chew on while they had dinner.

Happy with her freedom, the baby babbled something that sounded like *dog*, and Peanut obliging left her spot under the table to sit with Emari, who kicked her feet and patted the dog. Mel marveled at Peanut's patience but she'd taken to the baby from day one. It occurred to Mel that if and when she and Joe had kids, they were lucky to have such a benevolent dog.

Joe set extra places and they took their seats at the table. "How was Michigan?" Mel asked Tate.

"Amazing," he said. "We're going to crush it up there."

"Ahem." Angie cleared her throat.

"Sorry, silly me, thinking we'd talk business," Tate said. He winked at his wife to let her know he was kidding, and she rolled her eyes.

"Right, so Ray and the track," Joe said. He put a fist over his sternum. "Why do I feel my heartburn kicking in already?"

"No need," Angie said. "It was a very fortuitous meeting."

"Oh, really, how so?" Joe asked. He dished pasta onto his plate and passed the bowl.

"Because the man in the suit who was gambling really heavily and losing was none other than Doc Howard," Angie said.

Five

"No way," Mel said.

"Way," Angie said. "I told you there was something rotten about him."

"Just because the guy is at the track, doesn't mean he's up to no good," Joe said. "I can't believe I just said that."

"I don't know." Tate heaped sauce on top of his pasta. "From what Angie told me this guy has all the classic signs of an egomaniac. He's keeping Shelby isolated by firing anyone who gets too close to her, and he's clearly making some serious money off her if he has that much to gamble so early in the morning on the horses."

"He might be making serious money off Shelby," Angie said. "But he's also losing it. Ray said that he observed Doc Howard having words, not friendly ones, with Jerry Stackhouse."

Joe sat up straight. He stared at Angie. "Jerry Stack-house the loan shark?"

"Yup. Ray said they were cussing each other out and security had to tell them to take it outside."

"How does a guy who's only been in town for a few days have a connection to the local stakeman?" Tate asked.

"No idea, but I'm guessing from what Ray said that they met at the track. Now I want to see what Shelby's contract with Doc looks like," Angie said. "I need to spend more time with her before I can ask to see it without it seeming like I'm a weirdo but I really feel like there is some chicanery going on and I don't like it. This Christ-mas show, for instance. How is this supposed to help her career? She's singing carols but no originals. How does that make any sense?"

"Maybe he's trying to expand her fan base by having her sing classic songs, hoping people will then double back and buy her originals," Mel suggested.

"Does that seem like it would work?" Angie asked. "I mean I feel like we have a real Colonel Parker–Elvis dy-namic happening."

"Don't mention Elvis," Joe said. "I still have PTSD from that debacle in Las Vegas."

Mel reached over and patted his hand. "Don't blame Elvis. It's not his fault the women wanted to date him and the men wanted to be him."

"'Ambition is a dream with a V8 engine,'" Angie said.

"Elvis," Mel, Joe, and Tate said together. It wasn't a movie quote but it was still a favorite line from the king of rock and roll.

"Is there any way to find out if Doc Howard is in debt and, if so, to whom?" Mel asked.

Joe and Angie exchanged a speaking glance.

"He's made a connection," Angie said.

"We can ask him," Joe said. "But I don't want him to get overly involved. It never goes well when Ray helps. Never."

"Agreed." Angie nodded. "And he can't go anywhere near Stackhouse."

"Yeah, no, that'd be like setting a dog loose in a butcher shop," Joe said.

Mel laughed but it was a nervous one. Ray had a reputation for trouble and given that they'd previously been shot at together, she could testify that it was true. Also, she was very fond of Ray and didn't want to think of him in danger.

"What do you think he'll be able to do?" she asked. "Get a confession out of Doc that he's embezzling Shelby's money and gambling it away?"

"That would be ideal," Tate said. "But unlikely."

"Ray can buddy up to Doc," Joe said. "Be his friend and see what he has to say."

"If Ray can get Doc to talk about his business relationship with Shelby, that would be helpful," Angie said. "I'd like to know if he sees her as just a meal ticket or if he thinks she can break into the big time."

Mel nodded. She didn't like to think that Shelby, of whom she was becoming fond, was at the mercy of someone who was keeping her working just for his percentage. She'd seen Shelby's face when she said she wasn't going home for the holidays. She'd looked terribly homesick. Mel wasn't exactly thrilled that she was cooking for tons of people but at least she'd be surrounded by the ones she loved. There had to be a way to make that happen for

Shelby, too. It was Christmas. Surely they could find some holiday magic for their friend.

\' '/ '\ '

"Buenos días, chef," Oz greeted Mel as he entered the bakery through the back door in the kitchen.

"Good morning, chef," Mel returned. She was mixing a new batch of their Gingerbread Man cupcakes with cinnamon cream cheese frosting and the kitchen smelled amazing.

"I hear you're having everyone over to your house for Christmas dinner," Oz said.

Mel's head snapped up from checking the consistency of the cream cheese frosting in her KitchenAid mixer. "Where did you hear that?"

"Marty," Oz said. "He and Olivia are looking forward to it."

"He. And. Olivia." Mel could barely comprehend the words.

Oz frowned in concern. "Are you okay?"

"That depends. What are you doing for Christmas?" Mel asked.

"Dinner at my mom's," Oz said. "Best green corn tamales in the world. It just isn't Christmas without them."

"Any chance you'd want to be my sous chef on Christmas instead?" Mel asked.

"You mean slave in a hot kitchen all day instead of sitting on my butt watching football with my uncles and cousins?" he asked.

"Yeah, that," Mel said. "Football is so last year. Plus, you can work on your savory skills."

"So, we're not even baking? We're cooking the main course and sides?" he asked. He looked leery, as if the thought of the savory side of the kitchen was a foreign land he had no wish to visit.

"Yes, I have stacks of recipes from my mother and Joe's mother of expected dishes," Mel said. She knew her voice was overly bright and she likely looked a bit manic. "It's going to be so great!"

"You're scaring me," Oz said.

"Sorry." Mel tamped down her expression. "What do you say? Please?"

Oz heaved a sigh. "Fine. I'll be there."

"Great! Bring your knives," Mel said.

"That sounds ominous," Angie observed as she entered the kitchen from the front of the bakery. Shelby was with her, although with her hair up, sunglasses on, and wearing workout clothes she was practically in disguise. It did not stop Oz from recognizing her and he immediately lit up like he'd just discovered a brand-new flavor of frosting.

"Shelby, great to see you again," he said. "I don't know if you remember—"

"Hi, Oz," she said. She beamed at him and he looked like he might swoon.

"Can I get you—" he began but Angie interrupted him.

"We can't stay," she said. "Shelby is supposed to be at the gym."

"Oh, sure, yeah, okay," Oz said. He was clearly trying to hide his disappointment and failing spectacularly.

"Next time?" Shelby asked.

Oz nodded, looking encouraged that there would be a next time. He glanced at the time on his phone and said,

"I have to go. I'm working on a butterscotch bread pudding for the holiday menu at the resort."

"Feel free to bring that to Christmas dinner," Mel suggested.

"Consider it done," he said. "Ladies."

The three women watched him leave and Angie took a seat at the steel worktable and motioned for Shelby to do the same.

"Are you ready for tonight?" Mel asked. It was opening night and even though she wasn't performing, she had butterflies on behalf of Shelby.

"As I'll ever be," Shelby said. "I just wish my family could be here. Doc says I need to grow up, that this is the life I've chosen, but I don't think missing your family around the holidays means you aren't a grown-up. It just means you love your family."

"One more check in the column of why I don't like that guy," Angie muttered.

"He means well," Shelby said. "He didn't have to take me on as a client after Diana died, and it did cost him his marriage."

"Because he shoved his wife aside to represent you," Angie said. "Who does that?"

"Doc said Miranda wasn't a reliable performer anymore," Shelby said. "He tried to help her but she divorced him instead."

"Wasn't a reliable performer?" Mel asked. "What does that mean?"

Angie pantomimed drinking and Shelby nodded. "Doc said she started losing gigs because she was too inebriated to sing at a few of her shows. He sent her to rehab but she refused to stay and checked herself out after a few days."

"When you were represented by Diana and she was with Doc, did you ever see her perform?" Mel asked.

"All the time," Shelby said. "Miranda has an amazing voice. I never saw her drunk but I know that life on the road is hard. A lot of musicians turn to drugs and alcohol to combat the loneliness and, frankly, the boredom of life on tour."

"So you think she could have gone that route?" Mel asked.

Shelby shrugged. "It happens to a lot of entertainers. Traveling from city to city night after night can grind you down after a while."

"But you won't do that," Angie said. "Because you can just have a cupcake and know that everything will be better."

Shelby laughed. "It's true. There's nothing that a cupcake can't make better even if it's just a little bit for a little while."

"That should be our slogan," Mel said.

"I love it," Angie declared. "Let's tell Tate to fire our ad agency. We've got something way better."

Shelby laughed. "Right. Well, if my songwriting career comes to an abrupt end, I'll consider a pivot to slogan writing instead."

"Which reminds me," Angie said. "I saw the set list for your show and you're really not singing any of your originals?" She had that determined tilt to her chin that Mel knew so well. Shelby was in for a lecture whether she liked it or not.

"It's a Christmas show," Shelby said. "I haven't written any holiday songs."

"But how will the audience get to know you as Shelby

Vaughn if you don't sing some of your own material?" Angie insisted.

"Doc says no one wants originals that no one knows the words to during a holiday showcase."

"Well, he's wrong," Angie said. "I think you should work in a few originals."

"I appreciate your enthusiasm," Shelby said.

"But you want me to shush and mind my own business," Angie said.

"No . . . maybe," Shelby said. "I have a hard enough time meeting Doc's expectations. I don't want to believe I'm disappointing you, too."

"You could never," Angie protested. She threw her arm around Shelby's shoulders and gave her a half hug. "Tell her, Mel."

"You could never," Mel said. "And I know we don't know anything about showbiz but it seems to me that Angie is right. It'd be a shame not to let the audience see the real you at least for a song or two."

Shelby pursed her lips as she considered. "All right, I can promise to think about it but honestly I don't see where I could wedge another song into the set."

"It'll come to you," Angie said. "I know it will."

˅ ˎ ˏ ˎ

The VIP area was unlike any venue Mel had ever worked. The space they had toured a few days ago had been transformed into a winter wonderland with fake snow on the ground, a mini decorated tree on every table, twinkle lights strung across the ceiling, and holiday carols playing softly overhead.

There were roughly fifty VIP guests invited to the opening show, one of which was the hotel owner, Regina Bessette. Mel recognized her from her portrait, which was displayed in the lobby of the hotel. Regina appeared to be about sixty with long curly silver hair and a trim figure, and wearing a stylish sequined chemise in rose gold with matching stiletto heels with very pointy toes.

She greeted everyone in the room and paused by the Fairy Tale Cupcakes station, where Mel and Angie were serving the guests. Regina looked over their cupcakes as if searching for a fly in the icing. Mel tried not to be annoyed. They had arranged the cupcakes in very festive towers with twinkling lights and red and green curling ribbons giving their station a pop of color. Regina studied them, tilting her head and assessing the cupcakes from every angle.

"Why is this one so plain?" she asked. With a jewel-encrusted acrylic nail, she pointed at an Eggnog cupcake. "This other one has peppermint bark on it, and this one has a little gingerbread man cookie, and there's the pretty purple ones with gumdrops, but this one is . . . meh."

Angie glanced at Mel as if asking her permission to let the pushy woman have it. Mel suspected Angie didn't know that they were dealing with the owner of the hotel and she tried to subtly shake her head before addressing Regina.

"Well, Ms. Bessette, I can see where that cupcake looks plainer compared to the others but some people prefer a less-is-more approach to their confectionary and we do try to please all of our customers, much like you do with your hotel," Mel said. She heard Angie's sharp intake of breath and knew that she'd been right. Angie had had no idea who Regina Bessette was, so crisis averted. She hoped.

"It looks boring," Regina insisted.

"It's dusted with nutmeg, and I can assure you it tastes amazing," Mel said.

"That may be but it still needs some color, a little festive pop, with jimmies or something," she insisted.

"You mean sprinkles?" Mel asked.

"Yes." Regina snapped her fingers. "Now you're getting it."

Getting it? Mel tried not to be annoyed. She failed. Sometimes she just ran out of patience with people who thought baking cupcakes was no big deal like anyone could just whip up a delicious cake, slap some frosting on it, pour sprinkles on it, and call it a day.

"So, what did you have in mind? Quins? Dragées? Hundreds and thousands?" Mel asked. She felt Angie's hand on her arm, trying to rein her in.

"Quins? Dra . . . what?" Regina blinked. "What are you even talking about?"

"The many varied types of sprinkles that are available," Mel said. "I assumed you knew. No?"

Regina blinked at her again.

"You have your pearl-like balls, called dragées. They come in all sorts of colors. Then there are the flat round sprinkles called quins, also in many colors—very festive. The nonpareils, also known as hundreds and thousands, give texture to the frosting, adding a little crunch. Speaking of which, there is sanding sugar, coarse sugar, and traditional sprinkles, which you called jimmies. So, what would you put on an eggnog-flavored cupcake with a rum buttercream icing?"

Regina glanced away as if overwhelmed by the possibilities but not willing to concede her point as yet.

Mel and Angie exchanged a look and Angie said, "Can I plate one for you, Ms. Bessette? Despite being plain, the Eggnog seems to be the favorite of the night so far."

Regina looked at Angie as if she had offered her an illegal substance. "I don't eat sugar." Her voice was sharp and she sent them an outraged look as she strode away.

"Were we just insulted?" Angie asked. "I feel like we were."

"Nah," Mel said. Although secretly she felt exactly the same. "She probably has a medical condition and can't eat sugar." Angie stared at her. "Or something like that," Mel added.

"Ho ho ho!" Marty joined them at their table wearing a full-on Santa suit.

"What is that?" Angie asked. She waved a hand at his outfit.

"Me, pimping the Christmas spirit," Marty replied. "I'm just trying to liven things up a bit at our station."

"We don't need to liven things up," Angie said. "We are giving out free cupcakes. It doesn't get any better than that."

"Perhaps, but I don't think a little holiday cheer is out of order," Marty said.

"You're wearing a full Santa suit," Angie said. She poked him in the belly with her pointer finger. "That is not a little holiday cheer, that is an over-the-top attention-seeking ensemble if I've ever seen one."

"It is not," Marty said. "I can't help it if the spirit of the season runs through my veins." His gaze flitted over to the dressing room doors. "Has Shelby made an appearance yet?"

"She hasn't," Angie said. "But let me spare you some heartache and be the first to break it to you that she is not interested in a guy old enough to remember most of the last century who, in case you've forgotten, already has a very scary girlfriend."

"Aah," Marty gasped. "I am not interested in her in *that* way! What kind of a pervert do you think I am? She's young enough to be my . . . well . . . my very young daughter."

"More like your granddaughter," Angie said.

Marty waved a white-gloved hand at her as if she were a pesky mosquito.

"If you're not interested in her in *that* way, and thank you for not being a lecherous oldster, then what's with the getup?" Mel asked.

"If you must know, I feel that I could contribute to the show," Marty said. He began to sing and dance much like he had when he first met Shelby. When Mel and Angie didn't say anything, he spun around, turning his back to them and began to twerk his posterior. Over his shoulder, he cried, "See? I am total backup dancer material."

"Oh, no!" Angie cried. She held up her hand to ward off the sight. "No one needs to see that."

"What?" Marty stopped and turned back around. He planted his hands on his hips while trying to catch his breath. "I'd be amazing."

"Shelby's shows are three hours long," Mel said. "While I love your enthusiasm, I'm not sure you've trained enough to be able to sustain that length of a program."

Marty squinted at her. "What are you trying to say, boss?"

"That you'll stroke out halfway through the show and ruin it for everyone," Angie said. She turned to Mel. "Your diplomacy is lovely but I think we need to be blunt here."

"Blunt?" Marty asked. "Try hurtful."

"Direct," Angie corrected him. She moved out from behind the cupcake station and faced him. She placed her hands on her hips and they squared off, staring each other down.

"Mean," Marty argued. He leaned forward.

"Honest." Angie stuck her chin out.

"Cruel." Marty frowned.

"Enough," Mel said. She pushed her way in between them. "We have cupcakes to move. Why don't you each take a tray and work the room, while I man the table."

"I bet I unload more," Marty muttered.

"Oh, yeah, Santa pants?" Angie asked. "Game on."

Mel rolled her eyes and moved back behind the towers of cupcakes. She scanned the room and recognized several local politicians, a few regional television personalities, and much to her surprise, Jerry Stackhouse, the local loan shark.

He was in a slick suit, which did not hide his middle-aged paunch, with his dark hair combed back from his forehead as if it were a requirement of the mobster uniform. He was holding a martini and pacing around the room, looking very much like a shark circling in the water.

Technically, Jerry Stackhouse was in real estate, but no one believed that was where he made most of his money. After their dinner with Tate and Angie, Joe had shown Mel a picture of Jerry, on the off chance that her path crossed with Stackhouse's while Ray was working his newfound friendship with Doc Howard to see if he could discover how deep in debt Doc was to the stakeman.

What was Stackhouse doing here, though? Was he here to shake Doc down for money owed? Was he planning to demand it in public to humiliate Doc? Or was he just a fan of Shelby's and using his association with Doc to get the VIP treatment on the singer's opening night?

As Mel watched him, a teenage girl came up to him and grabbed his arm. She was a pretty girl with the same dark hair and wide-set eyes as Stackhouse. Mel assumed she must be his daughter. She was wearing a strapless red dress and heels, and her hair was styled in curls that bounced around her shoulders. She pointed at the cupcake station, where Mel stood, and said something to her father that Mel couldn't hear. He nodded and the two of them began to walk in her direction.

Mel glanced around the room to see where Angie was. She'd want to know that the loan shark was here and he was coming this way! Angie was in a far corner of the room, smiling as she handed out cupcakes to a festively dressed group of women. There was no way Mel could get her attention without causing a scene. Mel was on her own.

Six

Mel plastered a smile on her face. Not too difficult when the teenager bounced up to her station and clasped her hands and said, "These look amazing."

"Thank you," Mel said. "What can I get you?"

"What are the flavors?" Jerry Stackhouse asked. He stood behind his daughter, pondering the towers.

Mel ran through the flavors that Shelby had approved. The daughter, whom Stackhouse called Hayley, chose one of the Peppermint Bark cupcakes while he went for the Sugar Plum.

The Sugar Plum cupcake was new to the bakery this year. Mel had wanted to do something she hadn't seen any other bakery do. Sugar plums, which most people erroneously assumed were sugared plums, were actually a delicacy that dated back to the seventeenth century. Seeds covered in a sweet coating by a process called panning, which took several days to make layer upon layer of the hard sugar coating around the seed or spice until the delicacy was the shape and size of a small oval plum.

Mel had crafted her Sugar Plum cupcake recipe from a spice cake flavored with cinnamon, cardamom, nutmeg, and clove and topped it with a decadent vanilla buttercream, which she garnished with an assortment of festive candy and sprinkles, mainly spiced gumdrops, silver dragées, and purple quins.

Mel carefully plated their choices. She could feel her nerves ratchet up, which was ridiculous, because Stackhouse didn't know her from a potted houseplant. She watched him interact with his daughter and he seemed just like any other dad. She felt her spine relax a bit.

A stir of excitement began at the other side of the room as Shelby entered with a contingent of dancers. They were all dressed in sparkly red sequined Santa outfits trimmed with faux fur, and Mel suddenly understood why Marty thought he might blend in with the troupe. She glanced over at him with his faux big belly and full beard. Yeah, no. Not exactly a match.

"Daddy, she's here!" Hayley cried. "Can I go say hello to her?"

"Of course, that's why we're here, but mind your manners," he said.

"Yes, sir." Hayley shoved the last of her cupcake into her mouth and tossed her paper plate and napkin into the nearby trash can. Then she bolted across the room to meet Shelby.

Jerry Stackhouse watched her go and when she was out of earshot, he turned to Mel and said, "How's that hotshot prosecutor husband of yours doing?"

Mel's eyes went wide. She blinked and tried not to look surprised but she could tell she failed. Stackhouse picked up a red napkin from the table, pinching it between two fingers. It shouldn't have been a threatening gesture, quite the opposite—it was a napkin, after all—and yet it was.

"Excuse me?" Mel went for the bluff. When all else failed, she'd discovered that playing dumb usually bought her a few minutes.

"Joe DeLaura? Your husband? Surely, he's not that forgettable," Stackhouse said. He smirked at her as if enjoying her discomfort.

"How do you know he's my husband?" Mel asked.

He looked at her like she was a few sprinkles shy of a garnish. "You're kidding, right? What other prosecutor in the country has a wife who's been tied to so many murders? You're like your own true crime show or something."

"I am not tied to them," Mel protested.

"That's right," he said. He reached for another cupcake and Mel let him. He could eat the whole table full as far as she was concerned. She did not want to square off with a man with as dubious a reputation as Stackhouse. "You just happen to stumble upon dead bodies. A weird side hustle for a cupcake baker."

Mel glowered. This guy was getting on her nerves and she found her annoyance outweighed her intimidation.

"It's not like that," she said. "I can't help it if my occupation takes me to weird places." She raised her hands and gestured to the room they were standing in. "For example, if someone dropped dead right here right now, that would have nothing to do with me."

Stackhouse glanced around the room with a cautious expression. "Do you expect someone to die?"

"No!" Mel cried. "I'm just saying that if someone did, it wouldn't have anything to do with me."

"Except you just said you expected someone to die," he said. He put the cupcake he was holding down as if it might be poisoned and slowly backed away from the table.

"That's not what I meant," Mel protested.

"Hey now, no need to get riled," Stackhouse said. "I have no beef with you."

"Oh?" Mel asked. "Who do you have beef with?"

"No one, nope, no one at all," he said. He melted into the crowd and Mel pushed her bangs off her forehead and let out a long breath. That conversation hadn't gone at all as she'd expected.

"Are you all right?" Angie appeared at Mel's side.

"I'm fine," Mel said. She wondered if she should mention that Stackhouse was there. Before she could, Doc Howard approached.

"Listen, if Shelby comes over here, do not give her a cupcake," he said.

"I really don't think she's going to eat one right before the show," Mel said.

Doc was in another slick suit tonight and he crossed his arms over his chest and glared at Mel. "I'm not debating this with you." He pointed to the Sugar Plum cupcake on the table and said, "Put that away."

"It's not like we don't have several dozen cupcakes

still on display," Angie said. She met Doc's glare and raised it to a glower.

"It's fine," Mel said. "I'm boxing up cupcakes for the cast and crew for after the show. I'll just put it in one of those."

She picked up the cupcake and reached for the first box set aside for the show members. She'd put their names on them so that she made certain she didn't miss anyone. She popped the top on the lid and deftly put the cupcake inside. She closed the lid and noted that she'd already put Shelby's name on it. She figured Shelby would like the Sugar Plum cupcake, assuming Doc let her have it, which was doubtful.

Doc Howard didn't look too happy about that but Mel didn't think he had a right to tell Shelby what she could and couldn't eat. In fact, if he didn't let her have this one, Mel was going to sneak her another one. No one was denied a cupcake on her watch.

She felt that creepy tingling-up-the-spine sensation of someone watching her but when she turned to Doc, expecting it to be him, he was chatting up an older couple who looked quite wealthy. She scanned the room and saw Stackhouse, leaning against the opposite wall, watching her. When she met his gaze, he turned away.

Mel thought about crossing the room and calling him out but the auditorium bells sounded, alerting them that they had fifteen minutes until the Christmas extravaganza started. Shelby had arranged for them to sit in the first few rows with the paying VIP guests, and Mel was excited to see the show.

Shelby left the lounge with a big smile and a wave. She dazzled with her stage makeup on and her head of fat, bouncy blond curls. She was wearing a white gown with holly leaves and berries embroidered all around the hem. She looked amazing.

Mel, Angie, and Marty hurriedly packed away the cupcakes, saving the remainder for the show's after-party. With minutes to spare, they found their seats in the third row from the stage.

"Look at us," Marty crowed. "We're VIPs."

Mel glanced at the surrounding seats and saw Jerry Stackhouse and his daughter Hayley in the row in front of them and off to the right. Marty was right. They were in prime seating. She saw Jerry's head move, and afraid he'd catch her looking at him, she turned to the stage. The man had genuinely seemed afraid of her, which was so weird and kind of cool, but mostly weird.

The lights went down and a surge of anticipation rippled through the crowd. A lone beat, the tap of a drum, sounded and Shelby's backup dancers swooped down the aisles in a sparkling array of high kicks, lifts, and a medley of holiday songs that would lift up even the darkest of hearts. Marty started to twerk in his seat until Angie put her hand on his shoulder, holding him still. He sighed and sank into the plush chair.

When the dancers were all onstage and the crowd was at a fever pitch, the crimson curtain swooshed open and there on top of a lit-up staircase was Shelby. She was an ethereal beauty in her gorgeous gown, and she immediately began to belt out "White Christmas" much to the delight of the audience. Her voice was clear and strong and reached every corner of the auditorium.

The show was everything a Christmas extravaganza should be. It was impossible to feel anything other than happy and when Shelby took her bow with her dancers, the crowd roared their approval and demanded an encore.

Mel, Angie, and Marty were about to slip out to go set up their cupcake station, when the curtain parted and Shelby came out, all alone, with just her acoustic guitar. She'd had several costume changes and was now wearing a simple deep blue gown embellished with silver snow-flakes. Her long fingers moved over the strings of her guitar and she took a second to tune it. The entire audi-torium was silent, watching her as she stepped forward to a microphone that a stagehand hurriedly set up for her.

"Hey, y'all," she greeted the crowd. The applause was deafening. They loved her. "I was going to sing another Christmas carol for you but I think I'd like to sing one of my originals instead, if that's all right."

Mel turned and saw Hayley clapping her heart out. She wasn't alone. It seemed most of the crowd was eager to hear a Shelby original.

"Well, all right then." Shelby cleared her throat and began to strum the guitar. She smiled at them. She had been amazing tonight, crooning each holiday song with her whole heart but when she played her own song, it was as if she were conjuring magic. The ballad was about home and family and loved ones long forgotten. Mel thought of her father and felt her throat get tight. But be-fore the song could leave them all in tears, there was a twist in the narrative and Shelby turned it into a song about hope and second chances.

"Mercy, she is talented," Marty said. Mel glanced at him and noted that he was surreptitiously using his Santa beard to mop up a few tears.

"She certainly is," she agreed.

"This is what she needs to be doing," Angie said. "She has this audience enthralled."

Mel scanned the crowd. Angie was right. All except for one. Standing against the wall to the right of the stage with his arms crossed over his chest was Doc Howard and he looked furious.

Shelby threw her guitar pick out to the crowd and waved. Then she disappeared behind the curtain and the house lights came up. The show was over.

"Uh-oh, we need to be in the VIP room," Mel said. She elbowed Marty, who was still looking a bit emotional, and said, "Let's go!"

"I'm going," he said. "Just give a guy a second to get his feelings sorted, would you?"

"We don't have time for feelings," Mel said. "Get it together, Santa."

Marty popped up from his seat and said, "You're right. You're right. I know you're right. It's just that it was so—"

"Beautiful, I know," Mel agreed. "But Shelby hired us to hand out cupcakes so let's help her out by doing that."

Marty led the way out of their row and the three of them dodged around the crowd as they hurried back to the suite for the VIPs.

The guests were being held at the door while the bartenders and other food attendants set up. Mel, Marty, and Angie dashed in and set to work. They had plenty of cupcakes left and they stocked the tower, trying to make it festive by varying the flavors and colors. Angie and Marty loaded up trays with cupcakes so that they could work the room while Mel maintained her spot behind the table.

She glanced at the time on her phone. It was just after ten. Being a baker, she rose early in the morning to get the day's baking started and it was already past her bedtime. She knew the VIP suite stayed open until eleven and she really hoped she could stay awake that long. She stifled a yawn and braced herself for the incoming crowd.

The show must have given the audience an appetite because there was a nonstop rush on cupcakes that lasted forty-five minutes. Mel was concerned they'd run out of stock but the demand started to slow, and she thought they might just squeak through the night.

"My feet are killing me," Angie said. She put her tray down and collapsed onto a folding chair behind their station. "I'm never wearing heels again while carrying a tray full of cupcakes."

"You should have told me," Mel said. "We could have swapped out."

"No, you're the chief baker so if anyone wanted to ask questions about the cupcakes, you needed to be here," Angie said. She let out a big yawn.

Marty appeared out of the thinning crowd and he, too, looked worse for the wear. Judging by the sweaty sheen on his face, the Santa suit was a tad warm for the crowded room. As the party wound down and security ushered the remaining guests out, Mel began to pack up the few remaining cupcakes into paper boxes. She figured Shelby or some of the dancers or backstage crew would enjoy them.

The room was empty when Shelby stopped by their station. She looked shy when she asked, "All right, moment-of-truth time, what did you think of the show?"

"You were amazing!" Angie cried. She jumped up and

hurried around the table to give Shelby a massive hug. "It was the best holiday show I've ever seen."

"It's the only holiday show you've ever seen, isn't it?" Shelby asked.

"Well, yes, but that doesn't mean it's not the best," Angie protested.

"You really were magnificent," Mel said. "Everyone was. It was impossible not to be happy while watching. You've really tapped into that Christmas cheer."

"Really?" Shelby asked.

"Absolutely," Marty said. He stood up and Mel noticed he was sticking out his chest and sucking in his gut while giving Shelby his profile.

"Great outfit, Marty," Shelby said. "You really blend in with the show."

"Funny you should say that," Marty said. "I was thinking since you and I—"

"Shelby, a word," Doc Howard interrupted. It wasn't a request. Shelby turned and saw Doc standing behind her with a furious expression on his face.

Mel watched Shelby closely to see if she appeared afraid. She didn't. Instead, she tipped her chin up and said, "All right."

"In private," he said.

"Anything you have to say to me you can say in front of my friends," Shelby said.

Doc glowered at Angie, who flanked Shelby on one side while Marty stood on the other. Marty with the ball of his Santa hat flopping over his forehead was significantly less intimidating than Angie.

"Fine," Doc snapped. He raised his hands in exasperation. "What were you thinking?"

71

"In regards to what?" Shelby asked. She looked at him as if she had no idea what he was talking about but even Mel knew that Doc was likely furious that she had deviated from his order that she sing a holiday showcase with no originals. She wondered if Shelby was also buying herself some time by playing dumb.

"Oh, don't give me that innocent nonsense. You know what about," he said. He heaved a sigh and said, "You're the artist, Shelby, and I don't want to limit your creativity but the deal with the hotel was that you'd do a holiday show, and changing it up to close the show with an original song wasn't part of the deal."

"The audience loved it," Angie protested.

"Damn right they did," Marty chimed in.

"This isn't about the audience," Doc said. "It's about the contract with the hotel. But I'm sure with your advanced knowledge in music management you know that."

"Don't patronize me," Angie said. "If the audience is happy, then the hotel is happy, and clearly the audience was very happy. It doesn't take a degree in music management to know that." She turned to Shelby and said, "Don't let him intimidate you. Your instincts were spot on tonight, in fact, you should sing more originals and less holiday fluff and use the show to promote you, your brand, and win over new listeners. That's why a singer-songwriter has gigs, to promote their original material."

"Not if they were hired to perform holiday music it isn't," Doc insisted.

Angie took a step forward. She was half the size of Doc Howard but that didn't stop her. The inherently feisty Angie had grown up with seven older brothers, so it was virtually impossible for anyone to unnerve her.

"You're wasting her time and talent with this show," Angie said.

"Is that so?" Doc Howard asked. He looked completely befuddled, as if no one had ever dared to call him out before.

"Yes, it's so," Angie said. "What kind of manager doesn't have his singer perform their own work?"

"Are you actually questioning me?" Doc asked.

"Seems like a legit point to me," Marty said.

"No one asked you, old man," Doc snapped. "Shelby, I know this woman is your friend but I have to insist that you don't listen to her. She doesn't know anything about you or the business. She is putting things in your head that will violate your contracts and potentially destroy your career."

"Speaking of contracts," Angie said. "I'd like to see Shelby's."

"What?" Doc looked as shocked as if she'd asked him for a kidney.

"I have an entertainment attorney that I want to have take a look at it," Angie said. "Since you know the business so well, and I'm sure you'd never do anything to harm Shelby or her career, you don't mind do you?"

"Mind? Of course I mind," he snapped. "Not because there is anything wrong with the contract but because you're calling into question my ethics and standards, and I take that very personally." Doc Howard's face turned a vibrant shade of red, and his mouth opened and closed as if he'd continue his diatribe but was so offended that he was struggling to gather his thoughts.

Mel wondered if she should pour him a glass of water or get something stronger from the bar.

"Shelby, are you going to let your friend attack me like this?" Doc asked.

"She's just looking out for me," Shelby said. She leaned into Angie a little bit as if drawing strength from her diminutive friend. "I don't think that's a bad thing."

"Looking out for you is my job," Doc spat. "I'm your representation. I'm the one who negotiates your contracts and makes sure you get paid. Don't forget, my marriage ended because of you, Shelby, and this is the thanks I get."

"I'd say your marriage ended because you threw out the old wife who wasn't doing so well and traded her in for a younger model," Angie said.

"How dare you?" Doc cried. "Shelby is like a daughter to me."

"A daughter who isn't even allowed to sing her own material," Angie snorted. "Why? You have yet to substantively answer that question."

"Because the contract with the hotel specifically states a holiday show," Doc said.

"Then why is Shelby doing it?" Angie pressed. "This is a nothing burger of a gig. It's for has-beens or wannabes not for performers who are on the rise, which Shelby is. The auditorium only seats three thousand, and the fact that every show for the next two weeks sold out well in advance proves that she can perform in much bigger venues. So why is she here doing this schlock?"

Mel knew Angie wanted Doc to admit that he had a gambling problem. She was pushing him hard to admit it by calling into question his choice of this venue. But Mel was certain that Doc Howard wasn't going to crack. She was right.

"Shelby needs the money!" Doc shouted. "There, are you happy now? Your friend who you think you're helping by making me look bad is almost flat broke."

Shelby looked as if he'd just slapped her, so it was clear she had no idea about her own financial situation. Then she shook her head. To Mel's surprise, Shelby glared at Doc and demanded, "How am I broke?"

"Being on the road costs money," Doc said. "The buses, the roadies, the hotels, the food, your outfits, it all adds up."

"But the record label . . ." Shelby protested.

"Isn't paying for any of it," Doc said. He raised his hands and gestured to the suite. "Your sophomore album didn't hit the charts, and the label has lost faith in you. That's why you're here doing a Christmas show. I'm trying to keep your visibility up while paying your bills."

Shelby stared at him. "I want to see the accounts."

Angie nodded. "That's right. Prove what you're saying is true, Howard."

"Prove it?" Doc looked offended. He turned to Shelby. "You don't believe me? After all I've done for you, you spend a couple of days with this person, and now you don't believe me anymore. I guess we don't have the relationship that I thought we did."

Doc looked as dejected as a stray dog. Mel would have felt sorry for him if she didn't suspect it was an act. Shelby looked like she was weakening but Angie shook her head at her. Shelby stiffened her spine and drew in a deep breath.

"I want to see the accounts, Doc, *all* of the accounts," she said. She crossed her arms over her chest as if to emphasize that she would no longer be a pushover.

"It'll take me some time to gather it all," Doc said.

"You have until showtime tomorrow," Shelby countered.

"And if I don't?" Doc raised one eyebrow and stared at her, daring her to give him a consequence.

"If you don't, you're fired," Shelby said.

Seven

"You wouldn't dare," he said. He put a hand over his chest as if he felt her words like a shot to the heart.

"Try me," she countered. They stared at each other as if trying to gauge who held the power in their relationship at the moment. Both seemed to realize it was Shelby.

"Are you happy now?" Doc sneered. He took a step closer and loomed over Angie, who didn't budge an inch. She simply tipped her chin up in defiance.

"Oh, come on now. Have a cupcake and settle down," Marty said. He reached back and snatched one of the boxes Mel had packed earlier off the table and shoved it at Doc. "If everything is on the up-and-up, and of course it is, then you have nothing to fret about, right?"

It was the plainest statement of fact, leaving Doc without an argument.

Doc's lips compressed into a thin line. "That's not the point."

"Maybe not, but it's still true," Marty said. "It would be completely irresponsible of Shelby to turn over her business affairs to anyone without occasionally checking them over herself. If she really is a daughter to you, then you'd want her to be active in the business side of things and know what's happening."

"It's not that simple," Doc blustered.

"Sure it is. I have two daughters. I know exactly how it is. I mean, what if you dropped dead right now? Shelby would be in a pickle if she didn't know what was what. So, you're really being a good manager by making certain she's fully up to speed." Marty put his arm around Doc and hustled him to the door. "Now, have some carbs and sugar and get your paperwork in order. We'll see you tomorrow. All right. Bye."

With a hearty shove, Marty sent Doc through the door and slammed it shut behind him. Then he brushed his palms together as if he'd just taken out the trash.

Shelby wilted as soon as the door was closed. She turned to Mel and Angie. "I was too hard on him, wasn't I? I should have asked nicely. Mama always says you catch more flies with honey than vinegar."

"But who wants flies?" Angie countered. "No one, that's who."

"Fair point," Shelby conceded.

"You did the right thing," Mel said. "It's important for you to know what's happening with your career."

"And your finances," Marty said. "Don't forget that all of this is because of you and your talent. No one else is getting all of these people paid. You are."

"That's right," Angie said. "And just so you don't start to second-guess yourself the moment we walk out the door, there's something I need to tell you."

Shelby's eyebrows went up. "Sounds serious."

"Potentially." Angie sighed. "My brother Ray saw Doc at the horse track and he was having a heated discussion with Jerry Stackhouse."

"Oh." Shelby nodded. "I'm not following. Who is Jerry Stackhouse?"

"He's a local loan shark," Marty said. "Not known for tolerating people who don't pay their debts."

"And you think Doc owes him money?" Shelby asked.

"Maybe?" Angie shrugged. "But I honestly don't see how he can say you're broke when you're on tour for more than three hundred nights per year, playing to full houses. It doesn't add up."

"This is a nightmare," Shelby said.

"I take it you had no idea," Mel said.

"That Doc gambled?" Shelby shrugged. "I'd seen him at the tables at a few of the casinos that I played but I thought he was just killing time."

"More like killing your dime," Angie said.

Shelby sighed. "I don't know what to think. I trusted him. He fronted a lot of my career costs after Diana . . . well, you know. I owe him a lot of money."

"Have you had an entertainment lawyer look over your contract before?" Mel asked. "It seems to me that a professional might be able to figure out what to do. Also, we could find you a forensic accountant. Someone who could do a deep dive into the books and really see what's what."

"Doc would be furious," Shelby said.

79

"You're not afraid of him, are you?" Angie asked.

"Of Doc?" Shelby asked. "No, he'd never hurt me."

"One would argue that playing fast and loose with your money is hurting you," Marty said. His tone was gentle but his point was solid.

"Why don't you sleep at my place tonight?" Angie asked. "I don't like the idea of you being under the same roof with Doc by yourself."

"No, I'll be fine," Shelby said. "Even if there is some financial chicanery afoot, I know that Doc would never harm me."

"But would Jerry Stackhouse?" Mel asked.

Shelby looked at her in confusion. "But I've never met him. I'd never even heard his name until you all told me about his altercation with Doc."

"Maybe you haven't met him but he knows who you are," Mel said. "He was here tonight."

"What?" Angie cried. "Why didn't you say anything?"

"It's been a little dramatic around here," Mel said. "Besides I didn't want to mention it in front of Doc. But, yes, Jerry Stackhouse was here with his daughter and he made a point of saying hello to me and mentioning the fact that he knew my husband was Joe DeLaura the prosecutor."

"Well, that's creepy," Angie said. "Why would he mention that?"

"I don't know," Mel said. "He seemed obsessed with the fact that I happened to have been in the vicinity of some murder cases, like I had anything to do with them besides being in the wrong place at the wrong time." No one said anything. "It's coincidence," Mel said. Still, they were silent and not making eye contact. "Hey!" she cried.

"You're right," Angie said. She held up her hands in a placating gesture. "Sorry, definitely total coincidence."

"One hundred percent," Marty agreed.

Somewhat mollified, Mel said, "Okay then."

"Do you think Stackhouse was here to collect a debt?" Marty asked.

"I don't know. His daughter Hayley is clearly a super-fan of Shelby's," Mel said. "But did he use a connection with Doc to get VIP seating? Or was there another reason he was here, like shaking down Doc for money owed? Again, I don't know."

"That decides it," Angie said. "Come on, Shelby, let's go pack a bag for you. You're definitely not staying here tonight."

"We'll finish cleaning up and pick you up out front in fifteen minutes," Mel said.

"Sounds like a plan," Angie said. "Call me if anything goes sideways."

"Likewise," Mel said.

Mel and Marty watched as the two women left the VIP suite. Mel felt her anxiety spike and she glanced at Marty. He was still wearing his ill-fitting Santa suit and while she loved him dearly, if Jerry Stackhouse sent some goons back here looking for Doc or Shelby, Marty was not going to be able to "ho ho ho" his way out of it.

She glanced at the table where the cupcakes were boxed. A rolling cart was beside the table, and she would load the few remaining boxes onto it. They would drop off the leftover cupcakes at a women's shelter on the way home.

"Why don't you go ahead and get the car?" Mel asked. "I'll wheel these out and meet you in front."

"I don't want to leave you here alone," Marty protested.

The door on the other side of the suite banged open and two of the dancers came in. They were makeup-free, their hair up in ponytails, one a blonde and the other a brunette. They were wearing yoga pants and crop tops with zip-up hoodies. Mel would have looked like a wrung-out dishrag if she'd performed for three hours but they looked peppy and ready to dance some more.

They were also staring at the floor as they walked around, obviously looking for something.

"I'll be fine," Mel said to Marty. "I have company now."

"All right, but if you're not out in fifteen, I'm coming back to get you," he said.

Mel watched him go and finished loading up the cart. The dancers were still searching and she had a few minutes to spare so she crossed the room and asked, "Did you lose something?"

The slighter of the two dancers, the brunette, glanced up with tears in her eyes. "An earring. It was a gift from my parents. It matches this one." She pointed to the light blue sparkly stud earring in her right earlobe. "I'll just be crushed if I lost it."

"It's a small square aquamarine," her friend said. "I'm sure we'll find it."

Mel took her phone out of her pocket and turned on the flashlight app. She crouched down and set the light level with the industrial carpeting. She moved the beam across the floor, looking for a glint. The two women moved to stand beside her as all three of them searched the carpet.

"Oh, what's that?" the blonde asked. She pointed under one of the tables.

The brunette crawled forward partway under the table and patted the ground with her hand. "That's it!" She snatched up the earring, pinching it between her two fingers. She held it up and examined it. "I must have lost the backing to it, but that's easily replaced."

"See? I told you we'd find it," her friend said. She glanced at Mel. "I'm Abby and this is Sarah."

"I'm Mel." She pointed to herself.

Sarah glanced at Mel with a watery smile. "Thank you so much."

"No problem, I'm glad we found it," she said.

She watched as the two women left the suite. She returned to her cart and started pushing it towards the door. A ripple of unease shivered through her as she realized she was alone, which was ridiculous because as soon as she cleared the door, she'd be in the main part of the auditorium, where there were bound to be more people, cleaning up after the show.

She reached the door and grabbed the handle, planning to pull the cart through after her. The door was locked. Huh. Marty had just left through that door. Weird. She pushed the cart across the room and tried the door that the dancers had exited through. It was locked, too.

She felt her heart speed up. Every instinct she had told her this was not good. The dancers had just left mere minutes ago. That meant that someone had locked the door after them. But who? And why? How could they not know she was in here? The lights were still on.

Mel turned and scanned the room. The festive decorations mocked her as the red and green garlands shimmered in the overhead lights. The tables had been cleared of refuse, the linens taken to be laundered, the food and drink stations all packed away for the night.

The locked doors had to be a mistake. Probably, just a cleaning person had assumed everyone was already out and had locked all the doors. Mel had her cell phone, so she could just call Marty and Angie and ask them to have someone unlock the door.

Mel took her phone out of her pocket and called Angie. It rolled over to voice mail, which was weird. But maybe not. Perhaps Angie and Shelby were in the elevator and the call wasn't going through. That seemed most likely. She tried Marty. He didn't answer, either.

Mel didn't know anyone else on the premises of the hotel. Tate was watching baby Emari. Joe was at home, working on a case, so she didn't want to bother either of them. She also did not want to call any of the brothers as they seemed to make a bigger deal out of things than they needed to and she was just too tired for that. Unfortunately, she didn't have Shelby's number or she would have tried her.

Maybe she'd just turned the handle the wrong way. Mel tried the door handle again, moving it in the other direction. It wouldn't budge. She crossed the room and tried the other one just in case. Same result. She was locked in. Her chest felt tight even though she knew there was no reason to panic. Someone would come along. Heck, Marty had said he'd be back in fifteen minutes.

Still she paced the room while trying to reach Angie and Marty. No one was picking up. Was the hotel on fire?

Was everyone running for their lives and here she was completely oblivious and trapped and probably about to be burned to death? There had been a close call with fire before. She still had nightmares about it.

There were no windows in here. It was the first time she'd noticed that. Since the VIP room was in the bowels of the auditorium behind the stage and in between some utility rooms, it wasn't exactly elegantly appointed. Basically, she could be trapped in here and no one would know until they went to open the room tomorrow. Also, there was no bathroom. Knowing this was not helpful as Mel's bladder took this as a signal to panic.

"Mel!" a voice shouted through the door.

"Marty!" Mel hurried to the door that Marty had departed through just a few minutes before. "Help! I'm locked in!"

"What?" Marty jiggled the handle on the door. It didn't budge. "How did that happen?"

"I don't know," Mel said.

"What?" Marty shouted.

"I. Don't. Know."

"I'm going to see if I can find someone to unlock the door," he said. "Don't go anywhere."

"Ha-ha." Mel slumped against the door. Now that someone knew she was stuck in the room, she felt her anxiety wane. Marty would get her out and everything would be okay.

She tried calling Angie again to let her know what was happening. This time Angie picked up on the second ring.

"Hey, Mel, where are you?" Angie asked. "I thought we were meeting you out front."

"That was the plan," Mel said.

"Oh, no, what happened? Are you okay?" Angie asked.

"I'm fine," Mel said. "But I'm locked in the VIP suite."

"What?" Angie asked. "How did that happen?"

"No idea," Mel said. "One minute I was helping some dancers find an earring and the next I was locked inside."

"I don't like this," Angie declared. "I'm coming right now."

"No, you don't want to risk running into Doc again," Mel said. "Marty's on it. Don't worry. We'll be out front in a few minutes."

"Shelby says we're coming," Angie said. "We'll be right there. Don't move."

Seriously? Mel thought. As if she had a choice. She leaned against the wall by the door. She resisted checking the time on her phone. She didn't want to get stressed out about how much sleep she was losing because of this ridiculous situation.

"Mel, you still in there?" Marty's voice came through the door.

"The door is still locked," Mel said. "So, yes, I'm here."

"I have the head of security with me," Marty said. "He has a key."

"Great! Thank you." Mel felt bad about being surly but she really did have to use the bathroom now.

She could hear the jingle of keys and a man said, "Nope that's not it." She didn't recognize the deep voice, so she assumed it was the security guard. "Not that one. Nuh-uh. Huh, which one could it be?"

Mel jogged her leg up and down while trying to be patient.

"Give me those," Marty said. "It has to be on here, right?"

"Yeah," the other person said.

"Marty, where is Mel?" Angie asked.

"She's still in there," Marty said. "We can't find the key to get her out."

"Why is the door locked on the inside, too?" Shelby asked. "She should be able to open it on her side. This seems like it would go against the building code."

"It was intended as a storage room, not a lounge," the man with the keys answered.

"Should we break it down?" Angie asked.

Mel was only surprised that it had taken her this long to suggest the most forceful way to open the door, Angie being Angie and all.

"We may have to," the security guard said.

"I've got this," Marty said. "Everyone stand clear."

"Marty, no, don't—" Angie's words were cut off and a moment later a sickening thud sounded on the other side of the door followed by a low moan.

"Did you dislocate your shoulder?" Angie asked. "I told you not to do that."

"I just need a little more speed," Marty protested.

"No!" Angie and Mel shouted together from opposite sides of the door.

"What's the ruckus?" Although she'd only met him the one time, Mel recognized Jerry Stackhouse's voice. That couldn't be good. Had he been the one to lock her in the room? Maybe he was trying to intimidate her like when he mentioned her prosecutor husband. Or maybe he thought someone was going to die just because Mel was in the vicinity. He'd certainly seemed freaked out by her uncanny ability to come across dead bodies. He wasn't alone in that.

"The door's locked and we can't get it open," Shelby said. "Our friend is stuck in there."

"No one has a key?" Jerry asked. There was a rattling sound and Mel imagined the security person was holding up his keys. "We'll be here all night if we try to go through all of those."

"Which is why I was trying to break it down," Marty said.

"You're lucky you didn't break yourself in half." A woman spoke, but Mel couldn't identify her.

"Hey!" Marty protested.

"Regina, why is this door locked from both sides?" Shelby asked. So, it was the hotel owner, Regina Bessette. The way Shelby said her name, Mel got the feeling there was no love lost between the two women.

"Shelby," Regina returned. Her voice was equally as frosty. "Great show tonight."

There was a brief pause and then Shelby said, "Thank you."

"I especially enjoyed the final number," Regina said. "Very touching."

"I appreciate your saying so," Shelby said. She sounded wary and Mel didn't blame her.

"Trevor, how are you the head of security and you don't know which key to use on this door?" Regina snapped.

"This door isn't usually locked," the man answered. "Just give me a second." There was another rattle of keys and then a click and the door swung open.

Mel dashed outside, leaving her cart behind. She

didn't think that she was imagining that the air was cooler and fresher out here. Even though she felt several pairs of assessing eyes on her person and she probably should have played it cool, she sucked in a huge gulp of air. She didn't care. She was free.

"Mel, are you all right?" Angie grabbed her in a fierce hug.

"I'm fine," Mel said. "I just really need to use a restroom."

"There's one in my dressing room," Shelby said. "It's right over there."

She pointed to a door at the end of the hall, and Mel said, "Thanks." She hurried in that direction. With her luck, she half expected Shelby's dressing room to be locked but it wasn't. She turned the handle and pushed the door open. It was dark, so she reached for the light switch, hoping it was to the right of the door. It was and the overhead lights snapped on.

She stepped into the room and then jumped back with a yelp. Lying on the floor, his head resting in a pool of blood, was Doc Howard. As Mel took in the sight, she noted the box of cupcakes Marty had given him was on the floor beside him and clutched in his hand was one of their Sugar Plum cupcakes.

This was bad. So very bad.

Eight

"Help!" The cry came out softer than she'd intended but Mel couldn't seem to get enough breath for a full bellow. "Help!" The second attempt was no better so she staggered back out of the room.

Her friends were waiting for her at the end of the hall, as were Regina and Jerry and the security man. She tried to yell. Still nothing. She lifted her arm and waved. Angie gave her a puzzled look and waved back. Something in Mel's face must have clued her in that there was a situation.

"Mel, are you all right?" Angie asked.

Mel shook her head. This she could answer. "No. Call an ambulance."

"What? Why? Are you sick?" Angie hurried towards

her. Marty and Shelby fell in behind her with matching expressions of concern.

"Not me." Mel stepped away from the door and pointed into Shelby's dressing room. "Doc."

"Doc?" Shelby cried. She passed Angie and hurried into the room, stopping short when she saw Doc lying on the ground. "What happened?"

"I don't know," Mel said. She shivered and Angie's arm immediately went around her.

Shelby dropped to her knees beside her manager. "Doc. Doc, can you hear me?" She grabbed his hand and a scrap of fluffy white fabric, like the trim on the dancers' Santa outfits, fell out of his fingers.

Mel glanced at the others. Both Regina and Jerry looked alarmed while the security person Trevor was open-mouthed in shock. It took the man a moment to shake it off and he hurried into the room to assist Shelby.

"I know CPR," he said. He dropped into a crouch beside her and reached out to feel for a pulse under Doc's jaw. The pool of blood beneath Doc's head saturated the carpet. Both Shelby and the security guard ignored it. The guard frowned and moved his hand, pushing his fingers more firmly against Doc's jaw. He shook his head and then leaned forward and put his ear to Doc's chest. After a moment, he rocked back on his heels. "I'm sorry, Ms. Vaughn. He's gone."

"What do you mean?" she asked. She leaned forward. "Doc, can you hear me? You need to wake up. Come on, Doc. I'm sorry for what I said. I'd never fire you. I swear."

"Ms. Vaughn, he can't hear you," the security guard

said. He looked pasty pale and he swallowed as if he was about to be sick.

"No." Shelby shook her head. "Don't say it."

"There's no pulse or heartbeat, his chest isn't moving, he's not breathing. He's d—"

"No." Shelby backed away as if she could outrun his words. "This isn't possible. We just saw him and he was fine."

The security guard spread his hands wide. He glanced around the room. "Somehow he must have hit his head. Maybe he fainted and smacked his head on something on his way down. I don't know. I'm not an expert on this sort of thing but I do know he's no longer with us. I'm so sorry, Ms. Vaughn." His voice broke. It was clear he was fighting to keep it together.

"No, this is impossible." Shelby's voice was getting higher with each word. "I already lost Diana, I can't lose Doc, too."

Mel glanced at the others. No one seemed to know what to say to her. Not even Angie. Marty was on his phone calling for an ambulance while Regina went immediately into problem-solving mode.

She spoke to the security guard. "Trevor, we'll need you to stay here until the police arrive. Everyone else needs to leave the room. This is a potential crime scene and we don't want to compromise it."

"Crime scene?" Shelby asked. "What are you talking about?"

Regina's eyebrows went up. "The man is lying in a puddle of his own blood."

"But Trevor said he probably fainted and hit his head,"

Shelby argued. They all stared at her with varying degrees of sympathy. "He could have."

"Let's leave it to the police to determine, Shelby," Angie said. "I think you need to get out of here."

"I don't want to leave him," Shelby said. "I'll stay until the ambulance comes."

"Admirable, my dear," Regina said. "But the police won't thank you for it. You'd be better served leaving the room and finding someplace quiet to reflect upon your relationship with Doc and whether or not the police will consider you a suspect in his murder."

"Murder?" Shelby gaped at her. "What are you saying?"

"That man did not hit his head," Marty said. "He's in the middle of the room next to a soft chair. There's no sharp edges or corners that he could have hit his head on. It's pretty clear that someone wanted him dead and they killed him."

Trevor called for backup security personnel and stood outside the dressing room keeping it off-limits to anyone but the police and the crime scene unit.

"Are you all right?" Angie asked Shelby while they waited to talk to the police. "Sorry. Stupid question. What can I do for you?"

"You're doing it," Shelby said. "Just by being here and being my friend, you're doing it." She turned to Mel. "You both are."

"Happy to help," Mel said. Although *happy* wasn't

exactly the word she'd choose if she had full capacity of her brain, it was the best she could come up with, being freaked out and exhausted.

She'd called Joe and told him the situation. He wanted to come join her but Mel told him not to since her uncle, a detective with the Scottsdale Police Department, was here and would look out for her. Joe didn't like it but Mel diverted him by asking him to find out anything he could about Doc Howard's past, such as any jail time served, or potential enemies he might have had.

Mel, Angie, and Shelby were sitting on the edge of the stage in the auditorium. The police had told them not to leave the premises. Most of the show's staff had left for the night before Doc's body was found, making the number of people who needed to be questioned fewer than it would have been if the entire cast and crew were still in the building. So far, no one had reported seeing or hearing anything suspicious that could be related to Doc's death.

"Shelby! Shelby!" They all turned to see Cheryl, Shelby's stylist, racing towards them. Her eyes were wide and she had a bright green bandanna tied around her hair. She was wearing a white terry cloth Hotel Grande robe and slippers and she scuffed her feet across the floor, not bothering to pick them up.

"Cheryl!" Shelby pushed off the stage and raced towards her.

Cheryl hugged her tight. "Thank goodness you're all right. Erin, you know, the dancer who wears the snowflake costume, just banged on my door and told me what happened. I can't believe it!"

"It's horrible, Cheryl. Doc is dead and it looks li . . .

like . . . someone killed him." Shelby's voice broke and she sobbed.

Cheryl tut-tutted while she patted Shelby's back. "Oh, honey, I'm so sorry. I know you were fond of him, despite his overbearing nature."

"I just can't help feeling like it's my fault," Shelby said.

Cheryl drew back and stared at her. Her look was stern. "Now, Shel, why would you ever think such a thing?"

"Because Diana died and now Doc." Shelby raised her hands in the air as if asking the universe to explain why. "And the only thing they had in common was . . . me."

"Now you listen to me, Shelby Vaughn." Cheryl cupped Shelby's face, met her gaze, and held it. "Whatever happened to them has nothing to do with you. Nothing. They were simply your managers, which is a business relationship. You can't possibly know what they got up to in their personal lives, and I'd bet dollars to donuts that whatever got Doc killed was something he was doing that had nothing to do with you."

"Maybe." Shelby didn't sound convinced.

"There is no maybe about it, honey," Cheryl said. "You are the star, they are merely your employees, like me. If I got murdered would you think it was your fault?"

Shelby's eyebrows rose.

"I'm not saying I'm going to get murdered," Cheryl said. "I'm just sayin' if I did, it would be because the wife of the superhot wine salesman I met in the bar found out he was stomping grapes with me on the side." She gave Shelby an exaggerated wink. Shelby's lips twitched, and Cheryl said, "It would have nothing to do with you, okay?"

"I see what you're getting at," Shelby said. She hugged her tight. "Thanks, Cheryl."

"You're welcome," she said. "Now is there anything you need? Do you have to wait here? Or can you go to your suite and try to get some rest? I have some of those sleeping pills you take when you have to sleep on the tour bus. You could take one of those to help you relax."

"Oh, I don't think I'll be relaxing or sleeping tonight," Shelby said. "In fact, Angie invited me to her place for the night so I can get away from here for a bit."

Cheryl looked past Shelby at Angie and said, "You're a good friend, Angie. That's just what our Shelby needs, to put some distance between herself and all this. Don't you have a baby, though? Is this too much?"

"No, it's no trouble at all," Angie said. "Emari's been sleeping through the night for a while now."

Mel looked at Angie and noted that she twirled one of her long brunette curls around her index finger. This was Angie's tell. Whenever she fibbed, she twirled her hair around her finger. But why would she lie about Emari sleeping? Weird.

"Mel, can I speak to you for a second?" Detective Stanley Cooper, Mel's uncle, appeared in the doorway that led to the backstage area where the VIP lounge and the dressing rooms were.

"Sure," she said. She turned to the others and said, "I'll be right back."

"Find out what he knows," Angie said.

"I'll try but you know how Uncle Stan is," Mel said.

Angie nodded. She knew. Mel smiled reassuringly, or what she hoped appeared reassuringly, at Shelby. The poor thing looked wrecked and Mel knew that her last conversation with her manager had to be weighing heavily upon her at the moment.

Uncle Stan led Mel back down the hallway where the VIP suite and the dressing rooms were. He glanced over his shoulder at her. "You all right, being back here?"

"I'm fine," Mel said. She wasn't fine but she was better than Doc, so she didn't want to make a fuss.

"You've told me what happened," Uncle Stan said. "But I wanted you to go over what happened while you were in the locked room."

Mel repeated what she'd told him previously, trying to determine whether she'd left anything important out but she couldn't think of any new details.

"How long were you locked in?" he asked.

"Marty said he'd come get me if I wasn't out in fifteen minutes," Mel answered. "So, it had to be for longer than fifteen minutes but the two dancers were in there with me for a bit of the time at least, so maybe I was locked in for ten minutes?"

"Long enough for someone to bludgeon Doc Howard and run," Uncle Stan said.

"He was still holding the box of cupcakes and had one in his hand," Mel said. "Seems to me that means someone surprised him while he was choosing his cupcake. I mean how long does it take to crack someone on the head with . . . ?"

She let the sentence dangle, hoping that Stan would fill in the blank on what the murder weapon was. He didn't bite. Darn it.

She decided to be more direct. "Any idea what happened to him?"

"Yes." That was all Uncle Stan said. He frowned and glanced down the hallway where they'd left Shelby and Angie. "What do you know about Shelby's relationship with Doc Howard?"

"He became her manager when her previous manager Diana died in a house fire," Mel said.

"House fire?" Uncle Stan's eyebrows rose.

"Shelby was very close to her," Mel said. She didn't like the suspicious look on Uncle Stan's face. "She took Diana's death hard and Doc stepped in to represent her."

"But they didn't get along?" Uncle Stan asked. He was looking slimmer these days but he still patted his pants pocket looking for an antacid tablet. Despite Stan being a homicide detective, murder always gave him heartburn.

"I don't know about that," Mel said. "I only know that they had some creative differences and potentially some financial issues."

"What sort?" Uncle Stan asked. "Not the creative, the financial."

"Doc Howard said that Shelby was broke," Mel said. "That's why she's not home with her family this Christmas but is working through the holiday."

"So she's mad she had to work?" he asked.

"No, I mean, she misses her family, but she's fulfilling her contract," Mel said. "But she looked shocked when Doc told her she was broke. Apparently, she works three hundred days out of the year, so she can't understand how she's run out of money."

"That's a lot of time on the road," Uncle Stan said. "You wouldn't think she'd have time to spend what she earns."

"I don't think she was the one spending it," Mel said. "Angie's brother Ray saw Doc Howard at the track having words with Jerry Stackhouse."

"The loan shark?"

"And he was here tonight," Mel said. "He brought his daughter, who appeared to be a huge fan of Shelby's, to the show."

"I thought I saw him," he said. "Detective Martinez took his statement, along with the hotel owner Regina Bessette and the security guard. I can follow up with Martinez. It's certainly quite a coincidence that Stackhouse and Howard had words and then Howard ends up dead."

"But you don't believe in coincidences," Mel reminded him.

"No, I don't."

"I wish I had more to tell you, but I didn't see anything, given that I was contained in the VIP suite and all," Mel said.

"Do you have any idea how you got locked in there?" Uncle Stan asked. "It seems weird. Like if someone was locking up, wouldn't they poke their head in and check and see that the room was clear?"

"You'd think," Mel agreed.

A sound from Shelby's dressing room caught their attention. Mel craned her neck to see around Uncle Stan and caught a glimpse of a crime scene tech dressed in their Tyvek coveralls as they walked past the doorway.

"There's no chance that Doc accidentally hit his head, is there?" she asked.

Uncle Stan opened his mouth and then closed it. Mel

waited. She knew he was trying to figure out what to tell her, knowing that she had a propensity for getting involved in his investigations.

"There is nothing in the room that indicates that he fell and hit his head," he said.

"So, there's no blood on the corner of a table or anything like that?" Mel asked.

"Exactly," Uncle Stan said. "Whatever crushed the back of his head was removed from the room." Mel cringed. And Stan said, "Sorry. I forget you're not a cop sometimes."

"Because I'm so good at solving cases," Mel said.

"No, because you're always underfoot during investigations," he retorted.

A gurney was pushed through the door by an employee from the medical examiner's office. Strapped to the top was a black body bag. Doc. Mel glanced down the hallway to see if Angie and Shelby could see this. They couldn't and mercifully, the technician pushed the gurney in the opposite direction, to an emergency exit.

"We were told that the hotel owner, Regina Bessette, wants to keep this as quiet as possible," Uncle Stan said. "I understand the need to not upset the hotel guests but a man was murdered here. I don't know how she thinks the show is just going to go on like nothing happened."

"She doesn't actually think Shelby is still going to be able to perform, does she?" Mel asked.

"I'm just relaying the message we were told," Uncle Stan said. "I have no idea what she expects."

"Angie was already going to have Shelby stay with her tonight," Mel said. "Is it okay if she does? You're not going to arrest Shelby, are you?"

"If I was, she'd already be down at the station," he said. "According to Angie, Shelby was with her, so she has an alibi. I'll let her go for now."

"Good," Mel said. "She's a nice person and it makes no sense for her to have harmed Doc. I mean, she just found out about his gambling and asked to see the books. She didn't have any proof that he was gambling away her money, so why would she have hurt him?"

"Rage? Resentment? Revenge?"

Mel glanced at her uncle to see if he was serious. She couldn't picture Shelby exhibiting any of those emotions strongly enough to commit murder. Of course, Uncle Stan didn't know Shelby as well as Mel did. Uncle Stan was a career police officer and he tended to take a dim look at his fellow man. Mel supposed that thirty-plus years of catching bad guys would do that to a person.

Uncle Stan was her father's younger brother and had stepped into the father role when Mel's father had passed over ten years ago. Recently, he had begun dating Mel's mom and while it was a bit odd, it also felt right. Judging by the set of his chin, he had not been kidding when he suggested rage, resentment, and revenge as motives.

"Again, she didn't have proof that he was gambling with her money, so why would she be feeling any of those emotions?" Mel asked.

"Money makes people crazy." He shrugged. He wasn't wrong but Mel just didn't see it being the case in this situation.

"Not Shelby," Mel said. "The only thing that seemed to be bringing her down was working through the holiday and not being able to go home to Tennessee to be with her family."

Uncle Stan raised his eyebrows. "Do tell."

"Not like that," Mel said. "I didn't mean she would have bludgeoned Doc over it. She's just homesick, that's all. I think staying with Angie will be good for her. Life on the road has to be hard for a woman so young. Other than her stylist, Cheryl, she doesn't seem to have many friends. The dancers are all in awe of her because she's the big talent and I think Doc kept her somewhat isolated."

"What makes you say that?" Uncle Stan asked.

"He wasn't thrilled that she and Angie are such good friends," Mel said. "He really tried to put up some boundaries in the beginning to keep Angie at arm's length."

"Any idea why?"

"Control?" Mel guessed. "He and Angie really squared off about Shelby singing some originals in her show. He wanted it to be straight-up Christmas songs but Angie felt like Shelby was missing an opportunity to showcase her talent."

"I have to agree with Angie on that one," Uncle Stan said. "That is an unusual position for a manager to take."

"We thought so, too," Mel said. "It's another reason I think Shelby would do better away from here. There was a lot going on and things were tense."

"All right, let's go tell Ms. Vaughn she can go home with Angie. Come on," Uncle Stan said. "I'll walk you back. You look dead on your feet."

Mel stared at him.

"Sorry. No pun intended, I promise," Uncle Stan said.

They walked back up the hallway towards the auditorium, where Angie was waiting with Shelby.

As they cleared the door, Mel saw a dark-haired woman

standing in front of Shelby and shouting, "Did you kill Doc, too? Did he not make you famous enough overnight so you decided to murder him just like you did my mother?"

"Well, well, well," Uncle Stan said as they entered the room. "Who do we have here?"

Nine

"Hey!" Angie said. "I don't know who you think you are, but—"

"Angie Harper, meet Lisa Martin, Diana's daughter," Shelby said. She looked pale and exhausted. It was clear she was at her breaking point.

"Diana Martin, your manager?" Angie asked.

Shelby nodded.

The young woman was petite, even slighter than Shelby, and her dark hair reached almost to her narrow waist. She was wearing a minidress and very high heels. Her makeup was natural-looking, accentuating her full mouth and wide eyes. She was lovely, except for the frown that marred her forehead and the slight curl to her upper lip. She leaned forward into Angie's space. "I'll tell you who I am. I'm the daughter who was pushed aside for the conniving calculating singer that my mother thought was a phenom."

Shelby lowered her head and stared at the floor. She looked crushed. Mel hated that this woman was heaping on her at a time like this but she had no idea how to stop it. Even Angie seemed flummoxed.

"She was wrong. Look at you, belting out Christmas carols like a two-bit lounge singer." Lisa sneered. The contempt in her voice was sharp enough to cut, and Mel saw Shelby flinch.

"I'm sorry for your loss," Angie said. "But you need to leave. You're attacking the wrong person and I won't stand for it."

"Oh my god, don't tell me, let me guess. You're Shelby's new manager, aren't you?" Lisa asked. "Are you really so good that she'd murder for you?"

"I'm not her manager, I'm her friend," Angie protested.

Lisa threw back her head and laughed. It was humorless and she quickly became serious and said, "Shelby doesn't have friends."

"Clearly, that's not true," Angie said.

"I was her friend before my mother signed her, did you know that?" Lisa asked. "Shelby and I worked the pageant circuit together. Best friends. We even called each other 'sis,' as in 'sisters from different misters.'"

Mel went still. That was exactly what Shelby and Angie called each other. She glanced at Angie to see if this registered any alarm. It didn't seem to. If anything, Angie's face became even harder, her mouth tight and her eyes narrowed.

"So, you're angry because your mother saw that Shelby

was more talented than you?" Angie asked. It was a direct hit. Lisa's face turned an alarming shade of red.

"She's not," Lisa insisted. "She's just a better manipulator than I am. I mean, what sort of mother would send her daughter away to live with her father and his new wife so she could go on tour with her daughter's best friend?"

"I'm sorry," Shelby said. "When your mom offered to represent me, I didn't know that she just meant me."

"Liar!" Lisa spat. "You and my mother cooked it up together. 'How do we get rid of Lisa' was probably a nightly conversation between you two. And then what happened, my mother wasn't good enough for you? Your star didn't rise fast enough? So you murdered her, didn't you?"

Shelby shook her head. "I didn't, I swear."

"As if I'd ever believe anything you had to say." Lisa glared. "You murdered my mother and I'll be damned if you get away with it."

Mel glanced at Uncle Stan. He was watching the conversation intently as if trying to shuck the lies from the truth.

"I didn't murder Diana," Shelby said. "Whatever issues you had with her—"

"I didn't have any issues!" Lisa shouted. "We were very close. She was my best friend until you came along."

Shelby glanced away as if trying to keep herself from saying anything that might upset Lisa even more.

"You know, I got to know Diana pretty well a few summers ago," Angie said. "She didn't strike me as the sort of person who was easily manipulated. She was an excellent read of people, very kind but also quite firm, including not wasting her time representing someone who had no future in the business."

"How did you—?" Lisa blinked furiously as if trying to figure out how Angie had just disrupted her narrative so effectively. She frowned at Angie and asked, "Who are you?"

"I told you, I'm Shelby's friend," Angie said. "And while we're both devastated by Diana's passing, Shelby didn't have anything to do with it."

Lisa shook her head at Angie as if she thought she was too stupid to live. "You're just another sucker caught in Shelby's thrall. She'll betray you. Just like she's betrayed everyone who's ever cared for her."

"You're wrong." Angie's voice was as strong as steel. Her loyalty for those she loved never wavered. It was one of the things Mel admired most about her. Knowing that this altercation was going nowhere, Mel moved to stand on Shelby's other side.

"Shelby, Uncle Stan says you're free to go," Mel said. She glanced at Lisa, who was fuming, clearly feeling thwarted. Mel never could stand a bully and she certainly wasn't going to watch Lisa continue to badger Shelby when the singer was at her lowest.

"Wait, I have some ques—" Uncle Stan protested, but Mel whipped around and stared at him, interrupting his train of thought. Uncle Stan blinked. "You look just like your mother when you make that face."

"And?"

"Ms. Vaughn can leave with you and Angie," he said. He looked past Mel at Shelby. "I'll be in touch with you tomorrow if I have any more questions."

"Thank you," Shelby said. Her voice was soft.

"Who are you, Uncle Stan, and why do you have any say?" Lisa sputtered.

"Pardon me, where are my manners?" Angie said. "Lisa Martin, this is Detective Stanley Cooper of the Scottsdale Police Department."

Lisa let out a disgusted huff. "How very convenient that you're friends with the local police."

"Not friends," Angie corrected her. "Related."

"He's my uncle," Mel said.

"Of course he is," Lisa snapped. She shook her head at Shelby. "Your life is so charmed. Everything always works out for you, doesn't it? Even murder."

Shelby blanched and turned to Angie. "Can we go?"

"Of course, Marty is waiting with the car," Angie said. "Are you ready, Mel?"

"More than," Mel said. She turned to Uncle Stan. "I'll call you later."

"Please do," he said. "And if any of you think of anything you think I should know, call me immediately."

They all nodded and Mel gave him a quick hug.

"So that's it?" Lisa cried. "You're really just letting her walk away? You're as bad as the Vegas police when my mother died. They didn't do anything, either."

"Your mother's house was in Vegas?" Uncle Stan asked.

"Yes, that's where we lived . . . she lived," Lisa said. "The detectives said she died in a house fire and that it was an accident, but I don't believe it. My mother was dead for just two weeks and this . . . this killer . . . moved on to new representation." She waved her hand at Shelby, who shook her head.

"It wasn't like that," Shelby protested. "Doc Howard

came to me and offered to take over because I had no idea how to navigate the business. I didn't go looking for him."

"Right," Lisa scoffed.

"Enough," Angie said. "Come on, Shelby. You don't have to listen to this."

She took Shelby's arm and led her up the aisle towards the exit. Mel glanced at Uncle Stan and then at Lisa. "Who did you talk to in the Las Vegas police department?"

Lisa frowned. "An arrogant jerk of a detective called Manny Martinez. Why?"

"No reason," Mel said. She glanced at Uncle Stan, who met her gaze with an expression that clearly said, *Stop.*

"Ms. Martin, why don't you tell me what you know about your mother's death," Uncle Stan said. "Maybe I can get some answers for you."

"Phbth," Lisa huffed. "Sure you can." Despite the skepticism in her voice, she began to talk.

Mel left Uncle Stan to find out what he could. Meanwhile she planned to call her old friend Manny in Las Vegas and see what he remembered about the case. She absolutely didn't think Shelby had anything to do with Diana's death but she had to admit it seemed awfully suspicious to have two managers die in such a short span of time while representing the same client. Mel wondered if Shelby had an enemy she wasn't aware of. It would certainly explain why those closest to her kept dying.

She caught up to Angie and Shelby in the lobby of the hotel. Marty was waiting in an armchair by the front door. He had his arms crossed over his chest, and his head was tipped back. As she got closer, she heard the distinct sound of a dog growling. She glanced around the lobby but there were no dogs. It took her a beat to realize the noise was coming from Marty. He was snoring.

"Hey!" Angie tapped Marty's shoe with her foot. "Rise and shine, princess."

"What? Huh? Oh." Marty opened his eyes and then shook his head. "I was awake."

Mel smiled and held out her hand. "Let's go home."

Marty took it and let her pull him up to his feet. Together they left the hotel and stepped out into the night, taking Shelby with them.

Joe was still up and prepping for his court case when Mel arrived home. Together, they took their dog out to the yard and while Peanut did her business, Mel told him all of the events of the evening.

He hugged her close and asked, "Are you okay? That had to be terrifying."

"It was definitely awful," Mel said. "But I knew once I saw him that it was bad and the key was to call for help, so I did. I didn't get too close, which feels cowardly now, but it really was because I knew, I just knew he was beyond help."

"I'm sorry," Joe said. "How is Shelby taking it?"

"Pretty hard," Mel said. "Of course, it didn't help that almost immediately afterwards, someone accused her of murder." She told Joe about the fierce accusation from Lisa Martin.

"What is Lisa doing here if she lives in Las Vegas?" Joe asked.

"Stalking Shelby?" Mel suggested.

"Because she blames her for her mother's death."

"It certainly sounded that way," Mel said. "And it turns out that the detective she spoke to on the LVPD is none other than our old friend Manny Martinez."

"Uncle Stan's old partner," Joe said. "Small world."

"Yup."

"The one who was interested in you," Joe said. He gave her a look that said he hadn't forgotten his would-be rival for her affection.

Mel laughed. "Until he found a cupcake baker of his own."

"Is Stan going to reach out to him?"

"Definitely," Mel said. "Not that anyone believes what Lisa was saying. I mean Shelby murdering her old manager by burning down her house is pretty out there."

"You didn't like Shelby very much when she and Angie were bouncing around Los Angeles," Joe said. "What changed?"

"In my defense, I didn't know her. And at the time, I might have been a little worried that Shelby was coming between me and my best friend," Mel said. "Plus, the entire time Angie was dating Roach, I was left to deal with Tate."

"Heartbroken Tate was pretty awful," Joe agreed.

"He was an unshowered, scraggly, smelly man mess," Mel said. "He started scaring away customers. Marty had to threaten to hose him down if he didn't get it together."

Joe laughed. "I remember. He was hardly the suave investment analyst he'd been known to be at the time."

"I didn't expect to like Shelby," Mel admitted. "When Angie was with Roach, it was always 'Shelby this and

Shelby that' while I was stuck here holding down the bakery but now I can see why Angie became close friends with her. She's really sweet and for all her tremendous talent, very humble. I just don't see her as a murderer, which is backed up by her alibi. She was with Angie when Doc was murdered, so it can't have been Shelby."

Peanut barked at a leaf that fell from one of their citrus trees, and then got a case of the zoomies and booked it around the yard as fast as her Boston terrier legs could carry her. Mel and Joe exchanged a doting look.

"All right, putting aside your newfound fondness for her, I suppose the question is, Do you think Doc's gambling and the fact that he was likely embezzling her money and leaving her broke could have turned her into a murderer?"

"Again, no, because she was with Angie," Mel said.

"She could have hired someone to commit the murder for her," Joe countered.

"Meaning?"

"Just because she was with Angie when Doc was bludgeoned to death doesn't mean she didn't have something to do with it," he said. Mel opened her mouth to speak and he held up his hand. "Yes, I know you said she seems genuine but that doesn't mean she isn't psychotically ambitious."

The night air suddenly seemed to drop in temperature and Mel shivered. She hadn't thought about the possibility of Shelby hiring someone to kill for her. Joe was right. If Shelby was a stone-cold sociopath, she could keep up the facade of sweet innocence while someone did the dirty deed for her.

"I don't want to believe it," Mel said. Peanut finished her yard recon and trotted over to them.

Mel bent down and scratched the dog behind the ears, her favorite spot. "I suppose anything is possible, except Shelby didn't know about Doc's gambling until we told her tonight."

"Assuming she was telling the truth about that," he said.

"Right." Mel sighed. "But there are other people with motives. I don't want to get fixated on Shelby just because Lisa is trying to plant seeds of doubt. Why is Lisa even here? She lives in Vegas. What is she doing in Scottsdale? Unless she murdered Doc and is trying to frame Shelby to try and ruin her. It was very clear that she had issues about Shelby's relationship with her mother Diana."

"She's definitely worth looking at," Joe agreed. "Didn't you say Jerry Stackhouse was there, too?"

"Yes, sitting in the VIP section with his daughter," Mel said. "Doesn't that seem suspicious after he was seen arguing with Doc at the track?"

"Maybe Stackhouse really wanted tickets to the show for his daughter and that's what he and Doc were arguing about," Joe suggested.

"Maybe, but with Doc's gambling issues, it seems unlikely. Turns out there are several people who had a beef with Doc," Mel said. "Including his ex-wife, Miranda Carter, who he threw over for Shelby and who chewed him out in front of everyone during a rehearsal."

"The plot thickens," Joe said.

Peanut trotted past them and scratched at the back door.

"Business accomplished," Mel said to Joe and he smiled.

Joe opened the door for Peanut and they followed her into the house, where Captain Jack sat on the counter, where he wasn't supposed to be, waiting for the evening treats that had become a habit for their furry crew.

"I don't suppose I could talk you and Angie out of working the VIP suite for the rest of Shelby's shows?" Joe asked.

"Not likely, no," Mel said. "Angie won't abandon her friend and I won't abandon Angie."

"I figured," Joe said. "It's one of the things I love about you." He kissed the top of her head. "Try not to worry, cupcake, we'll figure it out."

\ ' \ \ '

"This is Joe's idea of 'figuring it out'?" Angie asked. She stared at her three brothers all in matching Santa outfits where they stood beside Marty, also in his Santa outfit, holding trays full of cupcakes.

"You know how Joe is," Mel said. "And I believe Tate was in league with him on this."

"Of course he was," Angie said. She tried to look annoyed but there was a small, very small, pleased smile on her lips. "I suppose it's nice to know they care."

"I'm trying to tell myself that," Mel said. "Ray, get your finger out of the cupcake frosting!"

"It was lopsided," Ray protested. "I was trying to even it out."

Mel took the Gingerbread Man cupcake that Ray had

poked off his tray and put it to the side. "You can eat it later."

"Or I could eat it now," he offered. "To keep from cluttering up your area."

"Later," Mel said. She whipped her head to the side, where Al and Paulie were holding trays of their own. "Don't even think about it."

Al slowly withdrew his hand, which had almost made contact with a Sugar Cookie cupcake.

"Smart move," Marty said out of the corner of his mouth. "Mel can be persnickety about presentation."

"I am not persnickety," Mel said. "I am merely saving the cupcakes for the people who actually paid for them."

"Given that we're doing this job and are dressed like this," Paulie said, "I feel that a little confectionary compensation is not out of order."

"Later," Mel said again. She gave them her best reproving look. "Do you really think I wouldn't reward you for this? Even though, for the record, this was not my idea."

The three brothers exchanged a pleased look and Marty rolled his eyes. "The doors are about to open. Can we get it together? Shelby could be in danger and we need to look out for her."

"I thought we were here to keep an eye on Mel and Angie," Al said. He was staring at the cupcakes on his tray as if trying to decide which one he would eat first when he was allowed.

"Well, of course, but we also need to protect Shelby," Marty said.

Despite there being no evidence that Shelby was a

target, Marty had decided that someone had murdered both of her managers to get to her. The whole situation was suspicious enough that Mel thought he might be onto something. It made sense. What if the target was Shelby and both of her managers had inadvertently died in her stead?

Uncle Stan was working that angle, looking for any stalkers in Shelby's life who might be planning to use her standing gig at the Hotel Grande as an opportunity to harm her. So far, he hadn't had much luck.

"Doors are opening," called a silver-haired man in a black suit. He was one of the hotel personnel in charge of the VIP suite and he had been on edge all during setup. Mel remembered that his name was Robert and he took his job very, very seriously.

"Places," Mel said. The brothers and Marty hefted their trays. They formed a line in front of the cupcake station but as soon as the doors opened, they would begin to work the room.

Mel and Angie moved behind the counter, where they would assist anyone who came directly to them for a cupcake. Tonight, they wouldn't be attending the show but would stay in the VIP room, along with the other vendors, until the second meet and greet was over.

"I'm nervous," Angie whispered as Robert opened the doors and people began to pour in.

"Me, too," Mel said. "But there's no reason to be. We have the brothers, and Uncle Stan has officers watching the crowd and Shelby specifically to make sure no harm comes to her or anyone else."

"I just can't believe she's back here tonight," Angie said. "They only gave her one day off after her manager was murdered. Shouldn't there be a bereavement clause in her contract or something? If she had the flu, they wouldn't expect her to be out there singing her heart out, would they?"

"Sadly, if she was about to give birth, I think they'd expect her to give birth during the intermission and get back onstage for the finale. It does seem to be a heartless business," Mel said. "I suppose Shelby could have refused. I wonder why she didn't."

"She said she doesn't want to get a reputation for being a spoiled diva."

"That doesn't even seem possible." Mel remembered how she felt after her father died. "I wish she could cancel the show and go see her family. I feel like she needs her people right now."

"Agreed, but she's afraid Regina, who put a lot of the money behind this show, will hit her with a breach of contract," Angie said. "Never mind that Shelby might get murdered, the show must go on. Am I right?"

"Shh, here comes Regina now," Mel said.

"Good, I'd like to give her a piece of my mind," Angie said.

"Which is why I'll do the talking," Mel said. She shoved Angie forward to help a couple while she moved to intercept the hotel owner.

Regina was standing off to the side with her arms crossed over her chest. She looked displeased. Without a greeting, she demanded, "Who are they?"

Mel followed the wave of her hand. It encompassed the DeLaura brothers and Marty, who were mingling with the crowd, delivering their cupcakes. "The Santas? They're our helpers."

"Why?" Regina asked.

"To keep the product moving during our limited amount of time in the VIP suite." Mel refused to debate her about the brothers and Marty being in the suite. They were working for the bakery and as far as Mel was concerned, that was the end of it.

"Huh, silly me, and here I thought they were on duty to keep Doc's murderer from his real target—Shelby."

Ten

"Excuse me?" Mel asked. She wasn't surprised by what Regina said so much as she was by the fact that Regina had thought of it.

"Don't look so shocked," Regina said. "It must have occurred to you that with both of her managers dying under suspicious circumstances the actual target is Shelby."

Well, obviously, that's what they were all worried about, but Mel didn't want to give that possibility any credence. Instead, she decided to push for more information from Regina if she could get it.

"But who would want to kill Shelby?" Mel asked, hoping she sounded mystified.

It must have worked because Regina rolled her eyes and said, "As I understand it, a lot of people have been tossed aside for her. That makes for some powerful motive."

"You mean Doc's ex-wife Miranda Carter," Mel said.

"For one," Regina agreed. "And her first manager—what was her name?—Diana Martin," Regina said, answering her own question. She didn't wait for confirmation but kept speaking. "Her daughter Lisa certainly seems to have an issue with Shelby."

"You know Lisa?" Mel asked. She plated a Gingerbread Man cupcake for a well-dressed woman, giving her a distracted smile.

"Lisa is a guest of the hotel if you consider that 'knowing' her," Regina said.

"Why?" Mel asked.

"Why what?"

"Why is she staying here, did she say?" Mel asked.

"I think your uncle the police detective will be asking her that," Regina said. "You should probably check with him."

Mel sighed. Uncle Stan wasn't about to tell her anything about the current investigation. He never did.

"I still say these could use more razzle-dazzle," Regina said. She pointed to an Eggnog cupcake. "They barely look edible."

Mel frowned as Regina took one of the offending cupcakes, clearly not put off entirely by its lack of pizzazz, and strode away, her beaded black caftan catching the light as she moved through the crowd.

"What's her deal?" Angie asked. "I overheard her mention Shelby's name."

"Honestly, I have no idea," Mel said. "I feel like there's more to Regina than we know. I wonder if Uncle Stan has looked into her background. Shelby said Regina put a lot of money into the show and is paying her very well to be in residency over the holidays. But why? Shelby is a star on the rise, and for the holiday extravaganza they didn't need a name, they just needed someone who could sing well."

"Maybe Regina was in cahoots with Doc. I can ask Tate to look into her financials," Angie said. "Perhaps she has a gambling problem, too."

"Maybe, but it doesn't feel right," Mel said. She met her friend's considering gaze. "I wonder how far Doc and Regina go back. I mean, there must be a reason that Doc chose this hotel to have Shelby perform a standing gig over the holidays. Why here and not Las Vegas or Branson or even Nashville?"

"Right?" Angie asked. "I've been wondering that myself. I feel like it had to be about money. Since Doc was in financial trouble, why wouldn't he have gone to the highest bidder and not a random tourist hotel in Scottsdale, which is not a venue known for live performances?"

"It all feels sketchy," Mel said. "And I'm not sure I agree with Regina's conclusion."

"Which was?"

"That someone killed Diana and then Doc because they're trying to get to Shelby," Mel said.

"It's not that out there," Angie said. "We've been worried about the same thing."

"I know but it's been bothering me because it doesn't make sense. It's not like Shelby travels with a bodyguard. She's very accessible. If someone wanted to murder her, they easily could have."

"Okay, that's chilling," Angie said. "But if they don't want to murder her, then what do they want?"

"At a guess? They want to destroy her," Mel said.

"They want to take away the one thing she loves, performing her music, and to do it they'll make her a pariah."

Angie's eyes went wide. "That makes sense. Because who is going to sign an artist whose management keeps dying?"

"Excuse me." A man in a suit waved to get their attention. "We'd like to get some cupcakes."

Mel shook her head to clear it and gave the man her best smile.

"Of course, what flavors would you like?" she asked. As she moved to the counter she leaned close to Angie and said, "Let's keep a close eye on everyone here."

"Suspects?" Angie asked.

"As Uncle Stan always says, everyone's a suspect until the killer is caught," Mel said.

Not many VIP guests lingered after the show. Mel wasn't surprised. She wouldn't linger, either, if a potential murderer was about. The crowd was diminished, too. Although the show had been sold out for weeks, only half of the auditorium was full.

Shelby arrived at the VIP suite after her last set, looking pale and tired. She greeted the people who had shown up with a bright, if a bit forced, smile and took selfies and signed autographs. She waved at Mel and Angie and started towards them, when she was intercepted by Miranda, Doc's ex-wife. Shelby's eyes went wide and she appeared to be nervous, clearly unsure of Miranda's intent.

"Oh, no, I am not having this," Angie said. She left the

cupcake station and with a purposeful stride approached the two women. She gave Shelby a side hug and said, "You were amazing tonight!"

Miranda glowered at her. She stepped towards Shelby and said, "You think you have everyone fooled but I know who you really are."

"What's that supposed to mean?" Angie demanded.

Miranda tossed her hair and pushed out her chest, looking like a drama queen from an '80s nighttime family saga. "Shelby Vaughn is a climber. She'll step over anyone to get to the top. If you're her friend, you'd better be careful. She'll stab you in the back just like she did me."

Shelby flinched. She blinked hard and said, "I didn't stab you in the back, Miranda."

"Didn't you?" she asked. "We were on the road together, you with Diana and me with Doc, and you oh-so-sweetly asked to meet him. A month later, Diana was dead, Doc signed you, and I was served with divorce papers."

"I had nothing to do with any of that," Shelby insisted. She was wearing a floor-length sequined dress in deep green. Her long blond curls were side parted, framing her face and giving her the air of a sexy ingenue.

"Didn't you though?" Miranda asked.

"Why are you here?" Angie asked. "You don't live in Arizona, you're no longer married to Doc, so what are you doing at the Hotel Grande?"

Miranda drew herself up, her lips puckered in a moue of displeasure. "That's none of your business."

"Perhaps not," Angie said. "But I'm certain my friend Detective Stanley Cooper would love to hear your explanation." She raised her arm, and Mel noticed that Uncle Stan had entered the room and Angie was signaling for him to join them.

"Rude," Miranda said. She glanced at Shelby, giving her a once-over. "We're not done."

"Yes, you are," Angie said. She and Miranda stared at each other for a beat, until Miranda had the good sense to walk away.

Uncle Stan arrived just as she left. "What was that about?"

"Doc's ex-wife seems to believe along with everyone else that I had something to do with Doc's murder," Shelby said. She sounded defeated. "I don't know what to do. I don't know how to prove my innocence."

"You don't have to." Angie stared at Shelby intently. She absentmindedly twined one of her long curls around her finger. "You were with me when Doc was killed so there's no way it could have been you. End of story."

Mel gasped. She had known Angie since they were twelve years old. She understood her on a cellular level. She knew when Angie was happy, sad, upset, depressed, or hangry. She also knew when Angie was lying, which she was right now. Fiddling with her hair was her tell and it gave her away every time.

She glanced at Uncle Stan. Did he know Angie was lying? She tried to keep her face free of expression. She didn't want to out her friend until she could get some answers from Angie herself.

"What have you learned about Doc's murder?" Angie asked Stan.

"You know I'm not going to talk about an ongoing investigation with you," he said. His face was mildly exasperated but he didn't appear to be suspicious, which Mel took to mean that he didn't know Angie had lied.

"I appreciate your professional dilemma but whoever murdered Doc might be after Shelby," Angie protested.

"Which is why I have officers watching over her," Uncle Stan replied. He turned to Shelby. "Don't worry. I have my best people assigned to you."

"Thank you," she said. She sounded weary, and Mel realized that performing on top of being homesick and having her manager murdered was clearly wearing her down. Angie seemed to come to the same realization.

"Come on, let's get you home," Angie said. She glanced at Mel. "Is it okay if I leave the brothers to help you with cleanup?"

"That's fine, get out of here," Mel said. She watched the two women leave along with two plainclothes officers who silently shadowed them, and then turned to Uncle Stan. "So, what have you learned about Doc's murder?"

"Not talking to you about it, either," he said. "What I do need to speak with you about is your mother."

Mel lifted her eyebrows. This couldn't be good. "What about Mom?"

"She's concerned that you don't have your Christmas tree up or any decorations on the house," he said. He sounded exasperated, as if this was a conversation he'd had to listen to at great length.

"How does she know? Has she been driving by my house?" Mel asked.

Uncle Stan pursed his lips.

"Has she been peering in my windows?"

Uncle Stan tipped his head back and studied the room's ugly popcorn ceiling overhead.

Mel hissed. "She has."

"You live in the same neighborhood," he said. "It's not like driving by is going out of her way or anything."

"Mom knows this is one of the busiest times of the year at the bakery," Mel said. "She's just going to have to be patient or come over and do the decorating herself."

"I'll tell her you suggested that," Uncle Stan said. He immediately started backing up as if he was making a getaway.

"No!" Mel said. "Don't. Last time she decided to clean for me, she rearranged all of my cupboards and it took me weeks to figure out where she'd moved my favorite coffee cup."

"The one shaped like a cupcake?" he asked.

Mel nodded. "It was in the garage in the box for the thrift store."

"Joyce doesn't like rogue dishware that doesn't match," he said. He sounded as if he had firsthand experience and Mel suspected his favorite coffee mug had gone the way of consignment as well.

"Clearly," Mel agreed. "Tell her that Joe and I are planning on decorating this weekend."

"That'll do . . . I hope."

"Lookee here, if it isn't the five-oh." Ray DeLaura, looking like a Santa via the Jersey Shore with his Santa coat unbuttoned to reveal a thick gold chain nestled in his chest hair, approached Mel and Uncle Stan.

Uncle Stan rolled his eyes. He and Ray had a long history that dated back to when Ray was a teenager and Uncle Stan was a patrol officer. "DeLaura."

"Solved the murder yet?" Ray asked. Mel knew he did this just to needle Stan.

"Gotten a real job yet?" Uncle Stan punched back. He gestured to Ray's outfit. "Or is this your new grift?"

"I'm undercover," Ray said.

"As what? Bad Santa?" Uncle Stan asked.

"Enough, you two," Mel said. "We have a lot of cleanup to do. Ray, get to work. Uncle Stan, keep my mom away from my house."

"Have you even met your mother?" he asked. Mel raised her eyebrows. "Fine, I'll try. I'm headed to the station if you need me."

Mel handed Ray a container to start packing up the leftovers. "Where are Al and Paulie?"

"They cruised out of here with some backup dancers," Ray said. "They said not to wait up, so I don't expect to see them again tonight."

"Oh," Mel said. "But not you?"

"I'm a happily monogamous man," he declared.

"Also, your girlfriend is a homicide detective who carries a gun," Mel said.

"That, too," he said.

Together they packed up the remainders. There weren't many cupcakes left, but the station needed to be wiped down and their cupcake towers, napkins, and other decorations packed away for the next night.

After Doc had been found holding a Sugar Plum cupcake, Mel had taken them off the VIP menu, as well as the bakery's, and replaced them with a Sugar Cookie cupcake. She didn't want to have a bad association of that particular cupcake—which every local news agency had felt inexplicably obligated to mention when reporting on Doc's murder—with her bakery.

Marty had left early as he was opening the bakery the

next morning, so it was just Mel and Ray who walked out to the parking lot together. It was late. Mel was exhausted. She knew this gig was temporary, so she planned to push through for Angie and Shelby, but truthfully, she couldn't wait to be back on her in-bed-by-ten schedule.

The cupcake van loomed ahead and they had almost reached it, when a male reporter popped out from behind it. Beside him was a cameraman and another person shining a glaringly bright light on them. Mel blinked and Ray threw up an arm, blocking his face from view. Mel didn't really think it was necessary as his wig and beard hid his face and in that moment she wished she were wearing a Santa suit as well.

"Melanie DeLaura." The reporter said her name, making it clear that he knew who she was.

"Any comment on the medical examiner's report that Doc Howard's murder was due to poisoning by one of your cupcakes?"

Eleven

"Back up," Ray barked at the reporter.

The reporter jumped. He likely wasn't used to being yelled at by Santa Claus, especially a Santa with his chest hair showing.

The reporter raised his hands in a gesture of surrender. "Hey, I'm just doing my job."

"Harassing a hardworking woman in the middle of the night is your job?" Ray asked. He gestured for Mel to climb into the van while he stepped forward with the leftover boxes of cupcakes from the evening. There were only a couple dozen, which would be dropped off at the local food pantry on the way home.

Mel watched as Ray stomped forward, forcing the reporter and cameraman back. He opened the side door to the van and placed the cupcakes inside before slamming the door shut.

"Not harassing," the reporter argued. "Merely inquiring."

"Which is why you had to jump out at her in the middle of the night?" Ray asked. He looked at the man as if he had the manners of an online troll.

"The news never sleeps," the reporter retorted. "And I've found most people respond more directly if I take them by surprise."

"Forcing the interview to be given under duress, which can hardly make for accurate journalism," Ray snapped. "Maybe if the news wasn't obsessed with sound bites for clickbait, it'd be more respected."

The reporter's face turned bright red and he thrust his mic into the van and shouted at Mel, "You can either talk to me now or face a crowd of reporters on your front doorstep tomorrow. How will that impact your business?"

Mel had been in the media's bright white-hot gaze before. She knew it was like a bad bout of food poisoning. It would pass—painfully, with some sweating, cursing, moaning, and complaining—but it would pass.

"That sounds fine," she said. She smiled at him as if he hadn't just accused her of poisoning someone. "Coffee and cupcakes at the bakery at eight?"

"I know I'll be there." Ray glowered.

The reporter took a hasty step back when Ray yanked the driver's side door open and climbed in. The reporter opened his mouth to speak and Ray fired up the engine, drowning him out. He stomped on the gas and they sped away from the hotel, leaving the reporter and his crew choking on their exhaust.

"That went well," Ray said.

Mel was already fishing her phone out of her purse. "Went well? Compared to what? A root canal? A backed-up toilet? A forest fire?"

"Yeah, all of those," Ray said. "I mean we got away without saying a thing."

"That's because there was nothing to say," Mel said. After pressing Uncle Stan's name and number, she put the phone on speaker.

"What's wrong, kid?" Uncle Stan answered on the second ring. She could hear the sound of the busy police precinct in the background and deduced that he was still at work, even though it was close to midnight. The case must be heating up, which would explain why the reporter showed up at the hotel.

"Nothing's wrong, exactly, but I really, really need to know how Doc died," Mel said.

Uncle Stan was quiet for a beat. She heard a shout in the background, then a laugh. The sound of a phone ringing and the clatter of someone typing on a computer nearby filled the void.

"Uncle Stan." Mel said his name the same way her mother did when she was unhappy. It practically made him do backflips to please Joyce. Mel was hoping for a similar reaction.

"We're not one hundred percent certain yet," he said. He was waffling. "The medical examiner hasn't weighed in officially."

"I'll take whatever percentage you are certain of," she persisted.

"Why are you asking now in the middle of the night?" he redirected.

"Because you didn't answer me earlier," she said. "Where are you?"

"Driving back to the bakery."

"It's late. You should get some sleep. We can discuss this tomorrow," he said. His tone was cajoling.

"Tomorrow I'm going to be busy fielding questions from a horde of reporters wanting to know what poison I used in the Sugar Plum cupcake Doc was holding," Mel said. "So, now would really be a better time for me."

Uncle Stan fired out a string of expletives that was impressive in both its volume and its physical impossibilities.

"Sorry, kid, that obviously wasn't meant for you," Uncle Stan said.

"Nice language, Cooper," Ray said from the driver seat.

"Shut up, DeLaura," Uncle Stan snapped. "Consider all of the rough language directed at you."

Ray laughed and the tension in the air eased a bit.

"Tell me what happened," Uncle Stan said.

Mel described the reporter and his questions, giving Ray full credit for chasing him away.

"He's fishing," Uncle Stan said. "The medical examiner hasn't made anything official other than the time of death."

"So the reporter was just speculating because Doc was holding a cupcake?" Mel asked.

"He had to be," Uncle Stan said. "The tox screens won't be in for a few more days at the earliest. We have zero evidence that Doc Howard was poisoned."

Mel took a deep breath and let it out. "I saw the body.

There was a huge pool of blood under his head. Poison doesn't do that."

"No, but being poisoned could make him susceptible to being clubbed and unable to fight back," Ray interjected.

Mel turned her head to look at him. Uncle Stan was silent on the phone but she could imagine he had one eyebrow raised in inquiry.

"I'm just sayin'," Ray said, breaking the silence.

"Right, well, I doubt there will be any reporters camped out at your front door tomorrow," Uncle Stan said with what Mel thought was more confidence than was warranted. "It sounds like this guy was making it up as he went along."

"I hope you're right," Mel said.

He wasn't.

"What are they all doing here?" Tate cried. He was standing at the bakery's front door, peering outside through the blinds like a reverse Peeping Tom. "It's like a swarm of killer bees out there."

"At a guess I'd say they are looking at us because they've discovered that Angie and Shelby are friends and they think we're a way into Shelby Vaughn's world," Mel said. "Uncle Stan assured me that there's no evidence that Doc was poisoned . . . yet. So that can't be it."

She crossed the bakery and stood beside Tate. Sure enough, the reporter who had warned her about the rumor was standing front and center with his cameraman beside him. Mel resisted the urge to be sassy and wave at him.

"This is our busiest time of year," Tate said. "They can't force our customers to run the gauntlet just to pick up their orders."

"Do you want me to call the brothers?" Marty offered. He was standing behind the counter, glaring at the window as if just daring the media outside to give him a reason to open a can of whup butt.

"Uh . . . no," Tate said. Mel suspected that her friend knew that while it was tempting to tap their testosterone-infused in-laws for help, it could also backfire spectacularly on them. Tate glanced at his watch. "I have to go to a meeting with a prospective franchise buyer. Two football players who are looking to have a cupcake business in retirement."

"I love that on so many levels. Go," Mel said. "So long as Shelby doesn't stop by and accidentally incite a frenzy, we'll be fine. I'm positive the reporters will get bored soon enough."

"I hope so. I don't want the bad publicity to mess up our deal with the football players." Tate sent an irritated glance at the window and said, "I guess I'll duck out the back. Angie should be here soon. She said she wanted to talk to you about something."

Mel nodded. This was good, as she had something to talk to Angie about as well. She followed Tate into the kitchen. When he slipped out the back door, she set to work making the cupcakes for tonight's VIP event. Shelby was paying them an exorbitant amount of money, something Mel now felt guilty about given that she knew Shelby was struggling financially, so she was pulling out all the stops on the cupcakes in an effort to be worthy. Of course, if people thought they were poisoned, there was no culinary magic she could employ to glamour away that stigma.

The phone in her apron pocket buzzed and she took it out and glanced at the display. When she read the name, she smiled. She slid her thumb across the screen to access the call and held her phone to her ear.

"Hi, Manny, how's Vegas treating you?" she asked.

"As busy as an elf in Santa's sweatshop," he said.

Mel laughed. She'd missed Manny's quick wit.

"How are Holly and Sidney?" she asked. Manny had moved from Scottsdale to Vegas a few years ago to be near his girlfriend, who also happened to own the first official franchise bakery of Fairy Tale Cupcakes.

"Great," he said. Mel could hear the warm affection in his voice and was happy for him. "In fact, I have a proposal planned for New Year's Eve."

"That's wonderful! And about damn time!" Mel said. Manny laughed.

"It took some convincing since Holly's a little skittish about marriage but her daughter Sidney is all in on the planning, so I think we can sway her." He sounded mostly confident with a dash of nerves.

"She'll say yes," Mel said. She paced around her kitchen, straightening her cooking implements as she went. "She'd be crazy not to."

"Thanks," he said. "I talked to Stan and he told me what's happening. Are you all right?"

"I'm fine," Mel said. "But I have a question for you."

"About the Martin fire, I'm guessing," Manny said. "I can only tell you exactly what I told Stan. There was no evidence of Diana Martin being murdered, despite what her daughter Lisa said. It appeared to be an electrical short in one of the ceiling fans that caused the fire. As far as the medical examiner could tell, Diana was asleep and never woke up."

"A freak accident then?" Mel asked.

"So it would seem," Manny said.

"You don't sound so sure."

"A death like that always feels wrong," he said. "Or maybe I've just been a homicide detective for too long."

"That's what makes you a good one," Mel said.

Manny grunted noncommittally and Mel changed the subject to his upcoming proposal. When they ended the call, Mel glanced around her kitchen, debating where to start with the day's baking.

She thought about Angie and her secrets and decided it had to be the peppermint bark. While the two candy coatings, chocolate and vanilla, melted in turn on double boilers on her stove, she used a rolling pin to smash up the peppermints, which she would sprinkle on top of the layers of melted candy.

The back door opened as she was in mid-swing, and she glanced up to see Angie, who looked at her with her eyebrows raised. "Anger management?"

"Maybe," Mel conceded.

"Tate told me about the press being parked out front," Angie said. She grimaced. "How's that working out with our customers?"

Mel shrugged. "That's not why I'm angry."

"Really?" Angie set her handbag in the small office tucked into the corner of the kitchen and then donned her apron and headed to the sink, where she scrubbed her hands. "If not that, then what?"

"You lied to Uncle Stan," Mel said. "Shelby wasn't with you when Doc was murdered, not the whole time."

Angie dried her hands on a towel and took the rolling pin from Mel. "What makes you say that?" She tried to sound offended but Mel could tell she was stalling.

"You're my best friend," Mel said. "I know you as well as I know myself. You totally fibbed."

Angie smacked the peppermint chunks that were still too large. Mel let her get it out. She knew Angie would tell her the truth but just needed a moment to pull it together. Finally, and mercifully before the candy was pulverized into uselessness, Angie put the rolling pin down. She moved around Mel to get the pot of melted chocolate and poured it onto the parchment-lined cookie sheet, spreading it with a spatula. She then lifted the cookie sheet and put it into the walk-in cooler to set.

When she came back, Mel was turning the heat on under the second double boiler, to melt the vanilla candy, which she would spread on top of the chocolate and then sprinkle with the crushed peppermint candy before the vanilla hardened.

"You're right," Angie said. "I wasn't with Shelby the entire time. I left her to call home, and Tate and I started talking about Emari and I lost track of time, so I don't know exactly how long we were in different rooms. But the whole thing is ridiculous. She was just packing a bag in her bedroom while I waited in the living room. I would have seen her if she left."

"Does her bedroom have a separate exit?" Mel asked.

Angie's chin shifted up at a stubborn angle. "That doesn't prove anything."

Mel shook her head. "Listen, I know Shelby is your friend, but you can't protect her by not telling Uncle Stan the truth. You have to tell him that she wasn't with you the entire time because if you don't and it comes out, she'll look guilty as all get-out."

"But she was right next door," Angie protested. "And just look outside. They're like sharks who smell blood in the water. If there is even a hint that Shelby might have had an opportunity to kill Doc, then the press will destroy her. You know this is true."

"I do," Mel said. "But when the truth comes out, and it always does, then lying to protect her will do much more harm than good. You have to tell Uncle Stan what happened and trust him to handle it."

Angie pointed to the double boiler. The vanilla had melted. Mel used pot holders to lift the inner metal bowl out of the larger pot of simmering water while Angie retrieved the chocolate from the cooler. Mel stirred the vanilla, letting it cool just a bit so it didn't melt the layer of chocolate as it was poured on top. As she spread the vanilla, Angie sprinkled the top with the crushed peppermints. Once they were done, Mel put the tray back into the cooler. When it was set, they would break the peppermint bark into pieces and use them to decorate the tops of the chocolate cupcakes frosted with mint buttercream.

"I'll talk to Uncle Stan," Angie said. "I never meant to lie. I just wanted to keep Shelby from harm. She's had a tough enough time of it as it is."

"I know," Mel said. "Your heart was in the right place."

"Hey, Mel." Marty popped into the kitchen through the swinging door. "There's a reporter out here who says you two spoke last night. He said to tell you he has a proposition for you."

Mel rolled her eyes. She did not need this today. "Tell him he can take his proposition and shove it right up his—"

"Good morning." The reporter appeared behind Marty. He looked as tired as Mel felt, with dark circles under his eyes and hair that looked as if it hadn't seen a brush or a comb in days. Mel refused to feel any sympathy for him.

"Hey, I told you to wait out front," Marty said. He looked like he was contemplating picking up the reporter and bodily tossing him out of the joint. This would have concerned Mel if Marty weighed more than a wet feather and the guy in question wasn't over six feet tall and, by the look of his biceps, very fit.

"Sorry, but I'm running out of time," the reporter said. "My editor wanted something turned in yesterday about the Shelby Vaughn situation and I've got nothing."

"Which is exactly what you're going to get from us," Mel said.

The reporter raised his hand in a stop gesture. "Just hear me out."

"There's only one word in that sentence that interests me," Mel said. She pointed to the door. "Out."

"Wait," he implored. "I have an idea."

"And you are?" Angie asked.

"Sorry." He stepped into the kitchen. He pointed to his credentials hanging off a lanyard around his neck and said, "Adam Previn."

"Well, Adam," Angie said. She crossed her arms over her chest, and Mel braced herself for the tongue-lashing her friend was about to unleash on the unsuspecting Adam.

"Let's hear what you have to say," Angie said.

Twelve

"What?" Mel and Marty cried at the exact same time. "Why?"

Angie blinked at them. "Because we need someone on our side." She looked at the reporter. "You are on our side, right, Adam?"

Something in her steady brown gaze must have alerted him to the seriousness of the question because he licked his lips, cleared his throat, and said, "Yes, absolutely. One hundred percent."

"So, what did you have in mind?" Angie asked.

"An exclusive interview with Shelby," he said.

Angie continued to stare at him. Mel thought she saw a bead of sweat trail down the side of Adam's face. He forced a smile and said, "Portraying Shelby as the poor young singer who lost both of her managers in less than a year."

"And how are you going to sell that angle when everyone wants to accuse her of their murders?" Angie asked.

"*Their* murders?" Adam's eyebrows bounced up on his forehead. He was clearly dazzled by the idea of a double homicide.

"As I'm sure you know, her previous manager, Diana Martin, died in a house fire and her daughter Lisa has been throwing around some very wild accusations," Angie said. "There's no evidence that Diana was murdered but the Las Vegas fire department does consider the fire to be suspicious."

"But nothing concrete has been proven, correct?" he asked.

"Correct," Angie confirmed. "Which is why it's so clearly a frame-up. Your job, Adam, is to find out who is trying to ruin Shelby and why."

"That's a pretty tall order given that, according to my sources in the department, even the police haven't been able to identify a lead," he said. He turned to Mel. "Your uncle chased us away from the precinct today. He sounded frustrated."

"Uncle Stan doesn't talk about his investigations with me," she said.

"Even though you have a reputation for being in the wrong place at the wrong time and have managed to solve several murders on your own?" Adam asked. "How does that happen to a cupcake baker anyway?"

"I wish I knew," Mel said. She glanced at Angie. "It seems to coincide with all of the special events we do."

Angie tipped her chin up. "You're not blaming me, are you?"

"Of course not," Mel said. "But in this particular case, Shelby is your friend and you did agree to provide the cupcakes for the VIP suite, so . . ."

"No, no, no." Angie shook her head. "We've helped out your friends in the past, which has landed us in all sorts of messes."

"You're exaggerating," Mel said.

"The Sweet Tiara Pageant," Angie shot back. "We only did that because your mom asked us to, and look where that got us."

"That was ages ago," Mel said. "And it was my mom. You can't say no to a mom, especially my mom. I mean, just look at how Christmas has gone sideways this year."

"Speaking of which, Olivia wanted to know what she can bring," Marty said. "She assumed you'd want her to cover dessert since you're . . ."

"Did she criticize my baking?" Mel asked, outraged.

"No, she'd never," Marty said. He didn't meet her gaze however. "She just thought that you might be too busy because of Shelby's show and all."

"Tell her I'm fine," Mel said. "I do not need her help." Realizing this sounded grumpy, she added, "Although it was nice of her to offer."

"Nice." Angie rolled her eyes.

"Hey, what's that supposed to mean?" Marty asked.

Adam's head was whipping in each of their directions as they squabbled about Olivia. Mel would have felt sorry for him but she could not have Olivia showing her up on Christmas Day with some over-the-top baked good from her rival bakery, Confections. No way. No how.

"It means what it means," Angie said.

"Which is?" Marty plopped his hands on his hips and frowned.

There was the sound of a counter bell ringing from the front of the bakery, and Mel said, "Looks like we have a customer."

Marty heaved a put-upon sigh. "Fine, but we're not done with this discussion."

He disappeared through the door, and Angie turned to Mel. "Oh, yes, we are."

"I heard that," Marty shouted through the swinging door.

Angie gave Mel a look and they both smiled. Mel knew that Angie adored Marty just as much as she did. He had become the face of the bakery and she had no idea what they'd do without him. Olivia still wasn't bringing dessert to Christmas dinner, however.

"Back to Shelby," Adam said. They both looked at him. It was clear after they'd been silent for a few beats too long that they'd lost the thread of the conversation. "You said you want me to see who is trying to ruin Shelby?"

"Yes." Angie nodded. "It's clear that someone is trying to destroy her career and they're taking out her managers to do it."

"Any idea who?" Adam asked. He looked hopeful.

"No," Mel said. "Which is the only reason we're bringing you into the loop."

"I can live with that," he said. He tapped his chin with his finger, pondering the situation. "If what you say is true and if I write an exclusive from that angle, then it might beat the bad guy out of the bushes so to speak. The last thing they'd want is public sympathy for Shelby. It will force their hand."

Angie turned to Mel. "I like the way this guy thinks."

Mel studied Adam. "How do you plan to go about this?"

"An exclusive interview with Shelby," he said. "Then I drop the story, painting her as a victim of misfortune, and see what happens."

"But doesn't your editor want a hit piece on Shelby?" Mel asked. "I mean isn't it all about getting readers to click on a story these days?"

"I'm not gonna lie, it is all about the clicks," he said. "Which is why misinformation is so rampant. News outlets love vitriol and performative outrage to get those clicks going. Facts are just not as entertaining."

"So, how will you get this approved by your editor?" Angie asked.

"Have you seen how many clicks a kitten rescued from a storm drain can get?" Adam asked. "Beats the ugly scandal news every time."

"Shelby is the kitten in this scenario, I take it," Mel said.

"Exactly." He pointed at her.

"I like it," Angie said. "I'll call her and set it up. If she says no, and she might, then that's that. No badgering."

"Got it," he said. "But a word to the wise?"

Mel and Angie nodded.

"Try and get her to say yes," he said. "Those other reporters do not care about a kitten in a storm drain and they'll drown her for traction on their bylines, no hesitation."

"I'll do my best," Angie said. Mel saw the doubt in her

eyes and hoped for Shelby's sake that she went along with it, as they were running out of options.

〴〵〴〵

Mel took the afternoon off to work on the house. She needed to get on top of this whole Christmas thing otherwise her mother was going to show up and deck her halls for her. It's not that Mel would have minded that so much, it's just that it made her feel as if she was failing at this whole holiday thing, and her pride was not up for the hit.

Captain Jack in mid-nap ignored her but Peanut was ecstatic to have Mel home. She raced around in a few circles that made Mel dizzy and then darted outside to patrol the yard. Mel set to work unboxing a few of the cartons her mother had sent over. One was as promised Joyce's Christmas china. Mel closed the box. Had the woman never heard of paper plates? For the number of people Mel was hosting, she feared it was the only viable option, but she'd get the fancy ones. She took out a piece of paper and a pen and started a list.

She then moved on to the next box. This was the Christmas tree decorations. Excellent. She and Joe didn't own enough of those to cover a tree. She glanced at the living room. First, she needed a tree. She added that to her list. She pondered the third box. This one was full of Christmas tchotchkes. She glanced around her serenely uncluttered living room. Because she and Joe had demanding careers, their home decor had never been a priority. She didn't have pictures on the walls, there were absolutely no knickknacks, and their aesthetic could best be described as "no one lives here." Of course, this meant Mel had plenty of places for the animatronic reindeer with the red light-up nose, the snowman who hugged his belly and giggled, and the Mr. and Mrs. Claus who ho-ho-hoed and then kissed each other.

Her mother had been collecting these animatronic stuffies since Mel was a kid. She checked each one before she set them on a table here and a shelf there to make certain that they were switched off. No one wanted to be ho-ho-hoed at two in the morning when they were going for a glass of water.

Feeling as if she'd made a solid start in the decorating, Mel played fetch with Peanut and attack the feather wand with Captain Jack before heading back to work. Before she departed, Mel left Joe a note on the counter, explaining the new additions to their decorating so he didn't freak out.

Mel met Angie at the bakery and together they loaded up the cupcake van with the VIP offerings of the evening. Marty was staying to watch the bakery as their other counter person, Madison, a sweetheart of a teenager who also ran their social media, was off for the evening.

"Are the brothers meeting us there?" Mel asked. She climbed into the driver's seat while Angie rode shotgun.

"Apparently," Angie said. She sounded annoyed.

"Is there a problem?" Mel asked.

"Only in that both Al and Paulie now want to bring the two dancers they met to Christmas dinner and my mom is furious with them," Angie said.

"Because the women are dancers?" Mel asked.

"I'd like to say that she's not that judgmental but I'm sure that's a part of it," Angie said. "Mostly, she's upset because Joe asked you to host as a favor to her and more people keep getting added to the guest list for Christmas dinner, which my mother, like yours, takes very seriously."

"Don't remind me," Mel said. She turned onto the street for the Hotel Grande. "Uncle Stan told me that my mother has been driving by my house and checking on my progress with her decorations."

"No, she didn't."

"Oh, yes, she did. We're talking about Joyce here."

"Silly me, how did I forget? We should just flee into the night," Angie said. "Emari is too little to know the difference. If we made a run for it on Christmas Eve, we could be beachside in Puerto Peñasco, Mexico, by lunch."

"Don't tempt me," Mel said. "Shrimp right off the boat and no battery-powered Christmas toys lighting up or singing at me? Sounds like heaven."

They both chuckled, knowing full well that they would never disappoint their mothers like that, tempting as it might be.

"Oh, I forgot to tell you," Angie said. "Shelby agreed to be interviewed by Adam Previn before the show tonight. I told her we would be there if she needed us. I figured the brothers could manage the cupcake station without us for at least a few minutes."

"Sounds good," Mel said. "How is Shelby holding up?"

"Sad, confused, and scared," Angie said. "About what you'd expect."

"Hmm." Mel could only imagine.

"She did bring her acoustic guitar with her last night

and when Emari was having an after-midnight melt-down, she sang her to sleep," Angie said. "Knocked Tate and me out, too. Best sleep I've had in ages."

Mel turned in to the hotel's parking lot. Angie texted her brothers, and Ray, Al, and Paulie, again wearing their Santa costumes, met them at the door. Angie explained about the reporter and Ray waved them off.

"Go," he said. "Make sure Shelby doesn't say anything dumb."

Angie gaped at him. "She won't."

"Eh," he grunted. "People get nervous and say stupid stuff in front of the media all the time. Go be her buffer."

"All right," Angie said. "We'll meet you in the VIP lounge as soon as the interview is over."

"If there's a photographer, try to get them to take a picture of her holding one of your cupcakes," Al said. He handed Mel a box with four cupcakes in it. "Major marketing there."

She glanced from the box to him. He wasn't wrong.

"Text us if anything comes up," she said. "We'll be right down the hallway."

"Roger that, boss," Paulie said.

Mel and Angie exchanged a nervous look. Yes, these were grown men and, sure, they were just passing out cupcakes, but Regina had been a real thorn in Mel's backside about the quality of Mel's product in the VIP lounge and Mel didn't want to get into an unpleasant situation with the hotel owner if she could avoid it.

"No shenanigans," Mel said. She made eye contact with each of the brothers and they all nodded.

"We've got this," Ray said. He made a shooing motion with his hands. "Go."

Mel and Angie hustled through the hotel to the auditorium. They shot down the hallway in a power walk until they reached Shelby's dressing room door. Angie rapped on the door, next to Shelby's nameplate, three times.

They could hear the rumble of voices on the other side and someone said, "I'll get it."

The door was pulled open and Cheryl, wearing an aqua smock tonight, stood there. "Well, hi there, girls. How are you?"

Mel glanced over Cheryl's head and saw Shelby sitting in front of the dressing room mirror with Adam, the reporter, perched on a stool off to the side. It appeared the interview had already started. Mel thought of Ray's warning and felt a pit of dread drop in her stomach.

"We're fine," Angie said. "Just checking on Shelby."

"Oh, she's doing much better," Cheryl said. She leaned out the door a bit. "She's even giving an interview. Doc never let her do that before."

"Really?" Angie asked. Mel and Angie exchanged an alarmed look. Why wouldn't Doc let her do interviews? Was Shelby bad at it? Had setting her up with Adam Previn been a terrible idea?

Angie took a step forward but Cheryl didn't step back. "Sorry, hon, she asked not to be disturbed."

"But it's me," Angie said. "I'm her friend. The one who set up the interview."

"I know," Cheryl said. "And that was a good thing you did. But just because you know a celebrity, doesn't mean that you are also a celebrity. I've seen this time and again with the people in Shelby's life." She shook her head as if the whole thing just made her sad.

"I don't think I'm a celebrity," Angie said. Her voice

was tight and Mel could sense she was losing her patience. While it was great that Cheryl was following Shelby's orders and not letting anyone walk in on her interview, they—Angie in particular—weren't just anyone, but there was no way to say this without sounding like a bragger.

"Hey, Shelby!" Mel called. She waved at Shelby over Angie's and Cheryl's heads. This was one of the few perks of being on the tall side of medium; she could command people's attention when necessary. She considered it a minor superpower and tried not to overuse it.

Thirteen

"Mel! Angie!" Shelby smiled at the sight of them. "Come on in. Adam and I were just about to get started."

"Thank goodness, we're in time," Angie said to Mel, who nodded in agreement. Their entire plan to have Adam draw out the killer would be for naught if Shelby said the wrong thing.

"Lucky us," Cheryl said. Mel glanced at her, wondering if she was annoyed, but Cheryl smiled and waved them into the room. "It's going to be a tight squeeze, I'm afraid. We're having to do the interview while I get Shelby ready."

"Not a problem," Mel said. "We'll just hug the back wall. You won't even know we're here."

Cheryl gave her a doubtful look but didn't argue.

"Hi, Adam," Angie called to the reporter from across the room. "We're just going to wait right over here."

Her voice was stern and Mel wondered why she didn't just say what she meant, which was a variation of *do not ask Shelby anything that might upset her or I will have to put a hurt on you.*

It was wonderful having a friend as loyal as Angie but it was also a teeny bit stressful.

Adam was no dummy. He saw the fire in Angie's eyes and looked suitably wary. Mel smiled at him, trying to let him know he'd be fine. Strangely, he looked even more alarmed than before. Hmm.

"Can you give me a little backstory for the piece?" Adam asked. He had a handheld digital recorder as well as his phone, which he was typing on. Mel assumed he was recording it as well as taking notes on the sorts of things a simple recording couldn't possibly capture.

"I can give you Shelby's backstory," Cheryl said. "I watched her grow up."

"Did you?" Adam asked, sounding intrigued. "Cheryl, right? What can you tell me about her?"

"Cheryl Hoover, with two *o*'s," the stylist said.

"Oh, I don't think Adam wants to hear about my life in the hills of Tennessee," Shelby demurred.

"Sure, he does," Cheryl said. She moved behind Shelby and began to tease her hair. "That's what gives you your—what do you reporters call it—your relatability."

"I'm pretty sure there aren't that many people who can

relate to a girl whose family lives in a tiny house on the outskirts of Memphis, attached to a junkyard where her dad crushes cars for a living."

"I don't know," Adam said. "That sounds pretty cool."

"Not if you're the car," Shelby said. She gave him a small smile as she glanced at him from under her long eyelashes.

Adam blinked, and Mel knew right then and there that like every other man who met Shelby, Adam was good and truly under the singer's spell. And the thing was, it wasn't as if Shelby flirted or played the sexy innocent. She was just her authentic self, who just happened to ooze charm out of her pores. There was something about her that made you like her and made you want her to like you in return.

It had taken Mel only a few days to become fond of Shelby and to want to help her. Angie's relationship with the singer made perfect sense to Mel now. There was just something about Shelby that made it impossible to dislike her.

"Oh, Shelby!" Cheryl laughed a big, loud, booming chortle that brought everyone's attention back to her. "You are so funny."

Adam shook his head as if the spell had been broken. He glanced at Cheryl and asked, "What was Shelby like as a child?"

Cheryl glanced at the mirror, where she met Shelby's gaze. Shelby looked curious as if she had no idea what Cheryl would say. Cheryl winked at her and said, "Don't worry. I only have good things to say about you."

Shelby laughed. "That's why you're my one and only." She turned to Adam. "When I first got signed to a contract, I was only sixteen. My parents didn't want me to go on the road alone, so we had a family meeting and since Cheryl's salon had just been destroyed by a flood and she was going to have to relocate, they asked her to be my chaperone and stylist."

"A family meeting?" Adam asked. He glanced at the two women. "Are you related?"

"No, we were neighbors," Cheryl said. "But it felt like family. My beauty shop was on the other side of Vaughn's junkyard, and Shelby and her brothers used to hang out there while their parents worked."

"It was safer than the junkyard," Shelby said. "My parents have a car-crushing business."

"In theory the salon was safer." Cheryl rolled her eyes. "Do you remember the time they got into the hair dye?"

Shelby pressed her lips together, trying not to laugh, while Cheryl was backcombing her roots.

Cheryl turned to Adam and explained, "One of them came out with his entire head the color of a cranberry. How that child did not get it in his eyes is a miracle."

Shelby lost the battle and burst out laughing. "Do you remember how we had to scramble to dye it back before my mom came to get us?"

Cheryl laughed. "We were partners in crime on that one. We managed to get it dyed back five minutes before Mary Ellen arrived."

"And Mary Ellen is your mother?" Adam asked.

"She is," Cheryl confirmed. "It's where Shelby gets her good looks from. Mary Ellen is the prettiest woman in our neighborhood, although now that you're all grown up, you're giving her a run for her money."

"No." Shelby shook her head. "My mama will always be the prettiest woman I've ever known."

Cheryl smiled fondly at her and then turned to Adam and asked, "Isn't she just the sweetest thing?"

"Refreshingly unspoiled," he said.

"Especially when you consider her mama's past," Cheryl said.

Shelby gasped and gave Cheryl a small shake of her head.

Cheryl nodded and said, "But never mind that, let me tell you the story of when Shelby performed for the first time at the Tennessee State Fair. She was only ten years old, and I did her hair in big bouncy curls but no makeup because she was too young for that sort of nonsense."

"You let me wear strawberry lip gloss," Shelby said.

"Now, honey, you were never supposed to tell anybody that I did that," Cheryl chided her with a smile. "The scandal!"

Shelby laughed, turned to Adam, and said, "You can see what a fierce chaperone she was. I never got away with anything."

"Unless donuts were involved and then I always gave in," Cheryl said.

"It sounds like you two are the best of friends," Adam said.

"Oh, we're more than that," Cheryl said. "We're family."

Angie looked at Mel and gave her a thumbs-up. Adam was definitely joining the Shelby fan base, which would only convince him that Shelby couldn't possibly be the murderer.

The interview continued and while Shelby was humble, Cheryl more than made up for her reticence with alternatively touching and humorous stories about Shelby's upbringing. Truly, with Cheryl feeding him stories about Shelby's childhood, painting her as an adorable tomboy with a big booming voice that stood out in the church choir, it was impossible not to be beguiled by the picture she painted. Cheryl made Adam's task of writing a sympathy piece about Shelby as easy as piping frosting on a cupcake. When Adam left the dressing room, he was positively dazzled by the singer.

As soon as the door shut, Angie stepped forward. "That was brilliant. He's going to write an amazing article about you that will bring the sympathy roaring in and no one will ever entertain the idea that you could be tied to Doc's murder in any way. I know it."

"You think so?" Shelby asked. "I was so nervous. He seemed very nice but I've had some nasty things written about me by some of the friendliest reporters. It makes you wary." She turned to Cheryl. "Thank goodness you were here. I absolutely would not have thought of most of the stories you remembered. You're the best. I have no idea what I'd do without you."

She hugged Cheryl tight. Cheryl returned it and then said, "Now, don't get all emotional. I do not want to redo that eye makeup. That cat eye is the best liner I've ever done."

Shelby sniffed and fanned her face with her hands. "You're right, as always."

A knock on the door interrupted them. The show's director poked his head in and said, "Shelby, time for a sound check."

"On my way." She turned back to the three of them. "Thanks, you guys. I couldn't get through this without all of you."

"Don't worry about it. Break a leg," Angie said.

Shelby nodded and slipped out the door. Cheryl let out a sigh and said, "I am going to rest my weary dogs." She sat on the couch and put her feet up. "Do you think I did enough background on Shelby to keep that reporter from digging any deeper?"

Mel frowned. "I think so; you were very detailed in your stories. But would it matter if he dug a little deeper?"

"It might," Cheryl said. She picked up a box of chocolates that had been sent to Shelby from a corporate admirer. Taking off the lid, she selected one and popped it into her mouth. While she chewed, she said, "I mean, given that her mama did seven months in prison for manslaughter, I thought that might be problematic."

Angie and Mel turned to look at each other with wide eyes and mouths agape. *Oh, no!*

"Why didn't anyone tell us about that?" Angie cried.

Cheryl shrugged and took out another chocolate. "You didn't ask."

"Is this why Doc didn't let her do interviews?" Mel asked. It all made sense now.

"Probably," Cheryl said. She put the lid on the box of chocolates and pushed it away. "He never said specifically but I figured that's what it was about. Shelby's fan base is big in the Bible Belt and he probably didn't want her image sullied by association."

"Manslaughter?" Mel asked. "How? Why?"

"Well, I told you Mary Ellen was the prettiest woman in our neighborhood, right?" Cheryl asked.

"Right," Angie said. She sounded impatient.

"Those sorts of good looks can bring out a powerful jealousy in some folks," Cheryl said. "Mary Ellen was just like Shelby when she was her age. Not just pretty, but smart and kind, too, making her popular with everyone from newborns to senior citizens. Well, that didn't sit right with Joelle Newton. She went and told everyone in town that Mary Ellen was having an affair with her husband Gary. As if Mary Ellen would have looked twice at that pea-brained waste of space."

"What happened?" Angie asked. Mel felt her stomach cramp. She didn't like where this was going.

"Well, the neighborhood loved Mary Ellen and didn't believe a bit of the nasty rumor. Several of the local men laughed in Gary's face when he said he could have Mary Ellen if he wanted her. That was a bad move as Gary decided he needed to prove that he could have her." Cheryl shook her head. "Head full of mashed turnip, that one. Anyway, he showed up drunk at Mary Ellen's one night when her husband was working late in the junkyard, and you can imagine what he tried."

Mel's lips felt wooden when she spoke. "He didn't succeed, did he?"

"Nah, Mary Ellen shot him when he kicked down her door and tried to strangle her," Cheryl said.

"So, it was self-defense?" Angie said. "How could she have been convicted of manslaughter then?"

"The judge was a poker buddy of Gary's father's," Cheryl said. "The prosecutor made it seem like Mary Ellen's reaction was extreme and that she could have reasoned with Gary. No one knew if he meant before or after he choked her out. It was a real 'boys will be boys' defense. There were eight men and four women on the jury. Mary Ellen didn't stand a chance."

"Well, hell," Angie muttered.

Cheryl picked up the box of chocolates and held it out to her. "Have one. You'll feel better."

"You might have mentioned this when we discussed having Shelby interviewed," Angie said.

"Shelby and I talked about it," Cheryl said. "The truth is if she's going to become the star we all know she can be, this story is going to come out eventually. Might as well deal with it now. Here's hoping Adam sticks to the fluff."

*   *   *

He did not.

As Uncle Stan paced in front of them in the kitchen of the bakery, Mel and Angie sat on their stools of shame at the silver worktable while Uncle Stan crunched antacid tablets between his molars and growled.

"Scale of one to ten, how much trouble are we in?" Angie said out of the side of her mouth. Before Mel could answer, Uncle Stan did.

"A lot, Mrs. Harper, a lot!" he barked.

Angie's eyes went wide. Uncle Stan never went formal when addressing her.

"We were just trying to help flush out the killer," Mel said. "We didn't know about Shelby's mom. And the piece Adam wrote about her was exactly what we wanted. It was smart and sympathetic and it really could have worked to get whoever is trying to ruin Shelby's life to—"

"To what? Expose themselves?" Uncle Stan cried. He raised his arms in the air. "If your theory is correct, and that's a big if, then this news storm is exactly what the person who is trying to destroy Shelby wants. Did you know that the trending news story today was from a tabloid positing that the ability to commit cold-blooded murder might be genetic?"

"I hardly think—" Mel began but Uncle Stan interrupted.

"Clearly."

"That was mean," Mel said.

"Sorry." Uncle Stan blew out an exasperated breath. "But you've jeopardized an investigation, put a person of interest at risk, and quite possibly blown any chance we had of catching the killer."

"We didn't know—" Angie protested.

"That the other news outlets would latch on to the story about Shelby's mother and twist it into clickbait?" Uncle Stan asked. "Of course they did."

"We're really sorry," Mel said.

"Don't apologize to me," he said. "You owe an apology to Shelby and her entire family. Can you imagine how her mother is feeling having her past dragged up again?"

Mel and Angie exchanged a rueful look, and Mel said, "We should go see Shelby."

"I tried to call her this morning," Angie said. "But she didn't answer."

"That can't be good," Mel said.

"No." Angie sighed. "Let's go over to the hotel and see if she's still speaking to us."

"It's early," Mel said. "She might still be sleeping."

"No one is sleeping," Uncle Stan said. "Not with this news making the rounds." He held up his phone and the display showed a picture of Shelby performing with a headline that screamed "Musician or Murderer?" What a horrible mess this had turned into. Mel had no idea how they were going to face Shelby, but she knew she was bringing cupcakes.

Mel and Angie arrived at the hotel and found Shelby in the auditorium. They slid into two seats at the back. They watched silently as Shelby performed and the sound man worked on the levels of her voice and guitar.

Shelby was onstage with her acoustic guitar, going over an original song. Mel hoped it was something they were planning to work into the show.

"I have no idea what to say to her," Angie said. "Do you think she's mad? I'd be mad."

"Mad?" Mel snorted. "You'd be volcanic."

"Like a Pop Rock," Angie agreed.

"A Pop Rock coming out your nose," Mel corrected her.

"We should sneak out before she sees us."

"No, no. We had no way of knowing that Adam would dig into her background, find out about her mom, and write about her," Mel said.

"Yes, but—"

"Maybe if Doc had told Shelby why she should never talk to the press, we would have been more prepared," Mel said.

"That's true," Angie agreed. "Still, what a disaster."

When Shelby's song finished, they joined the rest of the crew, who applauded. Shelby beamed at everyone and when she saw Angie and Mel sitting towards the back, she took off her guitar and put it on its stand.

She strode up the aisle towards them. Mel thought she'd be able to curb stomp them quite easily in those pointy-toed, hard-heeled cowboy boots of hers.

"Moment of truth time," Angie said.

Mel felt a little queasy. If Shelby was mad, she couldn't blame her, but she felt terrible causing a rift in Angie and Shelby's friendship. She had just been getting to know Shelby and she discovered the thought of losing touch with the singer if she fired them alarmed her.

"What are you two doing sitting all the way back here?" Shelby asked. "You should be in the VIP area." She turned and pointed to a section that was roped off. It was the same VIP seating they'd sat in on opening night.

"We weren't sure you'd want to see us," Angie said. "You have seen the news today, haven't you?"

"Why? We're not at war, are we?" Shelby asked. Her lips tipped up just slightly in the corners so Mel knew she was teasing, which was a good thing. No, great! It meant she wasn't mad.

"The article Adam wrote about you was nice, mostly," Angie said. "I hope it's okay that he found out about your mom and wrote about that, too."

"It was bound to happen, sooner or later. At least Adam wasn't a jerk about it. In fact, he made it sound like it was just another blow against me and my dreams. I actually watered up while reading it."

"So, you're not mad at us?" Mel asked.

"No! How could I be?" Shelby asked. "You're doing everything you can to protect me and I really appreciate it."

"But I called you this morning and you never picked up, so I was worried that you were upset that other media outlets have picked up your story and are not being . . . kind," Angie said. She chewed her lower lip anxiously.

Shelby shook her head. "Oh, I'm so sorry. No, I was writing a new song and I got caught up and I haven't looked at my phone in hours."

"You're writing?" Angie asked.

Shelby put her hand on her chest. "I don't know what else to do with all of this pain I'm feeling. First Diana and now Doc and I just don't understand why. I have to channel it somewhere or I'll drown in it."

Mel thought about the hours she spent in the kitchen after her father passed. She absolutely understood the need to do *something* when the grief overwhelmed. For her, baking had given her an outlet for all of her despair. Clearly, it was music for Shelby.

"Has there been any news from the police?" Angie asked. "I was hoping they'd have a suspect in custody by now."

"Me, too." Shelby's gaze scanned the theater as if looking for a threat. "It's very unnerving to potentially have a killer walking among us."

"Well, that's a very telling way to describe yourself," a voice said from the dark corner of the theater behind them. Mel, Angie, and Shelby all glanced in that direction. Lisa Martin stepped out. She was holding her phone and she held it up. "So many articles about you and your trashy family—"

"Hey!" Angie made to jump out of her seat but Mel grabbed her arm and held her back.

"Easy, we don't want Uncle Stan to ban us from the theater," Mel whispered. Angie grunted and fell back into her seat.

"Lisa, don't be like this," Shelby said. She sounded sad.

"Do you want to hear my favorite? It's from a newspaper in Tennessee, your home state, no less. 'One wonders if Shelby Vaughn is just an acorn falling at the feet of the oak and growing up to be a murderer just like her mama.'" Lisa lowered her phone and said, "Isn't that delicious?"

Fourteen

"Buttercream frosting is delicious," Angie said. "Lies? Not so much."

Lisa glared. "It isn't lies." She pointed at Shelby. "She killed my mother and now she's done it again."

"I didn't—" Shelby began but Lisa interrupted.

"I saw him, you know," Lisa said.

"The killer?" Mel asked.

Lisa looked at her as if she were mentally incompetent. "*No*, I saw Shelby's next manager. Terrence Nickels, the best music manager in the business, and he's here, staying at the hotel through the holidays, but I bet you already knew that, didn't you? Quite the coincidence that you're here . . . or is it?"

"I don't know who you're talking about," Shelby said.

Lisa threw back her head and laughed, but it was more evil Disney queen laugh than actual amusement. It made the hair on the back of Mel's neck stand on end.

"Yeah, sure," Lisa said. "Keep playing the ingenue. It's worked so well for you so far, why change it up now? But just so you know. I know who you are and I know what you did and I won't rest until you pay for it."

She sauntered away, tossing her long dark hair over her shoulder as she went. She was dressed in a curve-revealing number that caused people to turn and stare as she went by. She was obviously quite comfortable being in the public eye.

"Did you say that you were both represented by Diana but that Diana chose you and sent Lisa to live with her dad?" Angie asked.

"Yeah, I didn't really understand what was happening at the time," Shelby said. "Cheryl told me it was a custody thing with Lisa's father but years later Diana admitted that she felt that showcasing Lisa and me together was holding me back. It wasn't an easy decision for her but she had bills to pay and her own career as a manager to focus on. Lisa never forgave either of us."

"I can understand that," Mel said. "It had to feel like the worst sort of rejection from her mother and her best friend."

"I know," Shelby said. "If I could turn back time, I'd try and talk Diana out of it. Then maybe she'd still be alive."

Angie frowned. "Do you think Lisa killed her?"

Shelby wrung her hands. "I hate to think it, but she's so angry and it's been festering for years. I can't think of anyone else who would have wanted to harm Diana. You met her, Angie, she was the best."

"She really was," Angie agreed. "Of course, this is assuming that Diana was murdered. Just because she and Doc were your managers, and Doc was definitely murdered, doesn't mean that Diana was murdered, too."

"It's weird though, isn't it?" Shelby asked.

"It's coincidental," Mel said. "And if I've learned anything from Uncle Stan, it's that there are no such things as coincidences . . . generally speaking."

"Shelby, we need to finish going over the new song," the stage manager called from the stage.

"Sorry, I have to go," she said. "We're trying to get the new song in the lineup for tonight and we have to work out the choreography for the dancers. We're putting it in the middle of the show, so that should liven things up a bit."

"Excellent," Angie said. "I can't wait to hear it."

"Me, too," Mel agreed.

With quick hugs, Shelby hurried back down to the stage. She was in her casual attire. Jeans, boots, and an oversized sweatshirt, with a bandanna holding her hair back from her face. Mel realized that she had that indefinable "every girl" look. She doubted that she would even recognize Shelby on the street if she were to pass her. Wouldn't that be a perk for a murderer?

Mel shook her head. She did *not* just think that. Shelby was not a murderer. She and Angie decided to head back to the bakery but Mel wanted to make one detour in the hotel along the way. While Angie called her mother to check on Emari, Mel took the opportunity to approach the hotel's information desk.

"Hi, I hope you can help me . . ." She glanced at the man's name tag. "Mike."

The man, who looked to be in his late twenties, nodded and said, "Absolutely, what can I do for you?"

"I'm the personal assistant to Mr. Nickels," Mel said. She saw the man's eyebrows bob just once so she knew he knew whom she was referring to. Excellent. "He's staying in the . . . um . . . oh, drat . . . you know, the suite with the thingies . . ."

"The sunset suite on the top floor with the yellow sun umbrellas," he said. "The one with the view of Camelback Mountain."

"Yes, that's it," Mel said. "Nothing but the best for Mr. Nickels."

"Naturally," Mike said. "Now how may I assist you?"

"Mr. Nickels was wondering what your earliest tee time on the golf course is?" she asked, making it up on the fly.

"Six o'clock is our official earliest, but of course, we are happy to accommodate anything Mr. Nickels requires."

"Perfect, I'll let him know and be in touch," Mel said. "You've been very helpful."

"Anytime."

Mel crossed over to where she'd left Angie. "What are you up to?"

"How about a quick ride up to the top of the hotel?" Mel asked.

Angie's eyes went wide. "The baby is sleeping. I have time."

"Excellent," Mel said.

They strode across the marble-floored lobby to the

bank of elevators. There was one designated for the upper floor, and Mel pressed the button, hoping there was no additional security to gain access to the sunset suite.

They stepped inside and the doors closed. Angie turned to Mel and asked, "What's going on?"

"We're going to pop in on Mr. Nickels," Mel said.

"Are you insane?" Angie asked. "He's like the most powerful person ever and we're just going to knock on his door and say what?"

Mel held up the four-pack of cupcakes that they'd brought for Shelby as an apology but forgot to give her.

"We're delivering cupcakes?" Angie asked. She glanced at their outfits. They were both in their bakery attire, which was to say kitchen casual jeans and T-shirts with baking slogans on them. Mel's had a whisk and read *We Whisk You a Merry Christmas* while Angie's sported a rolling pin and said *This Is How I Roll.* Cute but not really meet "the man" appropriate.

Mel knew what Angie was thinking but she didn't care. She had no idea when they'd get this opportunity again and that was assuming Mr. Nickels was in at the moment.

The elevator opened up to a lobby with one door. The sunset suite apparently took up the entire floor. The lobby had a narrow black table against the wall. Beside it was a potted dracaena that had long green leaves and was taller than Mel. The lone door was stained glass with a very Frank Lloyd Wright pattern of rectangles. Beside the door handle was a buzzer. Before she could rethink it, Mel pressed it.

She didn't hear any noise but assumed that it made a sound inside the suite. It was midday during the week, surely they couldn't be waking Mr. Nickels?

Mel and Angie exchanged a look. This was clearly a dead end.

"Thanks for your time," Mel said. She turned to go and Angie followed suit.

"Not so fast," Miranda said. She held out her hands. "I'll take the cupcakes. Given my cooperation, I think I've earned them."

"That's fair," Mel said. She handed Miranda the box and was halfway to the elevator when she paused, and asked, "One more question. What will you do if Terrence wants to represent Shelby?"

Miranda flipped the top of the box and examined the contents. She chose a raspberry white chocolate cupcake and then closed the lid. She met Mel's gaze over the box and said, "He won't. I made sure of it."

She stepped back into the suite and shut the door.

"Is it just me or did that last sentence give you chills?" Angie asked.

"Oh, yeah." Mel shivered. "Let's get out of here."

They cruised in the elevator back down to the lobby. They stepped out and ran smack into Cheryl. Literally. Cheryl went one way and her handbag another. Mel tried to catch her before she fell but she was too late. Angie hurried to retrieve Cheryl's bag for her.

Cheryl lay on the marble floor in the middle of the lobby, trying to catch her breath after having the wind knocked out of her.

"Ms. Hoover!" Trevor, the head of security, dashed across the lobby towards them. Mel hadn't seen him since the night he unlocked the door when she'd been trapped in the VIP suite and she'd discovered Doc's body in the dressing room. She'd barely noticed him then, but

173

as he crouched down beside Cheryl, she noted that despite his short gray hair, he seemed quite fit.

"I'm fine, Trevor, or I will be." Cheryl turned to Mel and Angie. "Is there a fire, girls?"

"No, sorry," Mel said. "We didn't expect anyone to be in front of the doors. Our mistake."

"Yes, we're truly sorry," Angie said. She handed Cheryl her handbag.

The stylist glanced at them, hovering above her, then over at the elevator that led solely to the sunset suite. Mel could tell she was wondering what brought them out of that particular elevator. Mel was not a skilled fibber like Angie and her brothers, so she said nothing.

"Boy, did we take a wrong turn there," Angie said. She jerked her thumb at the elevator and blinked innocently. "Did you know there's a penthouse in this place?"

"Here, let's get you back on your feet," Trevor said.

Angie reached down and helped Trevor lift Cheryl up. Mel noted the muscles in Angie's upper arms and realized that hauling Emari around was making Angie fit. Hmm. Mel added this to the reason-children-would-be-good category of her mind and put it aside.

"Are you sure you're all right?" Trevor asked Cheryl.

"Just fine," she said. She patted his arm and winked. "I'm still young enough to bounce."

Trevor blushed a faint shade of pink and said, "Well, if you need anything, you just give me a shout, you hear?"

"Thank you. It's so nice to have a manly man around to help a girl out." Cheryl glanced at him from beneath her lashes and gave him a little finger wave. He blushed a deeper shade of pink and left them to return to his office behind the check-in desk.

As he crossed the lobby, Cheryl patted her hair back into place and said, "I find it always helps to have a strong man at one's beck and call, don't you think?"

Feeling as if agreeing would be the equivalent of sending the women's movement back a century, Mel chose to remain silent. She noted Angie did the same and opted to change the subject.

"What are you doing here?" Angie asked Cheryl.

Cheryl glanced between them. "If I tell you, you have to promise you won't tell Shelby."

"Absolutely," Angie agreed.

"Of course," Mel said. She wasn't sure what she was promising and felt a twinge of conscience that she slapped away.

Cheryl leaned in and lowered her voice to a whisper. "I heard a rumor that Terrence Nickels is in the building."

She stared at them and Angie cleared her throat and said, "The music manager?"

"Yes!" Cheryl cried. She glanced around the lobby, making sure no one could hear them. She reached into her handbag and pulled out her phone. "I was going to sneak up there and try to airdrop a video of Shelby singing onto his phone. Brilliant, right?"

"Well, that's assuming he has AirDrop on his phone," Angie said.

"Who doesn't?" Cheryl asked. "I mean what century are we living in if a guy like Terrence Nickels doesn't use the latest tech?"

"Valid point," Mel said. "But don't you think you should check with Shelby before you drop a file on someone who might get upset about it?"

"Why would he get upset?" Cheryl asked. "Shelby is amazing. He'd be damn lucky to sign her."

Angie and Mel exchanged a look, and Mel said, "We have to tell her."

"I don't like the sound of that. Tell me what?" Cheryl asked.

"Miranda Carter is working for Terrence Nickels," Mel said. "She'll never let him sign Shelby."

"No!" Cheryl cried. "How do you know this?"

Mel sighed. "Because we were just up there. We heard about him from Lisa Martin and we wanted to see for ourselves if he was here or if she was just messing with Shelby."

"And you spoke to him?" Cheryl asked.

"No, because Miranda answered the door in just a robe," Angie said. "Apparently, she's not just working for him, she's dating him, too."

"Oh." Cheryl's shoulders slumped. "I was so hopeful when I heard he was here that maybe he came to take a look at Shelby."

"No, according to Miranda, he's here because she wanted to rub Doc's face in the fact that she was dating and working for a man more powerful than him," Mel said.

A crowd of tourists filled the lobby, loitering around the lesser people's elevator. The women shifted to the side.

"I know you want to help Shelby," Angie said. "We do, too, but I don't think Terrence Nickels is the answer."

"I suppose not," Cheryl agreed. Her chin quivered. "What's going to happen to my baby? I'm so worried that she doesn't have representation and that someone is going to swoop in and ruin her career."

"First things first," Mel said. "We have to make sure she can't be tied to Doc's murder in any way, then we can worry about her career."

"But she can't be tied to Doc's murder," Cheryl said. She turned to Angie. "She was with you."

"Yes, she was." Angie didn't look at Mel. "But we need to get this murder investigation behind her so that she's not tainted by it."

"You're right," Cheryl said. She gave them a rueful smile. "I shouldn't meddle in Shelby's professional life. I need to stick to my gifts, which is hair and outfits. Despite the pain in my posterior, I think running into you two was a good thing. Can you imagine if Miranda found an airdropped video on Mr. Nickels's phone? She'd blow a gasket." Cheryl laughed and elbowed Angie. "It'd almost be worth it."

Angie laughed and Mel did, too. "Hopefully, Uncle Stan will have some information on Doc's homicide soon. Once Shelby is away from that mess, then she can look for a new manager."

"An excellent plan," Cheryl agreed. She glanced at her phone. "Ack! Look at the time. I have to go start getting ready for tonight's show. Bye, girls!" She blew them kisses and darted off in the direction of the auditorium.

"Can you imagine if Miranda had opened the door to find Cheryl up there?" Angie asked Mel.

"No," Mel said. "It would have been bad."

"So bad," Angie agreed.

Mel waited until they exited the hotel and were half-way across the parking lot before she asked, "You did tell Uncle Stan that you weren't with Shelby the entire time when Doc was murdered, didn't you?"

Fifteen

Angie glanced away. "I meant to."

"Ange, we talked about this," Mel said. She unlocked her Mini Cooper and they both climbed in. She'd bought the car when her last name was Cooper because it seemed cute, but now that she was Mrs. Joe DeLaura, she wondered if it was time for a change. Maybe a DeLorean like in *Back to the Future*. Did they even make those anymore? She shook her head. *Focus!*

"I know," Angie said. "It just seemed like I was making a big deal out of nothing and I didn't want to get Shelby in trouble."

"If she is the killer, you could be an accessory," Mel said.

"She didn't kill Doc," Angie said. "I know she didn't."

"Listen, I don't think she did, either, but you are putting yourself at risk by not telling the truth," Mel said. "If—and that's a huge if—she is somehow involved, you could get dragged into it. Even Joe won't be able to save you and the next thing you know you're only seeing your baby every other weekend in the jail yard."

"Are you trying to give me nightmares?" Angie demanded.

"That depends, is it working?" Mel asked.

"Little bit," Angie admitted.

"Good."

Mel didn't drive them right to the bakery. Instead, she parked at the police station, which was a few blocks over from the bakery in Old Town.

"We're going to see Uncle Stan now?" Angie asked.

"Yup."

"Fine."

Mel and Angie trudged into the police station. The desk clerk, Jaime, held out his hands and said, "What? No cupcakes?"

Mel smiled. "Next time. I promise."

"I'm going to hold you to that," he said. He jerked a thumb at the open office area behind him. "The big guy was just in the break room getting coffee."

"Thanks," Mel said. She led Angie towards the back.

"This is going to be so awkward," Angie said. "Can't I just text him?"

"No."

"Email?"

"No."

"Send a note with a carrier pigeon?"

"Stop." Mel glanced at her over her shoulder. "This

wouldn't be so weird if you'd just told him the truth at the beginning."

"I know but I was conflicted," Angie said.

"That sounds unhealthy," Uncle Stan said. He came out of the break room with a paper cup full of hot coffee.

"I thought Mom said no more coffee during the day because it gives you heartburn and insomnia?" Mel asked.

"Oh, it's not mine. It's for my partner," Uncle Stan said.

Mel lifted one eyebrow and gave him a dubious look.

Uncle Stan scanned the workroom until he spotted his partner, Tara Martinez. "Hey, Tara, I got you that coffee you asked for."

Tara frowned at him. "I don't drink coffee."

"See?" Angie said to Mel. "Everyone fibs." She turned to Uncle Stan. "You just sit down and enjoy your coffee. We won't mention it to Joyce. We promise. Don't we, Mel?"

"Yeah, sure," Mel said. "I didn't see a thing."

"Thanks, kid." Uncle Stan took a big satisfied slurp off his cup. "Say, how are the Christmas plans coming?"

"Fine," Mel lied. "Everything is under control."

"Great, so what can I do for you two?"

"I'm glad you asked," Angie said. Mel rolled her eyes. "When I told you I was with Shelby the entire time Doc Howard was murdered, I might have been a teeny bit in-accurate."

"You lied?" Uncle Stan asked. He looked shocked and a little disappointed.

"No," Angie said. "It's just there was a brief moment when I was in another room, talking to Tate on the phone and not with Shelby, who was in the next room packing her bag."

"Was there a separate entrance in the other room?" Uncle Stan asked.

Angie looked pained. "Yes."

"I can't believe you didn't tell me this," Uncle Stan said. He looked at Mel. "Did you know about this?"

"Mel told me to tell you," Angie said. "But I didn't want to get Shelby in trouble."

"If she didn't murder Howard, she has nothing to fear," Uncle Stan said.

"Are you kidding me?" Angie said. "Have you seen the horde of reporters, hounding us at the bakery just because we know her? She can't step out of that hotel or she gets mobbed. I didn't want to give them any fuel for their hit pieces."

Uncle Stan considered her for a long moment. "I appreciate your loyalty to your friend, but now I have to go and question her, just to be thorough, about the time she spent alone. How long do you think it was?"

"Twelve minutes and thirty-four seconds," Angie said. Uncle Stan raised his eyebrows. "That's the length of the call on my phone. I checked."

"That's a very tight time frame to walk out of her room, take the elevator downstairs, hurry to the auditorium, get to her dressing room, bludgeon Doc Howard, and then get back up to her room," Mel said.

"What floor is her room on?" Uncle Stan asked.

"Second floor." Angie sighed.

"So, not impossible then," he said.

"Except, if she had hit him with something, where did it go?" Angie asked. "Twelve minutes didn't give her a lot of time to commit the deed and hide her weapon, what-ever it was. Speaking of, has the medical examiner deter-mined what was used to hit him?"

"No." Uncle Stan shook his head. "And while they have ruled out poison, there was a very high level of sedative in his system. They didn't find the drug in the cupcake he was holding but he'd eaten half of it, so was the sedative in the half he'd eaten? Or did he take the drug before eating the cupcake? We don't know."

"But if it wasn't poison, that's good, right?" Mel asked. "Does it mean we're officially off the suspect list?"

"Yes—mostly."

"Do you think you could mention the no-poison thing at a news conference, because the reporters being in front of the bakery is getting old. Plus, they're eating all of our stock."

"I'll see if I can drop that info into the right ears," he said.

"Thank you," Mel said. She glanced at the clock. "We'd better go. You need to pick up Emari and I have some baking to do this afternoon before we have to get to the hotel for this evening's show."

"Be careful, both of you," Uncle Stan said. "There's a murderer out there and we have no idea what their end-game is."

After a harried afternoon of baking, Mel and Marty headed to the VIP suite. Angie wasn't able to make it tonight as the baby was fussing, and she was concerned that Emari was getting sick. Mel assured her that between Marty and the brothers—or, as she liked to think of them, "her Santas"—she had more than enough help.

Mel was just loading another tray for Paulie when she noticed a familiar figure leaving the VIP suite, not by the door for public access but rather through the staff exit that led to the hallway of dressing rooms.

Mel felt the hair on the back of her neck prickle. This could not be good. "Change of plan, Paulie, I need you to monitor the cupcake station."

"Bathroom break?" he asked, sounding sympathetic. "I got you."

Mel didn't bother to correct him. Instead, she nodded and headed for the door. She'd just crossed the threshold when she spotted Jerry Stackhouse enter Shelby's dressing room at the end of the hallway. It was a different one than the one she'd had before. After Doc's murder, they sealed off the old room and put her in a new one.

Mel hurried down the narrow passageway, passing stagehands and performers as they went to take their places. The curtain would be lifting in forty-five minutes and the hum of preshow adrenaline was beginning to fill the air.

The door to Shelby's dressing room was shut but she could hear raised voices, one of which had to be Stackhouse as it was low and growly. She didn't bother knocking but flung open the door and cried, "Shelby! Last call for cupcakes. What can I bring you?"

Everyone in the room turned to look at her. It took Mel only an instant to assess the situation as dangerous. Jerry was clearly threatening Shelby as he loomed over her in her makeup chair. Meanwhile, Cheryl was standing behind

Shelby brandishing a comb with the pointy handle sticking out like she'd use it on Stackhouse if she had to. Mel made her face blank and said, "Oh, sorry, am I interrupting something?"

"Yes," Stackhouse said.

"No!" Shelby cried.

Mel entered the room, leaving the door open behind her. "In that case, how can I help you, Shelby?"

Stackhouse glared but Mel wasn't afraid of him because she knew that Jerry Stackhouse was full of bluster. He'd shown his true self in the VIP suite when he all but ran from her.

"You just being here is all the help I need," Shelby said. "I'll think about what you said, Mr. Stackhouse."

"Make sure you do," Jerry said. "Doc owed me a lot of money and someone is going to pay it back. Since he worked for you, it seems to me, you're the likeliest candidate."

"Shelby doesn't have to pay Doc's gambling debts," Cheryl snapped. "That's not how that works."

"I don't care who pays me, so long as someone does," Jerry said.

Mel strode forward until she was standing beside him. "Hey, Stackhouse, I guess you were right about me."

"I don't know what you're talking about." Jerry sidled away but Mel followed.

"Sure you do," she said. "Don't you remember? You said people seemed to turn up dead whenever I was around." She turned and gave him a hard stare. "I wonder who'll be next."

Jerry scuttled back so fast, he tripped over a stool but kept right on going. "I'm not afraid of you."

"Are you sure about that?" Mel asked. She lunged and he yelped and ran out the door. She turned around to see both Shelby and Cheryl gaping at her.

"Are you two okay?" she asked.

"That was amazing," Shelby said. "He's terrified of you."

"Is that some sort of superpower of yours?" Cheryl asked. "Have you been holding out on us?"

"No," Mel laughed. "The night of the opening show, Stackhouse was here with his daughter."

"I remember," Shelby said. "He was one of the people milling around when Doc was found."

"Well, before that, he was in the VIP lounge. I remember because he asked me about my husband and then told me how weird it was that I'd been on the scene of so many murders. He wasn't wrong."

"But he tried to rattle you by mentioning it," Cheryl said. She shook her head. "Typical bully."

"I think so, but then I handed him a cupcake and implied that I had no idea how people got murdered near me," Mel said. "You should have seen his face. He put it down and—" Mel froze, remembering the moment.

"What is it, Mel?" Shelby asked. "You've got a weird look on your face."

Mel held up one finger as she tried to remember. She remembered that she had handed Jerry Stackhouse a Sugar Plum cupcake. He'd put it down and backed away when he was freaked out by her propensity for finding dead bodies, and she'd put it aside. Could it have been the same one in the box Marty had given Doc? Uncle Stan had said the tox screen was inconclusive because they couldn't determine whether the sedative in Doc's system was taken via the cupcake as the delivery system or if he'd ingested the drug another way and had then eaten the cupcake.

"I just remembered something," Mel said. "I'll follow up on it later." She focused on Shelby. "Did Stackhouse threaten you directly? If he did, you should tell Uncle Stan. Speaking of which, where are his guys who are supposed to be watching you?"

"They got called away," Cheryl said. "Something about an incident in front of the hotel."

"I don't like this," Mel said. She crossed the room and shut and locked the door.

"Even if there was an incident, one of them should have stayed with you unless they were told not to," she said. "It could be that Stackhouse set it up so he could threaten you in person, but I don't want to take any chances."

She took her phone out of her pocket and called Uncle Stan. When she told him what happened, he let loose a string of expletives and then told her to sit tight. He would send backup immediately.

Cheryl picked up a hot curling wand and asked, "Should we arm ourselves?"

Mel considered her for a beat. "No, I think we'll be all right but keep your guard up."

"What's happening?" Shelby asked. She didn't sound afraid just very weary.

"Uncle Stan would never have called your detail off," Mel said. "Not until the killer is caught."

"Oh." Shelby's eyes went wide.

A fist pounded on the door and they all jumped. "It's Detective Martinez, open up."

Mel would have recognized that surly female voice anywhere. She yanked the door open. "Martinez."

"DeLaura," Tara said. She and Mel had never gotten along but now that Tara was dating Ray, they tried. She was wearing her work uniform of khaki pants and a white dress shirt with a navy blazer over it. "What's happening?"

Mel told her about the security detail being called off at the same time Jerry Stackhouse just decided to pay a visit.

Tara nodded. She ran a hand over her hair, which was pulled back into a tight bun on top of her head. She turned to Shelby and asked, "Did he threaten you?"

Shelby looked at Cheryl and they exchanged a look of understanding. "Not directly," Shelby said. "There was no 'pay up or I'm going to break your legs' type of stuff. The fact that he was in my dressing room demanding the fifty thousand dollars that my deceased manager owed him felt threatening, but I can't say that he tried to hurt me or even said he would hurt me. He just said I'd be sorry if I didn't pay him what Doc owed him."

"So a vague bit of harassment. Lovely," Tara said. She took out her phone and called Uncle Stan. While she was talking, two officers showed up in the doorway. Tara ended her call and turned on them. "Outside. Now. I need to have a chat with you."

"I hope they're not in trouble," Shelby said. "They've been great about following us around without complaint."

"Well, that is their job," Mel said.

"I suppose but it's really been boring," Cheryl said. "I can't fault them for taking off when they thought there was some action."

"I don't think Uncle Stan is going to see it that way, but it's nice of you to do so," Mel said. She glanced out the door and saw Tara, with her hands on her hips, chewing out the man and woman who'd arrived moments earlier. They looked miserable but Mel supposed it was a teachable moment. When you were supposed to stay with someone as a bodyguard, you damn well stayed.

Cheryl had gone back to finishing Shelby's makeup. The star looked otherworldly with her big hair, makeup that made her features pop, and the formfitting red satin sheath she was wearing. All this and the woman could sing, too. Sometimes life felt incredibly unfair. Mel decided she needed a cupcake.

"I'm heading back to the VIP lounge before it opens," she said. "Have a great show, Shelby."

Shelby sent her a warm smile and a thumbs-up. Mel sighed. Of course, Shelby was sincerely nice, too. It really was too much.

Sixteen

Mel was sitting at her kitchen table, drinking coffee with Oz, while trying to fight off the panic that was slowly twining itself around her like an invasive vine.

Christmas was now just days away and the house wasn't any more decorated than it had been when she displayed her mother's collection of loud animatronic dolls. Her menu was all over the place as she tried to appease all of her guests' specific food wants and issues.

She knew she had to make her mother's prime rib, which, in order to feed over thirty people, she might need to take out a bank loan to afford. Then of course her brother Charlie would likely have a seizure if there weren't mashed potatoes and gravy. And then there was a peanut allergy to consider and two of their guests had gluten allergies, so she needed to provide carbs and desserts that they could eat. Thank goodness her sister-in-law Nancy insisted on cranberry sauce out of the can, as in it needed to maintain the actual shape of the can so it was sliceable.

"Why are you smiling?" Oz asked.

"Because I love my sister-in-law," Mel said.

"Random, but okay," Oz said.

"Low-maintenance people are my favorite people right now," Mel said.

He snorted. "'You're the worst kind. You're high maintenance but you think you're low maintenance.'"

"*When Harry Met Sally.*" Mel identified the movie quote. "Watch it, Ruiz, I've seen your kitchen standards at your resort job. You make Gordon Ramsey look like a cream puff."

Oz grinned. It was a slash of white teeth, showcasing his square jaw, deep brown eyes with arching brows, and thick head of dark hair. It was no wonder he was becoming such a local celebrity. He clearly had the "it" factor. Mel wondered how long it would be before he had his own cooking show, probably national. Move over, Guy Fieri.

"I take my profession very seriously," Oz said. He glanced at her under his lashes. "I did learn from the best."

"Aw," Mel said. "I'll forgive you the high-maintenance crack then."

"Seriously, what is our plan for feeding this many people with the variety of menu you have in mind?" Oz asked. "I don't want to freak you out but I have no idea how the two of us are going to accomplish this in mere days."

"We have backup," Mel said. "Olivia and Marty and Angie and Tate have all volunteered to help. And, of course, Joe."

Oz stared at her. "But as for the professionals, we're it?"

"'Fraid so," Mel said.

Oz heaved a sigh. "Let's break it down by what can be made ahead of time." He picked up the pen Mel had given him and started writing on the notepad in front of him. "Okay, if we crockpot the mashed potatoes, we can make those early and they'll be ready when it's time to eat. We're going to need a bigger oven than the one in your kitchen, so let's plan to use the bakery's ovens."

"Great idea," Mel said. "It's only a few minutes from here. The food won't even get cold on the drive."

"Another perk about living in the land of the sun in winter," he said.

They hammered out their shopping list and tried to designate who was cooking what and when. Mel glanced around her house and realized with the job at the Hotel Grande taking up her evenings and Joe prepping for a murder trial that was set to begin on January 1, they still hadn't managed to put up a Christmas tree. Her mother was going to have a stroke.

"Since Joe and I are both maxed out with work, tell me, how crazy would it be for me to ask the brothers for help with the decorations?" she asked.

"Without Joe or you available to supervise, pretty crazy," Oz said. "You know what they're like."

"I do, but I'm also in a pickle," she said. "I just don't have time and I don't want Joyce to be disappointed, for that matter I don't want Joe's mother to be disappointed, either."

"If you can get Tony to be in charge, it might be okay," Oz said. "Just not Ray, anyone but Ray."

"Yeah, Tony, you're right," Mel said. "He's a no-nonsense sort. I can totally trust him."

Feeling her stress level lower a smidge, she started on her shopping list.

"Why does he get to be in charge?" Ray whined.

Mel stared at him. She was standing in the garage with Al, Paulie, Tony, and Ray. Sal, Dom, and Joe couldn't make it. She had spent the rest of her afternoon after Oz left hauling out the decorations her mother had dropped off a couple of days ago, which she had stuffed into a corner of the garage to be dealt with . . . well, now.

"Tony is in charge because he . . . uh . . . well . . ." She stammered to a stop.

"Because I'm more responsible than you dopes," he said. Tony was the mysterious DeLaura brother. Tall, thin, and good-looking like the rest of them, he had a generic job description and worked in an industry no one really understood, but he had mad skills in technology and wasn't afraid to use them to, say, track his sister through her phone. Angie had loved that—not—among other ethically questionable choices.

"I wouldn't put it that way exactly," Mel said. She could see a brotherly beef starting and she didn't want to have anything to do with instigating that. "It's just that Tony is the most tech savvy and this is a lot of electrical stuff." Mel waved her hands at the enormous Tupperware bins.

Al and Paulie nodded in agreement and Al said, "She's right. This is a lot."

"And I need to get back to the bakery and let you all get started." She tossed the spare house key at Tony. "Lock up when you leave, and thank you. You're really saving me here."

"Well, you are hosting the entire family for Christmas dinner, it's the least we can do," Tony said. "Don't worry. We've got this."

Mel waved and climbed into her car. She felt a nervous flutter in her belly and thought maybe she should call them off. Surely, her house didn't need to be decorated in lights and whatnot for the day to feel festive. An image of her mother looking disappointed popped into her head. Mel started the car and drove to the bakery, hoping she didn't regret this.

The bakery was buzzing. Madison and Marty were working the counter while Angie was in the kitchen, packing up the cupcakes Mel had made early this morning before her meeting with Oz for the VIP suite.

Mel had called Uncle Stan last night to share her revelation about the Sugar Plum cupcake but he hadn't picked up, and she'd left a message asking him to call her. She didn't want to leave a voice mail accusing Stackhouse of poisoning the cupcake Doc had eaten, but she wanted to mention the moment with Stackhouse to Uncle Stan in case it warranted investigation.

Could it be that Stackhouse had slipped the sedative into the Sugar Plum cupcake thinking that Mel would eat the rejected cupcake, and if so, why? She wondered if it had to do with Stackhouse knowing that Joe DeLaura was her husband. Was he out to get revenge on Joe for something? Had Joe prosecuted him or one of his thug buddies? Had Stackhouse been planning to get revenge on Joe via Mel and it had gone horribly wrong when Doc ate the cupcake?

But if Mel remembered right, that particular box had been labeled for Shelby, so had Stackhouse drugged the cupcake to harm Shelby? Maybe to show Doc he could hurt her and force Doc to pay him so that he didn't take away his livelihood, namely Shelby?

Argh, why wasn't Uncle Stan calling her back? She called her mother just to see if she knew where Uncle Stan was.

"Melanie, so good to hear from you," Joyce yelled into the phone.

There was a loud banging noise coming from Joyce's end of the call. "Mom, are you all right?" Mel asked.

"I'm fine," Joyce cried. "They're just tearing out the cupboards for the kitchen. Hang on." The noise got much louder and then it became a muffled background sound. "I'm outside now. What is it, dear?"

"Do you know if Uncle Stan is in the office today?" Mel asked.

"He's in court," Joyce said. "Poor man, as if it isn't enough to have a homicide investigation over the holidays, he has to go to court, too."

Mel nodded. That made sense. If he was in court, he couldn't exactly call her back. "Okay, I'll try him again later. Thanks, Mom."

"Anytime," Joyce said. "How are the preparations for Christmas dinner coming?"

"Great," Mel said. It felt like less of a lie now that she and Oz had spent some time on the plans.

"You know, I'm happy to come over and help if you need it," Joyce said.

"I really appreciate that, Mom, but I think I've got it," Mel said. "It's going to be great. We're even getting on top of the decorating, too."

"Oh, that's wonderful," Joyce said. "Not to pressure you, but I drove by your house and there were no lights up and no tree in the window. It looked sad."

Mel closed her eyes and silently prayed for patience. "Well, it won't look sad much longer."

"That's good to hear," Joyce said. "Do you want me to text Stan to call you?"

"No, I already left him a message. It's nothing that won't keep," Mel said. "But thank you. Love you, Mom."

"Love you, too, honey," Joyce said. She ended the call at the same time Mel did.

Drat! Mel wanted to tell Uncle Stan about her suspicions now. Maybe she was just being paranoid but Stackhouse had been behaving oddly at the opening show. If he had been trying to get revenge on Joe for something, then what better way than to drug his wife and, what, torture her? Mel felt a shiver creep down her spine. Did Stackhouse really seem the type? Did anyone seem the type?

But if Stackhouse drugged the cupcake and Doc ate it by accident, then who murdered Doc and why? Did the sedative just give them the opportunity? Or did it turn a situation that wasn't supposed to be a homicide into one? If the police just knew what Doc had been hit with, they could narrow down the suspects. It was maddening, and Mel had enough on her plate at the moment, trying to host Christmas dinner.

"Mel." Angie waved her hand in front of Mel's face. "Hey, Mel, you all right?"

"Yeah, I'm just trying to reach Uncle Stan," Mel said. "I had a thought about the investigation."

"He'll love that," Angie said. Her sarcasm was as thick as Mel's buttercream. "Care to share?"

"Remember when I said Stackhouse approached me at the cupcake station on the opening evening?" Mel asked.

"Yeah," Angie said.

"He took a Sugar Plum cupcake but then when he reflected upon how many murders I've been connected to, he put it down," Mel said. She waited a beat and said, "Doc was holding a half-eaten Sugar Plum cupcake."

Angie gasped. "You think Stackhouse planted the cupcake? Wait, how could he possibly have known that Marty would hand Doc that cupcake? That you wouldn't just throw it out?"

"He couldn't have, except Stackhouse was milling around the cupcake station when Doc appeared, and I'm sure he must have heard me say that the boxes of extra cupcakes were marked for the cast and crew and others. Doc said not to box one for Shelby because she wasn't allowed to eat them."

Angie glowered. "Why? Was he afraid she might have a moment of joy in her life?"

"I think it was a weight issue," Mel said.

"The woman is as big as a pencil," Angie sputtered. "It wasn't about her weight. It was about control."

"Be that as it may," Mel said. "I think Stackhouse used the information to potentially spike the cupcake with the sedative, either to get to Shelby or Doc, I'm not sure."

"It feels like a reach but it's not like Uncle Stan has any other great leads that we know of," Angie said.

"We need to confirm which box Marty gave Doc. I didn't notice at the time I found Doc," Mel said. "I didn't even think about it."

"It could be that it wasn't Stackhouse," Angie said. Her eyes were wide. "If it was someone else who spiked the cupcake, assuming the sedative was in the cupcake, then Shelby might have been the target."

"Could be. Meaning Doc was just collateral damage and Shelby really was the target the entire time just like we feared," Mel said.

"Let's get to the hotel," Angie said. "We need to warn her."

Together they packed up the van and headed to the hotel. At this point, the security guards knew Angie and Mel on sight. They waved them in through the service entrance and Mel and Angie parked their cart beside their cupcake station. They were a half hour early, giving them time to go and talk to Shelby before the brothers arrived and the other vendors set up their stations.

"Should we just leave the cupcakes here?" Mel asked. "I mean, assuming someone put a sedative in the one Doc ate, what's to stop them from doing it again if we leave them unattended?"

"Good point," Angie said. "Wait here."

Mel pushed their loaded cart of boxed cupcakes behind the table. The cupcake towers and Christmas decorations were still in place from the night before. She watched as Angie crossed the room to talk to one of the hotel staff. They had an animated conversation that included a hair toss and a big smile from Angie. She strode back across the room to Mel.

"All set," Angie said. "I asked the guy over there to keep an eye on our cupcakes and not to let anyone near them and he agreed."

"Can we trust him?" Mel asked. "Do we even know his name?"

"His name is Lucas," Angie said. "He's been stationed in here to keep an eye on the room, so watching the cupcakes is no big deal, or so he said. Plus, I handed him a fifty."

"Okay." Mel glanced at her watch. "We don't have much time. Let's go find Shelby."

With a wave to Lucas, they left the VIP suite and hurried down the hallway to Shelby's new dressing room. Mel tried not to look at the old room, where she'd found Doc. She didn't want to think about how that might have been Shelby.

Angie rapped on the door and they heard a voice call, "Come in."

Shelby was seated in her makeup chair while Cheryl worked her magic. Shelby's hair was a mass of long fat curls, one of which flopped over her eye, and she blew it out of the way.

"Hi, guys," she greeted them. Her smile was warm and she looked happy to see them. "You're here early. What's happening?"

"Nothing bad, I hope," Cheryl said around the bobby pins she held between her lips.

"We're not sure," Angie said. She went on to tell them Mel's suspicion about Stackhouse hovering around, seeing the box that was labeled for Shelby, and putting the rejected and potentially spiked Sugar Plum cupcake in it.

Cheryl's eyes went wide. "I don't like this. You need to tell that uncle detective of yours and have that guy picked up or at the very least banned from the hotel."

"That would be great," Mel said. "But we have to prove it first. Right now, it's just speculation and a gut feeling that something was wrong about my entire interaction with him."

"I trust your gut instincts over cold hard facts any day of the week," Angie said.

"Thanks, but I don't think Uncle Stan sees it like that," Mel said. "We need proof."

"Like a confession?" Shelby asked. She frowned. "I could try and get him to say something to me. Maybe give him the opportunity to threaten me or something."

"Absolutely not!" Cheryl said. Her mouth was full of hairpins so it came out muffled. "We're not putting you in harm's way. Not for anything."

"I agree," Angie said. "It's entirely too risky. He's already threatened you to pay off Doc's debts or else."

"Do you think that was his plan?" Mel asked. She felt like they were onto something big.

"What? To impoverish Shelby with her manager's debts?"

"Potentially," Mel said. "Think about it. Shelby's money has been squandered by Doc. She is in all sorts of debt . . ."

"Don't remind me," Shelby said. "I'm feeling a depression coming on."

Cheryl gave them a dark look. "She has a show to do

in a few minutes. Try not to sabotage her right before she hits the stage."

"Right, sorry," Angie said. "Let's put aside your financial situation and think about how a loan shark would benefit from having you under his thumb."

"I think it's pretty obvious," Mel said. "I think Stackhouse saw how much money Doc was making off you and he probably figured he could do the same if he became your manager. So, maybe he wasn't trying to get the sedative to Shelby after all. Maybe he meant to drug Doc all along and when Doc got woozy, he clobbered him, planning to take his place as your manager."

Angie turned to Shelby. "I know you're grateful to Doc Howard for stepping in and helping you after Diana passed, but I have to say I think he was a real jerk, not to speak ill of the dead and all."

"Nah, he was a jerk," Cheryl said.

"Cheryl." Shelby's tone was disapproving. "I have come to understand that Doc was not the man I thought he was, but I still don't like to speak badly of him, especially when he's not here to defend himself."

Mel studied Shelby's face. Her expression was earnest. She meant what she said and despite the knowledge that Doc had been doing her wrong, she wouldn't badmouth him. Not yet. Not without proof. Mel respected that sort of loyalty.

"It's all speculation, but I'm still going to mention it to Uncle Stan just in case it supports any part of his investigation, details of which he is not sharing," Mel said.

There was a knock on the dressing room door and a stagehand shouted, "Thirty minutes to curtain!"

"Oh, we need to get back to the VIP suite," Angie said. "Break a leg!"

"Thanks!" Shelby said.

Mel settled for giving her a thumbs-up. Somehow wishing for a person to break anything, even if it was a good luck ritual in theater, felt so wrong.

They hurried down the hallway, around dancers and stagehands and a couple of the ushers, until they reached the suite. Just inside the door, tucked into an alcove, were Lisa Martin and Regina Bessette. Their expressions were intense as they stared at each other. To Mel, it did not look like a friendly chat.

Seventeen

"You need to go," Regina said. "Terrence Nickels is not interested in representing you, and lingering around the hotel isn't going to change that."

Lisa tipped her chin up. She was holding a glass of complimentary champagne from the bar at the far end of the VIP room, and she took a long sip. "No."

Mel slowed her walk, hoping to hear more. Angie did the same and she knew they were thinking the same thing. Mel glanced at the station and noticed that Marty and the brothers had arrived and had it all set up, the towers were fully stocked, and they were already moving through the room, bearing trays of cupcakes. Nice.

"Have you talked to Miranda?" Regina asked. "She's the only one who might be able to get you an interview with Nickels."

"I tried but I haven't been able to find her," Lisa said. "Shelby probably offed her like she did Doc. She destroys anyone who gets in her way."

"That's quite the wild accusation," Regina said. "Unless you have proof, I'd keep it to yourself, otherwise people might think you're projecting."

"I'm not. If something happened to Miranda, it's Shelby's doing," Lisa said. She then called Shelby several nasty names and Mel thought it was no wonder no one wanted to work with her, including her own mother. She immediately felt bad for thinking it, but she also didn't think she was wrong.

"Listen, I was tolerant about you coming here for the holidays, because I was friends with your mother, but I think you need to rein in your obsession with Shelby Vaughn. It's not healthy and, quite frankly, it's become annoying."

"But I hate her," Lisa said. "She took everything from me."

Mel didn't look at her but she could almost feel the fury pouring off the young woman.

"Not everything, darling," Regina said. "You still have me."

Mel glanced over to see Lisa nod, looking weepy, and she hugged Regina, albeit half-heartedly. "You're right. Thank you."

Regina patted her back and strode away. "You need to think about your future, Lisa, not be stuck in the past. Once Miranda surfaces, I'll see if I can talk her into getting you an audition with Terrence Nickels."

"Thank you, Regina. I knew you'd come through." Lisa slumped against the wall and watched the owner of the hotel walk away. When she turned her head in Mel's direction, Mel immediately pretended to be in an intense conversation with Angie.

"I don't see how we're supposed to accommodate their request," she said. Her voice was overly loud and she frowned as if she were consumed with a business problem.

Angie, quickly catching on, raised her hands in the air and said, "I don't think we have a choice. They're one of our best customers."

"Well, it's the holiday season and they just have to understand," Mel said. She was looking at Angie while walking and talking. Angie's eyes went wide but it was too late. Mel slammed into Lisa Martin, who had pushed off the wall right in front of her.

"You're not fooling me," Lisa said.

Mel felt her face get warm. And here she had thought she and Angie were giving very convincing performances.

"I have no idea what you're talking about," Mel said.

Lisa shook her head. Her dark hair caught the light overhead and Mel realized she was a very pretty woman, not an ethereal beauty like Shelby but still quite lovely. And if she could sing, it certainly stood to reason that she'd have expected her mother to help her achieve her dreams. Being passed over by Diana for her best friend had to have been devastating for Lisa. Mel felt a surge of pity for her.

"Don't!" Lisa snapped.

Mel gave her side-eye. "Don't what?"

"Don't you dare pity me," Lisa said. "I have more talent in my little finger than Shelby Vaughn has in her entire body and someday the entire world is going to know it."

"You just have to get rid of her first?" Angie asked. "Is that it?"

"Get rid of her?" Lisa blinked.

"Isn't that the plan?" Angie badgered. "You think if you can destroy her career by getting rid of her manager, then she'll fail and you'll what? Take her place?"

Lisa's eyes narrowed. "Are you accusing me of something?"

"You bet I—"

"Mel! Angie! Where have you been?" Al demanded. He stepped up to them, wearing his Santa suit and hauling a tray of cupcakes. "We're overrun tonight. Something came up and Ray couldn't make it so we're a man short. We need you at the station to prep the trays. Chop-chop."

"Al," Angie protested but Mel interrupted.

"He's right," she said. "We're here for a job. Have a nice evening, Lisa."

"Go to h—" Lisa began but Al shoved his tray in front of her nose. "Cupcake?"

Lisa slapped the tray away, tossing the cupcakes into the air. Al made a valiant attempt to catch them with his tray and he did catch a few, mostly frosting side down.

"She seems nice," he growled. The three of them dropped to the floor to pick up the casualties on the carpet while Lisa smiled and strode away.

"Not the word I would use," Angie said.

They loaded his tray and Al hustled back to the cupcake station to replace his damaged goods. Mel and Angie followed in his wake, navigating around the guests who were drinking champagne and taking selfies while they awaited Shelby's arrival.

"Lisa and Regina, what was that about?" Angie asked Mel.

"I have no idea," Mel said. "Did you know that Diana was friends with Regina? I mean, when you knew her from that summer tour, did she ever mention knowing someone who owned a hotel in Scottsdale?"

"No, and you would think it would have come up, given that I was flying back and forth a lot," Angie said. She moved aside to let a couple pass between them. "I thought Regina was friends with Doc."

"Me, too," Mel said. "When we asked Regina about Lisa before, she indicated that she only knew her as a guest of the hotel. She never mentioned being friends with Diana. Maybe she knew both of them. They were both managers, it could be Regina has a relationship with loads of celebrity representatives, especially any that perform here in her hotel."

"But it sounded like she and Diana were actual friends and not just business associates," Angie said.

"Yeah, I got that feeling, too," Mel said. They arrived at the cupcake station and it was mobbed. Mel started helping guests while Angie assisted Marty with loading up the trays for the brothers to carry.

It was about time for Shelby to enter, when Abby and Sarah, the two dancers whom Mel had helped find Sarah's missing earring, walked by. They were dressed as Christmas presents for the high-kicking opening number with Sarah in a green satin box with a red bow and Abby in the opposite, a red satin box with a green bow.

"Cupcake?" Mel offered. Surprisingly, Sarah nodded.

"Yeah, sure, I'll work it off by intermission, no doubt," she said. "Come on, Abby, don't let me go full carb-o-holic alone."

"You're such a pastry pusher, Sarah." Abby shook her head. She glanced at Mel. "Thanks again for your help the other night."

"Yeah, we never would have found my earring without you," Sarah said. "That was such a bizarre night."

"Because Doc Howard was murdered?" Mel asked. She plated the Sugar Cookie cupcake that Sarah pointed to and then did the same with a Peppermint Bark one for Abby.

"Well, that, for sure." Sarah took a bite and a look of bliss crossed over her face.

"But also it was crazy around here that day. You know the opening night manic energy that gets everyone over-amped," Abby said. She took a bite of her cupcake and her knees buckled. She bounced up and down. "Oh, that's soooo good."

Mel felt the same flash of happiness she always felt when her cupcakes brought a person joy. It was a very reaffirming line of work she was in. She shook her head. She had to keep on task.

"I've been meaning to find you both and ask you about the night we looked for your earring," Mel said. She paused to plate a cupcake for another guest before turning back to the dancers. "When you left, did you see any-one outside the room? Anyone just hanging around? Or a hotel worker, or security, anyone like that?"

They looked at each other as if they could jog each other's memory.

"You know the gray-haired guy who carries the big set of keys?" Sarah asked.

"Trevor? The head of security?" Mel asked.

Sarah shrugged. "I don't know what he does exactly, other than peek into our dressing rooms at irregular intervals." She frowned. "I did see him in the hallway, but I was so happy to have my earring back I didn't notice which way he was going."

"I don't remember him or anyone," Abby said. "But I was wiped out after my performance adrenaline fizzled. Why?"

"I got locked in this room after you two left," Mel said. She pointed to the doors. "They changed the locks the next day so that the doors can always be opened from the inside, but that night I couldn't get out."

"That must have been terrifying," Sarah said. "I hope . . ." She paused and sent Abby an alarmed look. "I hope we didn't accidentally do that to you."

"No." Mel shook her head. "According to Trevor, the security guard, it had to have been locked with a key from outside."

"Do you think someone locked you in on purpose?" Sarah asked.

Mel shrugged. She had no idea, despite having pondered this question constantly over the past several days.

"But why?" Abby asked. "It was after the show, right? Maybe they thought the room was empty."

"Or maybe they wanted to cause a distraction," Sarah said. "Wasn't that the same time that Shelby's manager was murdered?"

"Yeah," Mel said. "I had the same thought."

Both women put their cupcakes down as if they'd suddenly lost their appetites. Mel knew they were just realizing that they could have been locked in the suite, too, if they hadn't found Sarah's earring when they did.

"We'd better get ready for the show," Abby said. She glanced at Mel and said, "I'm glad you're all right."

"Me, too," Sarah said. She glanced quickly around the room. "But be careful. We're all just trying to get through the end of the show's run in a few days' time. There's something off about this gig. We've all felt it."

"Okay, thanks," Mel said. She tossed out the remainders of the dancers' cupcakes. She wished they'd seen someone, anyone, lurking outside the suite door, preferably carrying the murder weapon and loudly announcing that they were going to bludgeon Doc Howard. It would all be so much simpler then.

"Excuse me, may I have one of those adorable cupcakes with the gingerbread man on it, please?" A woman dressed in a sparkly Christmas sweater stood across the table from her.

"Absolutely," Mel said. She glanced at the petite woman with the short curly hair, kind eyes, and a warm smile and said, "Do I know you? You look familiar."

"Maybe, I'm Paula Wagaman from West Virginia," she said.

"Hey, we recently opened a franchise in West Virginia," Mel said. "Maybe I met you at the grand opening?"

"That could be," Paula said. "I have two grown children, both teachers, and sometimes we treat ourselves to a cupcake . . . or two."

"Well, it's nice to meet you, possibly for the second

time," Mel said. "And I couldn't agree more. Cupcakes are always a good idea."

The rest of the evening was uneventful. Cupcakes were handed out and consumed. The show was another smashing success, but Mel wondered about what Sarah had said. Did everyone working on the show feel as if something was off? It seemed like a reasonable response to a murder on opening night.

The brothers, Marty, Angie, and Mel packed up the cupcake station. Al and Paulie peeled off to go meet their new squeezes, while Marty drove the cupcake van back to the bakery. Angie was waiting for Shelby, who was still crashing at her house, and Mel was catching a ride in Angie's SUV with them.

Mel and Angie were waiting by the stage as Cheryl was in the dressing room with Shelby, helping her out of her final costume and makeup. A tall man about six foot four walked down the red-carpeted aisle towards the stage manager. Mel watched him approach the stage manager, Kyle Peters. She wondered if the man was another male groupie who thought Shelby might like to date him. There'd been a few of those over the past few nights. Creeps.

"Sorry, Mr. Nickels, I haven't seen Miranda in a while," Kyle said. "Not since she and Doc . . . well . . ."

His voice trailed off and Mel and Angie exchanged a look. This was Terrence Nickels. He was very tall, with a medium build, and turning gray at the temples. Despite his unassuming appearance, his suit was bespoke and he exuded a confidence and sense of power that no doubt came from being at the top of his industry.

"Mr. Nickels?" Angie, being fearless, approached him.

He turned around and looked her over. It was clear from his impatient expression that he considered her another wannabe singer, accosting him to listen to her demo.

"Yes, what?" he asked. His tone was abrupt.

"Sorry, I overheard that you're looking for Miranda," Angie said. She gestured between herself and Mel. "We saw her yesterday."

"Did you?" he asked. He gave her his full attention. "What time?"

"Midday," Angie said. "She answered the door to your suite."

"We took the wrong elevator by mistake," Mel said.

"I'm sorry, who are you?" he asked.

"Angie Harper and Melanie DeLaura," Angie said. "We own a bakery and have been providing cupcakes for the VIP suite during Shelby Vaughn's residency."

"Right, right." Mr. Nickels nodded. "Shelby Vaughn, Doc Howard's client. Miranda told me all about her and him."

"I know Miranda has issues with Shelby," Angie said. "But she really is talented and without representation right now."

"At any other time I'd be interested," Nickels said. "But right now I really need to find Miranda. It's completely out of character for her to take off without telling me, and I've come to . . . well . . . I care for her very much."

"When was the last time you saw her?"

"Last night at dinner," he said. "I had to work afterwards and she said she was going to go for a swim in the pool but she never came back."

"My uncle is a detective with the Scottsdale Police Department," Mel said. "If you want to file a missing person report."

"Thank you, but I already have," he said. "I've been checking with anyone who might have seen her or spoken to her. I know the police were interested in her whereabouts when Howard was murdered but she was picking me up at the airport."

"If we see her, we'll tell her you've been looking for her," Mel said. It felt unsubstantial but she didn't know what else to say.

"Thank you," Nickels said. "I'd appreciate it. I'm not leaving Scottsdale until I know where she is."

They watched him stride out of the auditorium and Angie turned to Mel. "Is it just me or do you have a bad feeling about this?"

"I have a very bad feeling," Mel said. "You heard Miranda. She was all in about Nickels, clearly gaga about him. There is no way she just up and left him. And Lisa mentioned to Regina how she hadn't been able to find Miranda. Something's wrong."

"That was my thinking, too," Angie said. "We should tell Uncle Stan and he can share it with whoever is leading the investigation to find her."

"I'll call him tonight when I get home," Mel said. "I don't want to do it here." She glanced around the theater. "You just don't know who's listening."

"Good plan," Angie said. They both waited, ill at ease, for Shelby to appear.

By unspoken agreement, when Shelby joined them, they didn't mention Miranda being missing. It served no purpose and Shelby was struggling enough with the loss of Doc and being homesick. Angie had set Tate on a mission to try to bring Shelby's family to town but they'd been reluctant to accept charity from strangers, and Mel hadn't heard whether Tate had successfully changed their minds or not.

They were driving through their neighborhood, towards Mel's house, when a bright glow filled the night sky.

"What do you suppose that is?" Angie asked.

"Oh, dear, I hope it's not a house fire," Shelby said. Her voice sounded strained and Mel imagined she was thinking about her previous manager's tragic death.

Angie turned her car onto Mel's street and Mel gasped. The glow was coming from her house but it wasn't on fire. It was bedecked, bedazzled, and bejeweled in a blindingly bright, over-the-top display of Christmas lights on steroids.

"Oh, my . . ." she breathed, running out of words.

Angie braked hard in front of the house.

"Well, this is some holiday cheer all right," Shelby said.

The three of them climbed out of the car and stood on the sidewalk, trying to take it all in. There were lights covering every inch of the house, several giant blow-up decorations, one of which was a family of snowmen that had a bell-ringing version of "Let It Snow" playing.

"I'm going to murder Ray," Mel said. "Scratch that. Let's go inside and start packing. We have to move. Our neighbors are going to kill us."

"Cupcake!" Joe called from the front door. He waved his arms—as if she couldn't see him in this manufactured daylight. It was almost eleven o'clock. The blow-up Santa on the roof kept shouting, "Ho ho ho!" and Mel was certain she saw the blinds in her neighbor's house twitch.

She hurried up the walkway to the front door, which was open.

"Joe, we need to shut this down," she said.

"Agreed," he said. "I've only been home for a few minutes. I thought the house was on fire when I turned onto the street, but I can't figure out where they plugged all of this in. I'm trying to get Peanut to do her business but she's afraid to come outside, and I don't blame her."

Mel looked at the outlet on their front patio. It was empty. "Let's deal with Peanut later. We have to make this stop."

"How did this happen?" Joe asked.

Mel sighed. "I suspect Ray 'knew a guy.'"

"Oh, no," Joe said.

"Yeah, I left Tony in charge, and I'm sure everything was fine when he and the others left, but Ray didn't make it to the hotel tonight because 'something came up,' and I suspect it was this." Mel hung her head in shame. She knew better than to leave Ray unattended. He always "knew a guy" and it never went well.

"Let's not focus on that now," Joe said. "Let's figure out how to stop the madness."

"We'll help," Angie said as she and Shelby joined them. She had to raise her voice to be heard over the snowmen.

"All right," Joe said. "Let's check all of the outside outlets first."

"We'll inspect the garage," Angie volunteered.

"I'll look in back," Mel said. She hurried around the side of the house and let herself into the backyard through the side gate. She knew there were a couple of outlets on the back side of the house. As she passed the Arcadia doors, she saw Peanut in her dog bed with her blanket over her head. Meanwhile Captain Jack stared out the window at her completely unfazed.

Mel had to hunker down to check the outlets along the back of the house. Both were clear. She glanced up at the doors and the windows to see if the brainiac who had done this had decided to plug the lights in using an outlet in the house. Nope. Everything was shut. She was about to walk back to the front when everything went off, plunging the yard and the house into silent darkness, which was a relief. Mel started to rise from her crouch to walk around to the front when a shadowed figure loomed out of the darkness, and dropped a thick cord around her neck.

Eighteen

Mel grabbed at the cord, but it was yanked tight, cutting off her air and making her see stars. She tried to remember what she'd learned in self-defense class but panic was making it hard to think. She couldn't shout. She couldn't breathe. She had only seconds to act.

With Doc's murder on her mind, Mel knew that whoever was bearing down on her was not just trying to scare her. They wanted her dead. She went limp, dropping all the way to the ground and dragging her assailant with her. Once on the ground, Mel used the last bit of strength she had to punch up as hard as she could. She heard the person emit an *oof* as the air exited their lungs. It had been a direct abdominal hit.

The cord around Mel's neck loosened as her attacker

staggered back to their feet. Mel yanked the cord from around her neck and sucked in a great gulp of air.

"Mel, where are you?" Angie called from the side of the house.

Mel's attacker took off running across the backyard and through the gate into the alley. Mel tried to get up to give chase, but her adrenaline was gone, leaving her feeling like a shaky puddle of goo.

"Mel!" Angie cried again. "Joe, she's not answering! Something's wrong."

Mel pushed herself up to her knees and tried to call out, but she couldn't manage it. As if sensing that she was in trouble, Captain Jack started to paw the window, and Peanut bolted out of her bed and charged the back door, barking all the way.

Two arms lifted Mel to her feet. She tensed, ready to fight, but it was Joe. "It's okay. I've got you."

Angie and Shelby appeared right behind him. "What happened?" Angie cried.

"I don't know," Joe said. He tossed her his keys and said, "Get the door."

Angie unlocked the door and snapped on the kitchen lights. She looked back at Mel being helped in by Joe and gasped. Peanut jumped around their feet. When Joe helped Mel into a chair, the dog pressed herself against Mel's leg as if to comfort her. Mel reached down and patted her head. Captain Jack hopped off the windowsill and jumped onto the table behind Mel as if he, too, was going to keep watch over her. Mel found this show of furry support to be quite comforting.

Joe took her face between his hands, kissed her forehead, and looked her over. "What happened, cupcake?"

Shelby stood behind Joe, her eyes huge, and she was holding a thick orange extension cord. Mel swallowed, trying to moisten her mouth, and pointed to the cord.

Her voice came out in a gruff whisper when she said, "Someone tried to strangle me with that."

Shelby dropped it on the table and raised her hands in the air. "I just tripped over it outside on the patio. I thought it had something to do with the lights."

Joe's fingers gently moved over Mel's neck. His voice was calm but his fingers shook. Mel could tell he was rattled but trying not to show it. "It's red and will likely bruise. Let's go to the hospital and have a doctor look at you."

Mel shook her head. "Water."

Angie thrust a glass into her hand as if she'd just been waiting for the order. "Here."

Mel took a careful sip and when it went down okay, she drank more.

"Joe's right, you need to get looked at," Angie said.

"No," Mel said. She wasn't going anywhere.

"Do not make me call your mother," Angie said.

Mel hoped she was kidding. Joyce would have the mother of all meltdowns. She reached up and squeezed Joe's hand, drawing his attention from her throat. "Call Uncle Stan."

"Right," he said. He took out his phone and called. He kept his voice low, but Mel could hear Uncle Stan in the background. He'd moved in with Mel's mother last year, so he was just minutes away. In fact, he'd probably be there before Joe ended the call.

A ruckus at the door made them all jump. Uncle Stan couldn't have gotten there that quickly. Joe was still on the phone with him. Mel felt herself tense, but would her attacker really come to the front door?

"Mel! Joe! Open up!" Ray's big booming voice sounded.

"Of course it's Ray," Angie said. She left the kitchen and hurried to the front door. Moments later, she was back with Ray in tow.

"What did you think of the lights? Pretty great, am I right?" he asked. "You were wowed, weren't you?"

Mel glanced at Joe. He ended his call with Uncle Stan and said, "He'll be here in a minute."

Joe took a long slow, calming breath and said, "Ray, while I appreciate your enthusiasm in decking our halls, so to speak, it's a little over the top, don't you think?"

"No, I think it's perfect," he said. "I'm just sorry I got here after the timer switched it off. I really wanted to see your faces."

"Timer?" Angie asked.

"Yeah, my guy set it up so it goes on and off automatically," Ray said. "Very handy."

"Very," Joe agreed. "And where would this timer be?"

Ray looked confused. "I have no idea. I was too busy adding lights on the roof. Tony's display was lame. Trust me, this is so much better. Now it has pizzazz."

Mel croaked, "Call your guy, Ray."

"What happened to you?" Ray asked. He backed away. "You're not getting sick are you? I don't want any of that. I have a very delicate immune system."

"No, she's not sick. She was almost just strangled," Joe said. He pointed to the extension cord. "With that."

"Holy sh—" Ray began but he was cut off.

"Kiddo, are you okay?" Uncle Stan strode into the

kitchen, wearing sweatpants, a hoodie, and two different sneakers. He leaned over her chair and hugged her.

"I'm okay," Mel said. And she was. Her voice was getting stronger and with this many people around her, she felt perfectly safe.

"What happened?" Uncle Stan demanded.

Mel glanced at Joe and nodded. He told Uncle Stan about arriving home and finding the house lit up like napalm, sending a look at Ray, who was staring at the ceiling. He then told Stan what happened from his point of view. Mel nodded to let him know he'd gotten it right.

When he was finished Uncle Stan looked at Mel and said, "What else?"

"It was dark, and I was crouched down checking the outlet," she said. "I only saw a dark shadow and then they dropped the cord around my neck. I managed to punch up and they let go, and when Angie called my name, they took off through the gate to the alley."

"I want to know every person that you've spoken to and every conversation that you've had over the past few days," Uncle Stan said. "It's clear that someone thinks you're getting too close to discovering something about Doc's death and they want to stop you."

Angie turned to look at Shelby. "Where did you go just now?"

"What do you mean?" Shelby asked. "I was with you."

"You weren't, though," Angie said. Her eyes narrowed in suspicion. "Just like you weren't really with me when Doc was murdered. You were in the other room. You could have slipped out and killed him and come back and I never would have known."

Jenn McKinlay

Shelby looked as if she'd been slapped. "Do you really think I murdered Doc?"

Angie didn't say anything.

"No," Mel croaked but both women ignored her.

"So, the whole 'sister from another mister' thing really doesn't mean that much to you, does it?" Shelby asked.

"I just want the truth," Angie said. "You were the one who walked in here with that." She gestured at the extension cord.

"Because I tripped over it outside," Shelby cried. She threw her hands in the air. "I can't believe this. I can't believe you think I would actually hurt Mel. I consider her my friend."

"Yeah, well, she's my best friend," Angie said.

"I see," Shelby said. She reached into her bag, took out her phone, and started scrolling through her apps. "I'll call for a ride and go back to the hotel."

Ray, Joe, and Uncle Stan glanced from woman to woman as if too cautious to say anything. Cowards, Mel thought. Then again, maybe it was the smart play.

Mel looked at Angie with wide eyes. She didn't really think this was a great idea. Angie tipped her chin up. She was clearly feeling stubborn about the situation. Mel couldn't blame her. She'd be equally as distraught if Angie were in danger. Still, her gut told her it wasn't Shelby who attacked her.

"Wait," Mel said. She reached up and put her hand on Shelby's. "I know it wasn't you. Stay here if you don't feel like going to Angie's."

"How do you know it wasn't her?" Angie demanded.

"It was dark, you couldn't see, and she was carrying that." She pointed to the extension cord.

"I found it," Shelby protested.

"Because the person I punched was soft in the middle," Mel said. She gestured at Shelby's fit body. "It wasn't her."

Angie expelled a relieved breath. "Thank goodness."

Shelby stared at her with one eyebrow raised.

"Listen, I'm sorry, I shouldn't have accused you of anything, I'm just so freaked out that Mel could have been—" Angie began but Shelby held up her hand in a stop gesture.

"You're forgiven," Shelby said.

"Just like that?" Angie asked. "I accused you of murder and you're just going to shake it off?"

"Yeah," Shelby said. Then she grinned. "Because I don't have such a short-term memory that I've forgotten that you've been by my side since all of this went down, lied for me, and let me live with you just to keep me safe."

"All true," Angie said. She opened her arms, Shelby stepped close, and they hugged.

"I'm really sorry this happened to you, Mel," Shelby said when they parted. "I feel like I'm responsible."

"No." Mel shook her head. "Whoever killed Doc is responsible."

"Exactly," Uncle Stan chimed in. His phone rang and he glanced at it and frowned. "Your detail wants to know why you haven't arrived at Angie's yet. Apparently, Tate is upset."

"Oh, I'll call him," Angie said. "Tell them we're on our way." She glanced at Shelby, who nodded.

"I'm going to add officers to your house. Mel and Joe, I want someone here as well."

"I'm here," Ray offered. "I can stay and keep watch."

"No!" Joe, Mel, and Uncle Stan said as one.

Ray blinked.

"We need you well rested to help out at the hotel," Mel said.

"Of course," Ray said. "I get it. I am the best Santa. I'll be off then. I'm still bummed I missed the lights."

"Call your guy and ask him where the timer is," Joe said. "Tonight."

"Got it," Ray said. "I'll text you."

He headed out the door with Angie and Shelby. Mel was relieved to see them all go. She just wanted to curl up into a ball and pretend none of this had happened.

"Come on," Joe said. "Let's get you checked out by a doctor or a nurse or anyone with advanced medical knowledge."

Mel hunkered low in her chair. She was tired and sore and didn't want to go anywhere.

"How about I send over a nurse friend of mine," Uncle Stan suggested. "She gets off from the hospital at midnight. I can have her swing by."

Mel nodded. "Yes, please."

"All right," Joe conceded. "But if she says you need to see a doctor, you go without arguing."

"Deal."

"How about I make us all some hot chocolate while we wait?" Joe asked.

Uncle Stan took the seat next to Mel's at the table. He rested his chin on his hand and said, "All right, kid, start talking. I want to know everyone you've spoken to over the past few days."

Mel sighed. Joe gave her no sympathy. "Don't look at me. If it was up to me, you'd be sitting in an ER right now."

Mel started talking, starting with Miranda Carter's disappearance.

\'∕∖\'

The nurse declared Mel fit. The police who arrived to look at the scene determined it would be better to do it again in daylight, when they could actually see the ground, but they did bag the extension cord and take it with them.

Mel didn't hear anything about the incident the next day, but she wasn't surprised because she had been chained to her kitchen in the bakery cranking out the special orders and keeping the display case stocked. When the last customer picked up their order, Marty shut and locked the door and they all collapsed into booths, exhausted.

The next day was Christmas Eve and it was agreed that Marty would man the shop on his own for a couple of hours, mostly to get the last of the special orders picked up. And then they were closed through the holiday. Mel wished she could just throw on her pajamas and binge on holiday movies, but no. From now until she called, "Dinner is served," on Christmas Day, she would be up to her elbows cooking Christmas dinner. The brothers would have to work the VIP suite tonight and on Christmas Eve on their own.

Mel was secretly relieved. She had almost fifty people to feed and no time to be dwelling on the fact that someone had tried to rub her out. She and Oz spent all of Christmas Eve prepping and cooking what they could in advance. They were just finishing up the cream cheese topping on the gelatin mold that Joyce insisted must be served when the light display came on outside. It was an abrupt explosion of light and sound that almost caused Mel to drop the mold.

"'Fudge . . . except I didn't say fudge,'" Mel said.

"*A Christmas Story.*" Oz identified the movie quote.

"How are we supposed to get used to that?" Mel asked. "It's like having a searchlight blast the house every night."

"At least you were able to set the timer so that it ends at ten and your neighbors haven't threatened to drive you out with pitchforks and torches," Oz said.

"Yet," Mel said. "The only reason that display is still up is because my mother went completely gaga over it. She thinks it's the greatest thing ever."

"It is pretty great," Oz said.

"Try living with it," Mel said.

She sent Oz home and began to clean the kitchen. Joe was late getting home from work and when she called and asked why, he said he couldn't turn into their street because of the traffic and had to park at Angie and Tate's house and was walking home, using the bike path that ran along the canal that went through their neighborhood.

Mel hurried to the window and saw a slow cavalcade of cars, as well as a mob of pedestrians, on the street in front of their house. Mel realized they had become one of those houses. The fun ones, who overdid it on holiday decorating, and they now had people lining up to admire their display.

She met Joe at the door with a beer for him and a glass of wine for her. Together they sat on their front patio, hidden behind an enormous blow-up Christmas tree, and watched the people watching their house.

"Ray is never allowed to 'help' us again," Joe muttered. Mel tapped her glass to his.

"I second that," she said. They were quiet for a beat and then she said, "Do you think I should go to the hotel and help out?"

"No." His voice was as abrupt as a door slam. "I don't want you anywhere near that place. Someone thinks you know something or that you are close to figuring something out, and I don't want you to give them easy access to you by hanging around in the crowd at the show."

Mel sighed. "You're right, I know you're right, but I just feel as if I'm letting Shelby down."

"You're not," he insisted. "The brothers can hand out the cupcakes you baked. Ultimately, that's all that matters."

He was right. Mel knew he was right. But she felt as if she should be there, yes, even if it was just to flush out the killer.

"I do not want my wife to be bait," he said. Married just over a year and he was already a mind reader. As if he knew Mel was about to protest, Joe added, "And I'm sure you'd feel the same if our situations were reversed."

He had her there. She definitely wouldn't want her husband to be at risk. It would devastate Mel to lose him.

"Come on, cupcake, let's just get through tomorrow," he said. He took Mel's hand and laced their fingers together while they listened to the very tinny version of "Let It Snow" that was coming out of the blow-up snowmen.

There was a stillness to Joe that made Mel glance at him. She had become familiar with this particular quiet in him. It usually meant he was brooding over a case.

"What are you thinking about?" she asked.

He turned to her with one eyebrow raised and said, "I'm wondering if it's too late to put Ray up for adoption."

Mel snorted and sipped her wine.

Nineteen

Mel enjoyed exactly forty-five minutes of Christmas morning. Sipping her coffee, while sitting on the couch with Captain Jack and Peanut, she and Joe exchanged gifts. She bought Joe a fancy watch to replace his old one, which had died a few weeks before, and he gave her a beautiful locket with a picture of Peanut on one side and Captain Jack on the other. He'd taken pictures of them at their most adorable and she loved it, as it represented the family they had built so far. The rest of the presents were, unsurprisingly, mostly for the pets.

Captain Jack went into a frenzy over his catnip mouse, which he batted down the hallway into the master bedroom, and Peanut settled in under the tree to chew her new toy. They knew she would be fully occupied until she ripped all of its stuffing out.

As they sat appreciating the quiet before the storm, eating the baked French toast that Mel had prepped the night before and baked this morning, she took a moment to be grateful for her life. She thought about the people she'd met over the past couple of weeks. There didn't seem to be much joy among them. Lots of anger, mistrust, suspicion, ego, and greed but not much thankfulness.

She leaned into Joe and said, "I appreciate you."

He kissed the top of her head and said, "Thanks, cupcake. I feel the same way. My life would be empty without you."

She felt her heart flutter. After all this time, all these years of pining for Joe DeLaura, he was her husband and he loved her. There was no doubt about it, she was blessed. She kissed him but before they could get distracted, the door opened and Angie and Tate strode in with Shelby and the baby.

"Merry Christmas!" Angie cried. She took in the sight of Mel and Joe on the couch and turned to Tate. "We should have called. I told you we should have called."

Tate shrugged. "Sorry."

Mel pushed off the couch. "No need. If we're going to serve dinner at three, we have to get cracking."

She went to get dressed while Angie and the others tucked into what was left of the baked French toast, hoping to fortify themselves through the day.

Oz arrived shortly after, and while Tate and Joe set up rented tables in the backyard, Mel, Angie, Shelby, and Oz began cooking. Mel felt like she was just getting her rhythm when Marty and Olivia arrived.

"All right, princess, what do you need help with?"

Olivia barked from the kitchen door. "Oh, and I brought an apple pie and a Black Forest roll cake. No need to thank me."

"Thank you?" Mel asked. She turned to stare at Marty but he appeared to have suddenly gone deaf.

"What was that, Joe?" He cupped his ear. "I think your husband is calling me from the yard." He scuttled out of the very busy kitchen before Mel could protest.

"Olivia, I appreciate your offer but we have it under control," Mel said.

"Really?" Olivia asked. She was spooning up a sample of the mashed potatoes out of the Crock-Pot and said, "These are gummy. You should toss them out and start over."

Mel gripped the handle of the carving fork in her hand until her knuckles turned white. She was about to say something, when Olivia cried, "No, no, no. That's not how you chop celery. It's all uneven. Here, let me."

She muscled Shelby away from her station, where she'd been tasked with chopping the various vegetables. Shelby met Mel's gaze and sent a slow wink. In that moment, Mel knew that she really liked the singer, who had undoubtedly made a mess of the celery to give Olivia something to do, and felt bad that she'd ever considered Shelby capable of murder.

The doorbell rang and Mel glanced at the clock. The guests would start arriving now. She smoothed her apron and took a look around her busy kitchen.

"It's going to be all right," Angie said. "You've got this."

Mel nodded. She glanced out at the backyard, where the non-cooks were congregating, and saw Joe excuse himself to come inside and answer the door. Mel's mother and Uncle Stan, her brother Charlie, and his wife and sons arrived at the same time as Cheryl. Mel's mother was beaming and it occurred to Mel that her mother might be tired of hosting Christmas every year. Hmm.

Joe's family arrived in bunches after that. It was an endless stream of greetings and chatter. The house felt full to bursting but it was a good feeling. Joe handed out drinks while Angie took over the appetizers. The timing on the dishes was working out and Mel began to think dinner might turn out all right. She had decided to serve it buffet-style on a long table in the backyard. She and Oz had done enough early prep that they hadn't needed the backup ovens at the bakery.

The tables that Joe and Tate had set up were decorated with rented red tablecloths, and Mel had used her mother's leftover Christmas village decorations as centerpieces. She and Angie had conceived the idea when mulling where to set up the light-up village. Each table sported a circle of batting that resembled snow and nestled on top were the quaint village pieces. Angie had figured out how to put a battery-operated votive into each one so that they did light up. Mel paused by the table that had the hand-painted ceramic library with some villagers singing outside of it. She had to admit it looked charming as did the other tables with the schoolhouse, a white church with a steeple, the mercantile, a movie theater, and all of the other buildings from Joyce's collection.

"Oh, Melanie, how darling," Joyce cried. She clasped her hands in front of her. "You used my village as centerpieces!"

"I'd like to take all the credit but I think Angie was

the one who thought of lighting them up with votive candles," Mel said. "Once the sun sets, they'll look amazing."

Joyce glanced at the tables. Then she frowned. "I think you have one extra table."

"Do I?" Mel glanced at the yard. Tate had been in charge of renting the tables. Maybe he'd been afraid their mutual in-laws would morph into more as the DeLauras tended to do.

"Well, better too many seats than too few," Joyce said. She patted Mel's arm. "I'm sure dear Joe will get it sorted out."

"Sorting is his gift," Mel said. She lifted her wineglass to her lips.

Angie came outside. "Okay, so I was going to mention this to you but when you were almost murdered, I figured I'd wait."

Joyce's head snapped in Mel's direction. "Almost murdered? What is Angie talking about?"

"It's a euphemism," Mel said. She fingered the scarf she'd tied around her neck. "You know, like 'that slayed me' means something is really funny, 'almost murdered' means you're crushing it. Right, Angie?"

"Right! Totally!" Angie said. She lifted one of her curls and twined it around her finger.

"Oh, Angie, honey, you always do that when you're fibbing," Joyce said. She turned to Mel and asked, "And since when have you started wearing neck scarves?"

She reached up and gently tugged the festive green scarf Mel was using to hide the bruising on her throat. Joyce clapped a hand over her mouth and gasped. "Melanie Cooper DeLaura, what happened to you?"

Uncle Stan had just stepped out into the backyard but

at the sight before him, he turned on his heel to head back into the house.

"Don't you dare, Stanley Cooper," Joyce said. "Now what happened? When did it happen and why didn't anyone tell me?"

Charlie, Mel's brother, was standing behind Uncle Stan. "Mom, did I tell you the boys made your Christmas gift all by themselves? They're inside very eager to have you open it."

"That's nice, Charlie," Joyce said. "Don't use my grandsons to try and save your sister and your uncle, very bad form."

"Right." Charlie glanced at Mel and Uncle Stan. "Well, I tried. Good luck, you two."

"Help me," Mel hissed at Joe.

"But your mother loves me," he protested. "I'm 'dear Joe.' I don't want to ruin that."

"That's exactly why you need to save me," Mel said. "She'll forgive you anything."

Joe opened his mouth to argue, when the back door opened and a middle-aged couple and two teenage boys stepped outside. Mel frowned. She knew the DeLaura family was large but she was quite certain she'd met everyone who was coming to dinner today. Who were these people?

"Hello, sorry to interrupt." The woman spoke. She was petite with shoulder-length honey-blond hair that was just turning gray at the roots. She was a beautiful woman and the man beside her appeared to be about the same age as her, his face handsome but weathered, his expression wary as if he was uncertain of his welcome. The boys were teens in the middle of the awkward stage.

They were tall and thin with braces and acne but their similarity to Shelby made their identity clear right away. These had to be the Vaughns.

Mel knew that Tate and Angie had been trying to get them here for Shelby, but when she hadn't gotten an update, Mel had assumed it didn't work out. She was delighted to have been wrong. She stepped forward with a smile.

"Welcome, Mr. and Mrs. Vaughn," Mel said. "We're so glad you could join us."

The woman beamed at her, and Mel realized it was from her that Shelby got the sparkle in her eyes.

"Mama? Daddy?" Shelby was standing by the fire pit with Marty and Cheryl. She handed Marty her glass and broke into a run.

The Vaughns opened their arms and swept their daughter into a hug. There were tears and laughter, and Shelby's brothers looked mortified to be the center of attention but also happy to see their sister.

"But I thought you couldn't make it," Shelby said. She took the tissue her mother handed her and blew her nose. "This is the best Christmas gift ever."

"You can thank your friends," Mary Ellen Vaughn said. "They arranged for someone to watch the house and the pets."

"And the business," Mr. Vaughn added.

"And they bought our plane tickets," the older brother chimed in. He glanced around the backyard with the citrus trees and view of Camelback Mountain. "I can't believe I'm in Arizona."

"We've never been out of Tennessee," his younger brother said.

Shelby turned around and looked at Angie. "You did this, didn't you?"

"I had some help." Angie pointed at Tate. "But, yes, we knew how homesick you were and how much you wanted your family to be here to see your show."

"Oh, that's right! You'll get to see the show!" Shelby clapped. "That will make today just perfect."

"We think so, too," Mary Ellen said. Her smile mirrored her daughter's and it was clear from the sheen in her eyes that she was feeling all the feels to be with her daughter for the first time in a long while.

"Well, hello, Mary Ellen, Jack, boys." Cheryl joined their group. "Merry Christmas. How wonderful of you to come all this way."

"Hi, Cheryl," Mary Ellen said. "It's so good to see you."

Mary Ellen stepped forward to hug Cheryl, and Mel noted that they were of an age, but while Cheryl was dressed in a glittering silver chemise with substantial diamond earrings, Mary Ellen was in a simple but elegant navy blue dress with a delicate gold chain around her neck and a plain wedding band on her finger. If Mel didn't know better, she'd have thought Cheryl was the mother of the up-and-coming singer.

"It's too bad Shelby's show is sold out," Cheryl said. "I don't know where we would get tickets for you."

Mary Ellen's face fell and her husband patted her on the back and said, "Maybe we can watch from backstage."

"I think that's against the fire code," Cheryl said. She sounded regretful.

"Well, this stinks," Angie said. She turned to Mel. "Can they hang out with us in the VIP lounge?"

"Absolutely," Mel said. "You can't see the show from there but you can hear it."

"Better than nothing," Jack said.

Cheryl looked annoyed and Mel got the distinct feeling she wasn't happy about the Vaughns being here, but that seemed out of character for the gregarious hairdresser, so Mel assumed it was just the surprise of having them here.

"Aw, I really wanted to see the show," the older of the two brothers said. "I heard you fly in on a wire during one song."

Shelby laughed. "I do, Sammy, and it's terrifying, every single time. Maybe you and Jack junior can watch from the rafters."

"No," Mary Ellen said. "Absolutely not. Too dangerous. I'd be a nervous wreck."

"Aw, Mom," the boys protested together.

"Boys, that's enough," Jack said. "Your mother is right."

"What's this I hear that four tickets are needed for tonight's show?" Ray joined the group. "I just happen to have VIP seats for everyone." He held up a fistful of tickets. "I managed to buy out the entire VIP section tonight. We're all going."

"Raymond Dominick DeLaura," Joe said. "How did you manage that?"

Ray's grin was impudent and he said, "I know a guy."

Mel narrowed her eyes and said, "His name wouldn't be Jerry Stackhouse, would it?"

"Might be," he said. "And it could be that he'd been shaking down a certain music manager who is no longer with us for tickets to the VIP suite. I told him he had to give me all the tickets or I was turning him in."

"Ray!" Uncle Stan barked and Ray flinched. They stared at each other for a tense moment and Stan said, "That is complete genius. Looks like we're getting dinner and a show, everyone."

Ray grinned and handed four tickets to Jack Vaughn. "Merry Christmas, my man."

Jack gaped at him. "Are you sure?"

"Absolutely, it's the season of giving," Ray said.

"And that's why we don't actually give Ray up for adoption," Joe muttered so that only Mel could hear him.

Mel laughed. "He does have a very big heart."

"Problem solved," Cheryl cheered. "But that's the story of your life, isn't it, Mary Ellen?"

Angie raised one eyebrow and looked at Mel. So, it wasn't just her getting a weird vibe off Cheryl then. Mel shrugged and Angie's frown deepened.

If Cheryl was being testy, Mary Ellen didn't seem to notice. She put her arms around her family, pulling them all close, and said, "I am a very lucky woman, if that's what you mean."

Oz popped his head out of the kitchen door. "Chef, I need you."

"Oh!" In all the ruckus, Mel forgot she was on duty. She kissed Joe quick and dashed into the kitchen. They had an hour to get everything out to the buffet table, piping hot all at the same time.

Much to Mel's surprise, Olivia proved to be a huge help in the kitchen and the extra hands made the meal possible. Mel caught Marty watching them work from the kitchen door and she gave him a thumbs-up. He grinned.

Someone had set up a Bluetooth speaker outside and they listened to Christmas music while they hustled dish after dish onto the buffet table, where Joe and Tate arranged the dishes and set up the plates and silverware.

Mel saw her mother watching them with a smile, so she assumed the fact that she hadn't used her mother's china but had rented the plates and silverware from the same party supply company that had provided the tablecloths was okay.

"Is there anything I can help with?" Cheryl stepped into the kitchen. She was holding a martini in one hand, which she carefully set down on the counter.

"I think we're good," Oz said. He was wielding an enormous prime rib, while Angie carried out the Gorgonzola ravioli and Marty the porchetta.

Olivia brought out her newly cooked mashed potatoes, and Joe carried out the asparagus and a massive bowl of salad. Tate doubled back for the enormous basket of rolls and Mel felt as if she could breathe. She smiled at Cheryl.

"Excuse me." She stepped into the living room, where a few guests lingered. "Dinner is served." She then went to the front door and opened it, finding Shelby's brothers, her nephews, and several of the DeLaura teens all loitering on the patio furniture, looking at their phones.

She cleared her throat and a few of them looked up. "Dinner is ready."

The boys popped up, leaving the girls to follow. It was nice to see that food overruled whatever was streaming, trending, or going viral. As the crowd of guests made their way into the yard, Captain Jack hid while Peanut decided to assist with cleanup of any food that might be dropped.

Joe carved the prime rib while Tate served the ravioli and Oz the porchetta. There was a lot of good-natured laughing and joking, and Mel leaned against the wall of her house, appreciating that for the moment her duties were done.

Uncle Stan joined Mel where she stood. He smiled down at her. "You did it, kid. Your mother is so proud she could bust."

"Not gonna lie," Mel said. "I'm very relieved. With three hundred and sixty-four days between now and next Christmas, that would be a long time to listen to disappointment."

Uncle Stan laughed. "You could never disappoint her." Mel looked at him and he added, "You know, since you married dear Joe." They both laughed.

"Not to be a holiday buzzkill but there's still no suspect for Doc Howard's murder?" Mel asked.

Uncle Stan shook his head. "Unfortunately, no. I really wanted this nailed down before Shelby finishes her residency and leaves."

"Because you think she had something to do with it?" Mel asked. She couldn't believe that he could think Shelby capable of murder.

"No, so she could be free and clear," he said. "She's a real talent and I didn't want this to taint her career."

"Has there been any word on the whereabouts of Miranda Carter?" Mel asked. Uncle Stan shook his head. "Do you think her disappearance is related to Doc's murder?"

"She was his ex-wife and they were at odds," he said. "Did she kill him and then vanish? I don't know."

"It doesn't seem likely, does it?" Mel asked. "I mean she was so invested in her new career and in showing him up. She struck me as a woman who thrived on winning not destroying."

"And she had an alibi for his murder that was solid," Uncle Stan said. "Unless . . ."

"She discovered who his killer was and they went after her?" Mel guessed.

"Exactly," he said. "There were a lot of people who wanted Howard dead, but who wanted it the most?"

Mel couldn't shake Uncle Stan's question. It spun around her brain all through dinner. Although she smiled and laughed and chatted with all of their guests, she felt Uncle Stan's question scratching at the back of her brain. *Who had wanted Doc dead the most?*

Twenty

The dinner broke up when Shelby had to leave to go to the theater. Uncle Stan had let the officers on her detail go have dinner while Shelby was under his watch but when it was time for her to go, the officers arrived to escort her. Her family and Cheryl went with her, and Mel started to clean up.

"Melanie, why don't you go ahead to the hotel," Joyce said. "Angie mentioned that you were working the VIP suite again tonight, and I am more than happy to take care of the cleaning here. We can get it started and still be there in time for the show."

"Oh, no, that's too much," Mel said. Although, truth-fully, she was eager to get to the hotel and see if there had been any news about Miranda.

"Not at all," Joyce said. "I have plenty of help." She

gestured behind her where Joe's mother stood as well as the rest of the DeLaura family. Maria was tying on an apron and made a shooing gesture with her hands.

"You go," Maria said. "We will clean and I will stay and watch the baby."

Angie kissed her mother's cheek and passed off Emari. "Thanks, Mom. We won't be late."

"Hold up," Joe said. "I'm going with you."

"Me, too," Tate cried. "We can take the brothers' places and pass out cupcakes."

"You can take Al and Paulie's places," Ray said. "But you're not taking mine." He was already dressed in his Santa suit with his chest hair and gold chain on full display.

Al and Paulie started to protest but Mr. DeLaura handed them each a trash bag and pointed to the backyard and that was that.

"Do you think I'll have that kind of authority over Emari when she's older?" Tate asked Angie.

She looked at him. "No, you can't even put her in time-out when she's pitching a fit."

"It's true," he said to Mel. "That kid owns me."

Mel and Joe exchanged a smile. Tate was the world's biggest pushover for his little girl, but Mel didn't consider that a bad thing, not at all.

They stopped by the bakery and loaded up the van with the last batch of cupcakes for Shelby's final show. Because Oz had helped with dinner, Mel had insisted he take the night off, same with Marty. They were going to attend the show like regular VIPs. With Joe and Tate and Ray on board for the suite, they would be just fine.

The hotel was buzzing with holiday cheer. Mel saw

Regina in the lobby, greeting guests. She looked resplendent in a purple strapless gown with her hair pulled back with pearl-tipped hairpins. When she turned and met Mel's gaze she made no acknowledgment of her and turned back to her guest with an overly loud laugh.

"That was rude," Angie observed.

"Agreed," Mel said. "I have to be honest. I am thrilled that tonight is it. I'm ready to put this gig and the Hotel Grande behind us."

"Me, too," Angie said. "No more long-running events—ever."

They hurried to the VIP room while Tate and Joe ducked into the men's room to change into their Santa costumes. The doors wouldn't open for a bit, and they set up the cupcake towers and boxed extra cupcakes for the cast and crew for the final time.

When the doors opened, Mel studied the guests as they entered. She wondered if Doc's killer would be in attendance. Since they hadn't been caught, would they come to Shelby's final show to enjoy some twisted thrill in knowing they'd gotten away with murder? She searched the crowd for Lisa Martin, Shelby's childhood best friend who clearly had a grudge, and the loan shark Jerry Stackhouse, who had to be furious with Ray and who still wanted Shelby to pay off Doc's debts. She would have searched for Miranda, too, but she didn't think Doc's ex-wife would suddenly appear. Mel's gut told her there was something wrong about Miranda's disappearance. It just didn't feel right.

Shelby's parents and brothers arrived. They chose their cupcakes but Mel noted that Mary Ellen picked at hers, just nibbling, not really eating.

"Did you want to try a different flavor?" Mel asked.

Mary Ellen cringed. "Sorry, no, the cupcake is delightful. I'm just so nervous. We haven't seen Shelby perform in years, and I forgot how nervous it made me to have my baby up there onstage in front of everyone, you know?"

"I can imagine," Mel said. "But you don't have to fret. Shelby is a pro."

"That's what Cheryl said." Mary Ellen nodded. An expression of sadness flashed over her face. "Sometimes I feel like Cheryl is more her mama than I am. I missed so much when I . . . well, I had to go away for a while and when I returned, Shelby had already started performing."

"You being here means everything to Shelby," Mel said. "She was so desperately homesick, thinking that she wouldn't see you for the holidays."

"Yeah?" Mary Ellen asked.

"Yeah."

"That's good to hear," Mary Ellen said. "When Cheryl told us that they wouldn't be coming home with us after the show, I was so disappointed, but Mr. Nickels is the best and if he wants to represent Shelby, then I guess we have to let her return to Los Angeles with him."

"Mr. Nickels is going to represent Shelby?" Mel asked. She was shocked. He'd been so adamant that he wouldn't.

"According to Cheryl, and she should know," Mary Ellen said. "That's the hard part about having children, I suppose, you can't stand in the way of their dreams even when those dreams take them away from you."

"I suppose not," Mel said. She thought about Mr. Nickels and his refusal to manage Shelby. What had changed? She decided to go and find out. "If you'll excuse me."

"Of course," Mary Ellen said.

Mel looked for Joe but he was passing out cupcakes on the other side of the room, as was Tate. Angie was helping three customers at the station, and Ray was loading up more trays. Mel decided to try to catch Shelby before her entrance into the VIP suite.

She didn't want to believe that Shelby had anything to do with Doc's death or Miranda's disappearance but she couldn't forget how excited the singer had been to hear that Terrence Nickels was at the hotel. Could Mel and Angie have been wrong? Could Lisa Martin be right? Could Shelby have murdered to get the representation she wanted not just once but twice?

The hallway was busy and Mel skirted around dancers and stagehands and a couple of musicians. She rapped on Shelby's door and the singer called out, "Come in."

"Hey, Shelby," Mel said as she entered. "I was just wondering if you wanted me to put aside any cupcakes for you for after the show?"

"Oh thanks, Mel, that's really nice of you." Shelby was sitting on the couch, strumming her guitar. She put it down and stood up and stretched. "That would be amazing. It's a long trip back to Tennessee."

Mel tipped her head to the side. "Tennessee?"

"Yeah, since I'm at loose ends, with no representation and all, I've decided I'm going home with my family for a long rest. Don't tell my mama. I want it to be a surprise."

"Of course," Mel agreed. "Does everyone involved in the show know this is your plan?"

"I've told everyone who needs to know," Shelby said.

"I'm really sad about Doc and I think some time at home will give me a chance to heal. I never really had that chance after Diana died, so I'm hoping to process that, too," she said. "Cheryl insists it'll kill my career, but I just don't care."

Mel glanced around the room. One of Stan's officers was in the corner of the room. He waved at Mel, who waved back. Other than that, they were alone.

"But I thought you were headed to Los Angeles to be represented by Terrence Nickels," Mel said.

Shelby shook her head. "You mean the guy Miranda works with now? She made it pretty clear that she would never let that happen."

"You spoke to Miranda?" Mel asked.

"Cheryl and I ran into her a few days ago," Shelby said. "She said straight out that she told Terrence she'd leave him if he represented me. She was very pleased that he chose her. Honestly, he's a bit intimidating. I can't say that I'm sorry he passed on me."

Mel felt her heart beat hard in her chest. She leaned close to Shelby and said, "I need to know exactly when you had that conversation with Miranda."

Shelby looked surprised. "Oh, I don't know, maybe two days ago. It was late, after my show, and she was on her way to the swimming pool."

"It was just before Miranda went missing then," Mel said.

"She's missing?" Shelby asked. Her eyes were wide. "I've been so busy with the show. I didn't know. I hadn't heard." She frowned. "She has to be okay, right?"

"No one knows." Mel glanced around the dressing room. "Where's Cheryl?"

Shelby glanced at the door. "She just left. She said she forgot something upstairs but she'd be back before the show starts."

"Ms. Vaughn, it's time for your appearance in the VIP suite," the stage manager called through the door.

"Time to go," Shelby said. "Please keep me in the loop about Miranda. Despite everything that happened, I do care about her."

"I will."

"Thanks again, Mel, for the best Christmas in a long time."

"Of course," Mel said. She stepped out of the room with Shelby and the officer assigned to her.

Shelby set off down the hallway but Mel didn't. Shelby paused and asked, "Aren't you coming?"

"In a bit," she said. "Go get 'em." She still couldn't say, *Break a leg.* Shelby smiled, showing her dazzling slash of white teeth. With a wave, she was gone.

Who had wanted Doc dead the most? Stan's question popped into Mel's head. Was it Jerry the loan shark he owed money to? Lisa, the daughter of Shelby's first manager, who believed Doc was responsible for her mother's death? Shelby, who was fighting for creative control of her show? Or Miranda, the bitter ex-wife who wanted revenge for being tossed aside? Or none of the above?

The answer had been staring her right in the face for days. But how could she prove it? She glanced down the hallway towards the VIP room. A gray-haired man in a security uniform slipped out of a side door, glancing over his shoulders as he locked it behind him. Trevor.

Mel remembered Cheryl saying that she valued having a strong man at her beck and call. Mel put her hand to her throat. Had Trevor been doing someone's bidding when Mel was nearly strangled?

She hurried to the door that he had just locked, and tried the handle, confirming that she couldn't get inside. There had been something so suspicious about his actions that Mel knew he was hiding something in that room. But what?

Mel saw one of the stagehands hurrying towards the auditorium. She waved him down and asked, "Do you have a key to that room?"

He sent her an annoyed look. "Lady, we have a show starting in thirty minutes."

"I know but Shelby said she left something in there, and I promised I'd get it for her," Mel said.

He reached into his pocket and pulled out a massive set of keys. "This is what they gave us for this area when we arrived. If there's a key for that door, it's one of these. I'm in the sound booth. Get those back to me when you're done and good luck."

He tossed the keys at Mel and hurried away. Mel snatched the keys out of the air. Their sharp points bit into her palm and she opened her hand to see at least thirty keys of varying sizes. She sighed.

One by one, she tried the keys while trying to keep an eye out for Trevor the security guard. It would be hard to explain what she was doing as she didn't think he'd be as gullible as the sound tech.

Finally, on the sixteenth key, the lock turned with a click. She pulled the door open and the eye-watering smell of industrial cleaner punched her in the nose. The illumination from the hallway gave her just enough light to see that it was a supply room. Her shoulders drooped.

She didn't know what she'd expected but cleaning supplies wasn't it. She grabbed a heavy bottle of bleach and used it to prop the door open. She was not going to get trapped again, especially not in here.

There was a string dangling in front of her and she pulled it, lighting up the room with the single bulb overhead. Steel shelves were stacked with supplies. Discouraged, she turned to go, when she saw a movement behind one of the shelves.

"Is someone in here?" she asked.

There was a scuffling noise and she sucked in a breath, fearing that the highest probability was that it was a rat. She forced herself to step forward and peer around the large shelving unit. She braced herself for the sight of a whiskered rodent, but it wasn't. Sitting on a pile of towels, in a robe and swimwear with her hands and feet bound and her mouth taped, was Miranda Carter.

"Ah!" Mel cried and rushed forward. She yanked the tape off Miranda's mouth. "Are you all right?"

Miranda gasped, sucking in great gulps of air. "Thank you. I was beginning to think I was going to die in here."

Mel glanced at the zip ties around Miranda's ankles and wrists. "Who did this to you?"

"Trevor, the head of hotel security, grabbed me when I was leaving the swimming pool," Miranda said. "I have no idea why. He's been moving me around the building, from room to room, but he hasn't hurt me in any way. He's even fed me and let me use the bathroom. Weird, right?"

Mel frowned. It was weird. Why would Trevor do this to Miranda—unless he was doing it for someone else? If her suspicions were right, there was only one person it could be.

"Is there a problem in here?" a man's voice called from the doorway. Mel tensed, fearing it was Trevor, but one of the officers who had been shadowing Shelby stepped into the room.

"She's Miranda Carter, the woman who's been missing," Mel said. "Do you have anything to cut her loose?"

The officer stepped forward, taking a knife from his utility belt. At the same time, he used the radio on his shoulder to call Uncle Stan.

"Mel, is Terrence okay?" Miranda asked. "If someone did this to me, it could be to get to him."

"I think you're right," Mel said.

"Please go check on him," Miranda said. Her face was white and she grimaced as the officer sawed at the zip ties around her wrists. "I'm afraid for him."

"All right," Mel said. "Tell the detective when he gets here where I'm going."

Miranda nodded.

Mel pulled her phone out of her pocket. She opened her contacts and pressed Joe's number. He answered on the second ring, "Cupcake, where are you?"

"No time to explain," Mel said. "Meet me at the elevators in the lobby."

"What?"

"Hurry!" Mel cried and then she started to run.

She reached the lobby and ran right to the elevator for the sunset suite. She pressed the button, willing it to arrive. The button stayed lit and she paced back and forth. The Christmas sweater she'd thought was so festive earlier now itched and she pulled the high collar away from her neck as she couldn't get enough air.

"Mel! What's going on?" Joe crossed the lobby, coming

towards her, still in his Santa suit and carrying a tray of cupcakes, as the doors opened.

"I'll explain on the way. Come on!" Mel grabbed his arm and guided him into the empty elevator. Inside she pressed the button.

"What's happening?" he asked. He shifted the tray to his other hand.

"I found Miranda Carter tied up in a cleaning closet."

"What?" He looked at her in surprise.

"And I think I know who murdered Doc Howard," she said. "In fact, I think I know who murdered Diana Martin, too."

"Who?" Joe asked.

The elevator dinged and the doors slid open. Standing in front of them was Cheryl Hoover. She frowned at them, looking furious, but it vanished so quickly Mel almost thought she imagined it.

"Cheryl," Mel said. She gave Joe a raised-eyebrow look, hoping he understood that she was answering his question.

"Mel?" Cheryl said. "And . . . Joe? What are you two doing up here?"

"We were sent here to make a cupcake delivery," Mel said. "Crazy, right? But what Mr. Nickels wants, he gets."

Cheryl stiffened. "He's not here. There must be a mistake."

Mel shrugged. "I don't know about that. I just know we were sent to the sunset suite and told to bring cupcakes. Excuse me."

She went to step around Cheryl but the stylist moved into her path. Her voice was tight when she said, "I told you. He's not here."

Mel glanced at the stained glass window. Through the lighter-colored rectangles, she definitely saw movement. "I think you're mistaken. I can see someone moving in there."

"I'm sure it's just the cleaning people," Cheryl said.

"Then they can answer the door and let us leave the cupcakes for Mr. Nickels," Joe said. His voice was reasonable but firm. He stepped around her and approached the door.

He had his hand on the knob when Cheryl cried out, "Ow, oh, ow!"

Mel and Joe turned to look at her.

"I think I've twisted my ankle," she gasped. "Please help me."

Mel looked at Joe and shook her head. Joe turned the knob, which was unlocked, and pushed the door open. Sitting on the couch, bound with duct tape and zip ties just as Miranda had been, was Terrence Nickels. He flailed, clearly signaling his distress, and Mel knew that was the motion she'd seen through the glass.

Joe dropped the tray of cupcakes onto the table by the door and strode into the suite. Mel went to follow him but a movement out of the corner of her eye brought her attention to Cheryl, who was frantically pressing the elevator button as if willing it to open faster.

"Oh, no, you don't," Mel cried.

The doors opened and Cheryl jumped in. Mel ducked in after her. The doors slammed shut. Cheryl lunged for the button that would send the elevator down but Mel blocked her.

"It was you," Mel said. "You're the one who slipped Doc Howard a sedative. What did you hit him with?"

"You're crazy," Cheryl scoffed. "Why would I do that?"

"Two reasons, one was because he was going to re-place you with someone younger," Mel said. "Someone who didn't keep Shelby cut off from her family, friends, and fans."

"I don't—"

"You do," Mel said. "And because you think Shelby is your daughter and you will do anything to get her to the top, including murdering the managers who aren't getting her there fast enough. That's why you killed both Doc and Diana, isn't it?"

"You're insane," Cheryl said. "You have no proof."

"I do though," Mel said. "He's tied up in the sunset suite and she was bound and gagged in a cleaning closet on the first floor."

"Miranda is alive?" Cheryl gaped.

"Why do you think I'm talking about Miranda?" Mel asked.

Realizing her mistake, Cheryl charged. She knocked Mel to the side and pressed the down button. The doors slid shut and the elevator was cruising down to the first floor. Mel knew that if Cheryl reached it, she would dis-appear into the crowd and never be seen again. She reached for the other woman, trying to grab her, but Cheryl was quick on her feet and eluded her.

The elevator stopped and the doors opened. Mel jumped in front of them, blocking the exit. Cheryl tried to get around her but Mel grabbed the sides and refused to let go. Cheryl hunched over and rammed Mel with her shoulder right in the gut. Still, Mel didn't let go.

"Let me out!" Cheryl screamed.

"No."

"Help! Help! She's holding me hostage!" Cheryl screamed into the lobby. Mel didn't dare take her gaze off Cheryl to see if anyone was coming to Cheryl's aid.

"You murdered Doc Howard," Mel said. "Admit it."

"Shut up!" Cheryl cried.

"He was going to get rid of you so you got rid of him first. After all, if you aren't Shelby Vaughn's stylist, who are you?"

"Leave me alone!" Cheryl cried. She took a swing at Mel, her fist slamming into Mel's elbow as if she could get her to release the door. Not a chance.

"That's not what happened," Cheryl said. "It was an accident."

"How is cracking a man's head open an accident?"

"He wasn't the best. Shelby deserves the best," Cheryl said. "I was trying to help her. I heard Terrence Nickels was going to be here and I wanted to get her signed with him but Doc wouldn't let her out of her contract. He wouldn't even let her sing her originals because he didn't want Terrence to hear how good she is."

"Is that why Nickels is tied up in his room? You were trying to force him to sign Shelby?" Mel asked. "Did you kidnap Miranda as leverage?"

"No," Cheryl said. "I have no idea what you're accusing me of. I think you're cracking under the holiday stress, Mel. You really need to take a vacation."

"What were you doing in Nickels's suite, Cheryl?" Mel asked. Her arms were straining and she knew she couldn't ward off Cheryl's attacks for much longer. Where was Uncle Stan? He should be here by now.

"I wasn't doing anything," Cheryl protested but it sounded like a lie. "I was never even in his suite."

"Oh, Cheryl." Mel tried to make her voice sound full of pity. She was going in with a bluff and she could only hope that she'd picked up some fibbing skills from Angie after all these years, because she really needed Cheryl to believe her right now. "Don't you get it? Trevor already gave you up. He told us everything when we found Miranda."

"I don't believe you!" Cheryl cried.

"He's been moving Miranda from room to room," Mel said. "You told him to get rid of her, didn't you? But he couldn't do it."

Cheryl visibly paled but she shook it off. "You can't prove anything."

"The sedative you give Shelby on the tour bus was found in Doc's system." Mel continued to bluff. She had heard Cheryl offer the sleeping aid to Shelby after Doc's murder. It only made sense that she'd used it on Doc. "You drugged him before you hit him, didn't you? It's the only way you could overpower him, and you had Trevor lock me in the VIP suite to cause a distraction. It worked. You were able to bludgeon Doc and then run back upstairs to your room with no one the wiser."

Cheryl was sweating, her face pink and her breath short. "You don't understand."

"I think I do," Mel said. "My friend is a detective in Vegas and I'm going to have him check the medical examiner's records for Diane Martin. I'm betting they'll find traces of the same sedative in her system on the night of the fire. That's why she slept through the blaze you set, didn't she?"

"No." Cheryl shook her head.

"Yes," Mel countered. "It's over, Cheryl."

"But I did it for Shelby. Don't you see? She's my daughter and my best friend. I'd do anything for her. I even flooded my own salon so that I could go on the road with her," Cheryl cried. Big fat tears rolled down her cheeks and her shoulders shook with sobs. "She's my entire life."

"Oh, no, Cheryl, no."

Cheryl gazed past Mel with a stricken look on her face. Mel turned around to see Shelby standing there with her parents and Uncle Stan.

"You're mine," Cheryl said to Shelby. "You're my daughter. Not hers." She pointed at Mary Ellen. "She didn't raise you. I did."

"Cheryl!" Mary Ellen gasped. "What are you saying?"

Mel saw two officers on either side of the lobby. If Cheryl tried to run, they'd grab her. Mel glanced at Uncle Stan, who tipped his head to the side to indicate she should move. Mel started to ease away.

"Don't even think it," Cheryl snarled through gritted teeth. She grabbed Mel by the arm and jammed her clutch purse up against Mel's side. Cheryl pushed Mel forward, leaving the elevator behind, allowing the doors to close. "I have a gun in here and I am not afraid to use it."

The watching crowd collectively gasped.

"Let Mel go," Shelby said. "She didn't do anything to you."

"Oh, didn't she?" Cheryl asked. "Always asking questions, going up to the sunset suite, sniffing around where she didn't belong. She just couldn't let it go."

"If by 'it' you mean Doc's murder, then, no, I couldn't let it go," Mel said. "Is that why you tried to strangle me in my own backyard? To keep me from figuring out what you'd done?"

Uncle Stan's eyes went wide and he shook his head at her, clearly trying to tell her to shut up for fear that Cheryl might actually shoot her.

"I have no idea what you're talking about," Cheryl said. She tipped her chin up. She was going to deny it all to the bitter end.

"Right, just like you have no idea how Diana burned to death so that Doc Howard could become Shelby's new manager and when he proved to be not good enough, Doc ended up sedated and bludgeoned in Shelby's dressing room?" Mel asked.

"Cheryl!" Shelby cried. Her eyes were enormous. "Is it true? Did you do those horrible things?"

"Take it back," Cheryl hissed in Mel's ear. "Or I'll shoot you for the sheer joy it will give me to shut you up once and for—"

Thwack! Her grip slackened and Cheryl slumped to the ground. Standing in the open elevator, holding an empty cupcake tray, were Joe and Terrence Nickels. The two officers swooped in and grabbed Cheryl and her purse and hauled her to her feet. Joe tossed the tray aside and scooped up Mel in his arms.

"You all right, cupcake?"

"Never better," Mel said. She'd never meant it more.

Miranda ran into the lobby right into Terrence's arms. Behind her was the officer who had cut her loose, leading Trevor, the head of security, in handcuffs.

"Tell them." The officer nudged Trevor.

"Don't you do it," Cheryl moaned. The two officers

had zip-tied her hands and she was leaning heavily against one of them, while the other checked her purse for a gun. He glanced up at Uncle Stan and shook his head.

So, holding a gun on her had been a bluff. Mel wished she felt more relieved but instead she was just queasy.

"Best save yourself now, Trevor," Uncle Stan said. "Ms. Hoover is going down for murder. Trust me, you don't want to be tried as an accomplice."

"I had nothing to do with the murder. She did it!" Trevor cried. His voice was low and he was staring at his shoes, glancing up only occasionally as if he couldn't bear to meet anyone's gaze. "She drugged Doc with a cupcake and then hit him on the back of the head with Ms. Vaughn's guitar."

"My Fender?" Shelby squeaked. "Is that why it's been missing? You told me we left it behind."

"Cheryl had me take it to a repair shop in Old Town," Trevor said.

"Shut up, Trevor." Cheryl stomped her foot but he ignored her.

"I have the claim receipt from the day after the murder," he said. He glanced at Uncle Stan. "If you need it."

"That would be helpful," Uncle Stan said.

"Why would you help Cheryl with this?" Shelby asked Trevor.

Mel didn't think it was possible but Trevor's head went even lower as his face darkened with shame. "She said if I helped her, she'd see to it that I got to be a part of your show. All I ever wanted was to be onstage. I figured this was my only chance, so I helped her cover up Doc's murder. But then Cheryl wanted me to kill Ms. Carter and make it look as if she'd run off with another man, but I couldn't do it."

"Thank god," Terrence said. He hugged Miranda close and buried his face in her hair. "I don't know what I would have done if I lost you."

Mel felt Joe's arm slide around her back as he pulled her into his side. "I know exactly how he feels."

"I'm okay." Mel leaned against him. "And we caught Doc's killer."

Uncle Stan began reading Cheryl her rights. "Cheryl Hoover, you're under arrest for the murder of Doc Howard."

"You're making a mistake," Cheryl protested. "Stop! You can't do this! Shelby, help me!"

Shelby turned away from her, stepping into the arms of her parents, who shielded her from Cheryl's fit.

Uncle Stan talked over her and when he was done, he turned to his officers and said, "Take her in and book her for a double homicide, attempted murder, kidnapping, and aggravated assault. I'll be right behind you." He glanced at Trevor. "Take him, too. I want to hear his story from the top."

"You won't get away with this!" Cheryl resisted while they led her outside but it was a losing battle. They all watched through the lobby window as the officers led her to the waiting squad car. Trevor was taken to an adjacent car, but unlike Cheryl, he followed his arresting officer like a placid sheep.

"What is the meaning of this?" Regina Bessette arrived in the lobby. She glared at Shelby. "Aren't you supposed to be onstage?"

"Yes, ma'am, but—"

"There are no buts in show business," Regina said. "Get yourself onstage right now. The show must go on."

Shelby looked at Uncle Stan. He waved for her to go. "I suspect we'll be busy at the station for a while but I'll want to interview you as soon as your show is over."

"Yes, sir," Shelby said.

The Vaughns looked at Stan and he sighed. "Yes, go ahead, but the same goes for you."

Shelby's parents hurried after their daughter.

"And me?" Mel asked.

"Can tell me everything that happened right now," he said.

Mel told him about her conversation with Mary Ellen where Shelby's mom told her that Shelby would be leaving for Los Angeles, and then her conversation with Shelby about going home. Mel explained that in that moment she realized that it was Cheryl who actually drove Shelby's career, that it had been Cheryl all along since Shelby was a child. She also reminded him of his observation that they needed to figure out who wanted Doc dead the most, and it was then that she realized it had to be Cheryl.

When she saw Trevor come out of the cleaning supply closet and then found Miranda tied up inside, everything clicked and she knew that Cheryl had gotten Trevor to help her with her scheme. Cheryl felt she had to kill Doc just as she'd murdered Diana for the sake of Shelby's career. She wanted Terrence to think Miranda had left him. Then he wouldn't feel conflicted about signing Shelby. In fact, Mel was betting there was probably a contract in Cheryl's purse. A contract Terrence had obviously refused to sign, which was probably why Cheryl had tied him up.

In her frustration, she'd thought she could force him to represent Shelby.

Uncle Stan had taken Cheryl's handbag from the officer who retrieved it when she was knocked down. He opened it and glanced inside. He pulled out a sheaf of papers.

"And you would be right," he said.

"I'd look in there for a sleep aid, too," Mel said. "Shelby told me that Cheryl always gave her something to help her sleep on long overnight bus rides. I'm betting that's the sedative she used on Doc and potentially Diana."

"Well done, Mel," Uncle Stan said. "But please don't scare the daylights out of me like that again. When Joe called and said you were trapped in an elevator with Doc's killer, I about had a heart attack."

"Sorry," Mel said. She turned to Joe and said it again. "Sorry."

"It's all right," Joe said. "I knew you'd be okay. I just had a feeling."

Mel smiled.

"All right, I'm going to have more questions for you two but I want to start upstairs with Mr. Nickels and Ms. Carter." He glanced over his shoulder at the couple. "Are you up to an interview at the moment?"

"Yes." Miranda nodded. "I'll do anything that will help put that psychopath behind bars."

Terrence nodded in agreement and they stepped into the elevator with Uncle Stan, who hit the button. As the doors started to close, he said, "We'll talk after the show."

Mel nodded. "I'll be here."

The doors shut and Joe pulled her into his arms for a comforting hug. "Are you all right?"

"I'm fine," Mel said. "Nothing a cupcake can't cure at any rate."

"Well, it's a good thing you're with me," he said. "I'm a VIP, you know."

Mel laughed and together they made their way to the suite to have a cupcake and tell their friends that the murder of Doc Howard had been solved.

The entire cast and crew retired to the VIP suite post-show. It hadn't been planned but after the events of the night, the hotel owner, Regina Bessette, took it upon herself to order food and drink for everyone.

Uncle Stan had left for the police station but came back to finish his interviews. Much to Mel's surprise, Lisa Martin, Miranda Carter, and Terrence Nickels were in attendance at the after-party. Shelby had brief and what appeared to be intense conversations with both women before they left. When she returned she sat down beside her mom and put her head on her mother's shoulder.

"I feel like this is all my fault," Mary Ellen said. "I was so scarred from being tabloid fodder myself that I backed away from the world you were living in and let Cheryl take over instead of stepping up. I'm so sorry, Shelby."

"Me, too," Jack said. "I should have been more involved while your mom was away but I didn't know how."

"It's not your fault," Shelby said. "We all trusted Cheryl. She was our friend and neighbor. She was family. Honestly, I should have realized something wasn't right when she was weird about me going home for visits, having friends. Even on this trip she didn't like my hanging out with Angie."

"She was trying to keep you closed off," Mary Ellen said. She shook her head. "We should have noticed. We just assumed you were living your best life and were . . ."

"Were what?" Shelby asked.

"Ashamed of us," Jack said. "We're not rich or educated. Your mother went through that hellish experience with Gary Newton."

"I've been thinking about that," Shelby said. "Wasn't Cheryl best friends with Joelle Newton?"

"Back in high school, sure," Mary Ellen said. "But they grew apart." Her voice sounded unsure.

"Unless Cheryl decided to have you removed from the picture and used Joelle to do it," Shelby said.

"Oh, my." Mary Ellen gasped. She turned to her husband. "If that's true then I lost seven months of my life because of her, and Gary Newton lost his life."

"Giving her just enough time to swoop in and become a second mama to our daughter and sons," Jack said. His face went dark with fury. "I will not rest until she pays."

"She will, Daddy, she will," Shelby said. "I'll make sure of it. I just can't believe it. After all these years, I trusted her completely."

"We all did, honey," Mary Ellen said. She glanced across the table where Mel and Joe sat, and said, "I can't thank you enough. If you hadn't realized what was happening, Shelby would be on her way to Los Angeles and we'd be headed back to Tennessee. We'd never know that our baby was being essentially held hostage by a murderer."

"I just got lucky," Mel said. "If I hadn't run into you

when I did and then talked to Shelby, I would never have realized that Cheryl was the key. She played everyone against each other until she got caught in her own lies."

"What do you think her plan was?" Angie asked.

"Judging by the papers we found in her handbag, I think she was going to coerce Terrence into representing Shelby and then she was going to take Shelby back to Los Angeles, keeping her away from her family. I'm sure she told Mary Ellen and Jack about the deal because she wanted them to leave, and she was likely waiting to tell Shelby until after she had locked Nickels down."

"Of all the conniving, sneaky, no-good—" Angie was just getting warmed up. Tate put an arm around her trying to soothe her.

She'd been horrified that Mel had been in danger. So much so that she'd begged Uncle Stan to just give her a minute with Cheryl. Uncle Stan had refused, although it looked like it pained him to do so.

Just about everyone who'd been at Christmas dinner was in the VIP suite, mixing and mingling with the performers from the show. Despite the chaos before the performance, it had been the best show of the entire run. And the relief that the murderer had been caught made the atmosphere almost buoyant.

Surprisingly, Ray, of all people, tapped the side of his glass with his spoon, then rose to his feet and started to sing, "*I don't want a lot for Christmas . . .* "

A chorus of groans filled the room, but he persisted, singing the second line of the famous Mariah Carey holiday song in a surprisingly pleasant baritone. With a grin, Shelby jumped up from her seat and joined him, and the rest of the room followed suit.

The next thing Mel knew the entire room erupted into song and someone started banging out the tune on an old upright piano in the corner. She saw Uncle Stan singing to her mom, who was laughing. Her brother Charlie and his wife were singing and dancing as were most of the DeLauras. Tate was twirling Angie, while Olivia dipped Marty. Oz had a dancer on each arm and they were both singing to him. The Vaughns as a family were all holding hands and singing, even Shelby's brothers. Mel turned to find Joe standing there with his arms open. She stepped into him and together they swayed, singing along with the rest of the party.

"Merry Christmas, cupcake," Joe said.

Mel sighed and rested her head on his shoulder. "Merry Christmas, Joe, and for the record." She paused, waiting for the song to kick in, and then she sang, *"All I want for Christmas is you."*

Joe smiled and then he kissed her. Despite the craziness of the day, the near-death experiences, and capturing a murderer, Mel realized that having all of her loved ones together, safe and sound and happy, made it the best Christmas ever.

Acknowledgments

First, I have to thank reader Paula Wagaman, who entered the contest to name the next Cupcake Bakery Mystery. She came up with the title *Sugar Plum Poisoned* and it is just so perfect. Thank you, Paula! I hope you enjoy being a character in the story.

As always, much gratitude to the team that makes this series such a joy to write every year—Kate Seaver, Christina Hogrebe, Amanda Maurer, Daché Rogers, Jessica Mangicaro, Kim-Salina I, Jennifer Lynes, Angelina Krahn. It is an amazing thing to keep a series going for fifteen books and I simply could not do it without all the marvelously talented professionals working behind the scenes. Thank you all so very much.

I also want to thank my assistant, Christie Conlee, for her endless enthusiasm and positivity. You are a wonder! Much love to my menfolk, Chris, Beckett, and Wyatt, for their limitless supply of encouragement. And, finally, for the readers. I would be nothing without all of you, and I never take that for granted. Thank you for coming along on this ride with me! The best is yet to be (I hope)!

Recipes

Sugar Plum Cupcakes

A spice cupcake frosted with vanilla buttercream.

1¾ cups all-purpose flour
1½ teaspoons baking powder
½ teaspoon salt
1 teaspoon cinnamon
¼ teaspoon cloves
½ teaspoon nutmeg
½ teaspoon allspice
¾ cup butter, softened
¾ cup brown sugar
½ cup sugar
4 eggs, room temperature

3 teaspoons vanilla extract
½ cup milk

Preheat the oven to 325 degrees. Put paper liners in the cupcake pan. In a medium bowl, whisk all of the dry ingredients: the flour, baking powder, salt, and spices. In a large bowl, mix the butter and sugars together until fluffy. Mix each egg in one at a time. Add the vanilla and the milk, and beat until well blended. Using a spatula, fold the dry ingredients into the wet until thoroughly mixed and smooth. Fill each liner three-quarters full. Bake for 18 to 22 minutes or until the tops are golden brown. Allow to cool completely before frosting. Makes 18.

Buttercream Frosting

½ cup (1 stick) salted butter, softened
½ cup (1 stick) unsalted butter, softened
1 teaspoon vanilla extract
4 cups sifted confectioners' sugar
2 tablespoons milk

In a large bowl, cream the butter and the vanilla. Gradually add the confectioners' sugar, one cup at a time, beating well on medium speed and adding the milk as needed. Scrape the sides of the bowl often. Beat at medium speed until light and fluffy. Pipe onto the cooled cupcakes in big swirls using a pastry bag.

Garnish with a variety of sprinkles and holiday candy like peppermints or spiced gumdrops.

Eggnog Cupcake

An eggnog-flavored cupcake with rum
buttercream.

1¼ cups all-purpose flour
1½ teaspoons baking powder
¾ teaspoon nutmeg
¼ teaspoon salt
6 tablespoons butter, softened
¾ cup sugar
1½ tablespoons vegetable oil
1 teaspoon vanilla extract
2 large eggs, room temperature
½ cup eggnog

Preheat the oven to 350 degrees. Put paper liners in the cupcake tin. In a medium bowl, whisk the flour, baking powder, nutmeg, and salt, and set aside. In a large bowl, cream together the butter, sugar, and oil until light and fluffy. Add the eggs one at a time and then the vanilla, mixing until well blended. Alternately mix in the dry ingredients and the eggnog, beat on medium speed until smooth. Fill the cupcake liners two-thirds full and bake for 16 to 20 minutes, or until a toothpick inserted in the center comes out clean. Makes 12.

Rum Buttercream Frosting

½ cup (1 stick) salted butter, softened
½ cup (1 stick) unsalted butter, softened

1 teaspoon rum extract or 1 tablespoon rum
4 cups sifted confectioners' sugar
2 tablespoons milk

In a large bowl, cream the butter and rum extract or rum. Gradually add confectioners' sugar, one cup at a time, beating well on medium speed and adding the milk as needed. Scrape the sides of the bowl often. Beat at medium speed until light and fluffy. Pipe onto cooled cupcakes in big swirls using a pastry bag. Grate fresh nutmeg on top and garnish with a cinnamon stick.

Peppermint Bark Cupcake

A chocolate cupcake with peppermint buttercream garnished with bits of peppermint bark.

1½ cups all-purpose flour
¾ cup unsweetened cocoa
1½ cups sugar
1½ teaspoons baking soda
¾ teaspoon baking powder
¾ teaspoon salt
2 eggs, room temperature
¾ cup milk
3 tablespoons vegetable oil

1 teaspoon vanilla extract
¾ cup warm water

Preheat the oven to 350 degrees. Put paper liners in a cupcake tin. In a large bowl, whisk together the flour, cocoa, sugar, baking soda, baking powder, and salt. Add the eggs, milk, oil, vanilla extract, and water. Beat on medium speed with an electric mixer until smooth, scraping the sides of the bowl as needed. Scoop into the paper-lined cupcake pans and bake for 20 minutes or until a toothpick inserted in the center comes out clean. Makes 18.

Peppermint Buttercream Frosting

½ cup (1 stick) salted butter, softened
½ cup (1 stick) unsalted butter, softened
1 teaspoon peppermint extract
4 cups sifted confectioners' sugar
2 tablespoons milk

In a large bowl, cream the butter and peppermint extract. Gradually add the confectioners' sugar, one cup at a time, beating well on medium speed and adding the milk as needed. Scrape the sides of the bowl often. Beat at medium speed until light and fluffy. Pipe onto the cooled cupcakes, and garnish with pieces of peppermint bark.

Peppermint Bark

1 dozen crushed candy canes
1½ pounds chocolate candy, chopped

1½ pounds white (or vanilla) candy, chopped
1 teaspoon peppermint flavor

Line a rimmed baking sheet with wax or parchment paper. With a rolling pin, smash the unwrapped candy canes in a plastic bag. Set aside. Melt the chocolate candy in a double boiler, occasionally stirring, until completely melted and smooth. Spread evenly onto the wax paper. Refrigerate to harden, approximately 20 minutes. Melt the vanilla candy in a double boiler, stirring in the peppermint flavor, until completely smooth and melted. Spread evenly on top of the chocolate candy. Sprinkle the crushed candy canes evenly across the top. Refrigerate until thoroughly hardened, approximately 30 minutes. Break into pieces of varying sizes.

Sugar Cookie Cupcakes

A fluffy vanilla cupcake topped with buttercream and sugar sprinkles.

1½ cups all-purpose flour
1½ teaspoons baking powder
¼ teaspoon salt
½ cup butter, softened
1 cup sugar
2 eggs, room temperature

3 teaspoons vanilla extract
¾ cup milk

Preheat oven to 350 degrees. Put paper liners in a cupcake tin. In a medium bowl, whisk together the flour, baking powder, and salt. Set aside. In a large bowl, cream together the butter, sugar, eggs, and vanilla. Alternately add the dry ingredients and the milk, mixing until smooth. Fill the cupcake liners two-thirds full. Bake for 17 to 21 minutes or until a toothpick inserted in the center comes out clean. Makes 12.

Buttercream Frosting

½ cup (1 stick) salted butter, softened
½ cup (1 stick) unsalted butter, softened
1 teaspoon clear vanilla extract
4 cups sifted confectioners' sugar
2 tablespoons milk

In a large bowl, cream the butter and vanilla. Gradually add the confectioners' sugar, one cup at a time, beating well on medium speed and adding the milk as needed. Scrape the sides of the bowl often. Beat at medium speed until light and fluffy. Pipe onto the cooled cupcakes in big swirls using a pastry bag. Garnish with colored sugar or sprinkles of your choice.

Gingerbread Cupcakes

A dense gingerbread cupcake with cinnamon
cream cheese frosting.

1½ cups all-purpose flour
½ teaspoon baking soda
2 teaspoons ground ginger
2½ teaspoons cinnamon
½ teaspoon nutmeg
½ teaspoon ground cloves
½ teaspoon salt
½ cup butter, softened
½ cup dark brown sugar
2 eggs, room temperature
½ cup molasses
1 teaspoon vanilla
½ cup milk, room temperature

Preheat oven to 350 degrees. Put paper liners in a cupcake tin. In a medium bowl, whisk together the flour, the baking soda, the spices, and the salt. Set aside. In a large bowl, mix together the butter, brown sugar, eggs, molasses, and vanilla. Alternately add the dry mixture and the milk until just combined. Fill the cupcake liners three-quarters full. Bake for 18 to 21 minutes or until a toothpick inserted in the center comes out clean. Cool completely. Makes 12.

Cinnamon Cream Cheese Frosting

8 ounces cream cheese, softened
1 stick unsalted butter, softened
½ teaspoon vanilla extract
1 tablespoon cinnamon
3 cups confectioners' sugar

In a large bowl, beat the cream cheese, butter, and vanilla until smooth. Add the cinnamon. Gradually add the confectioners' sugar and beat until the frosting is smooth. Put the frosting in a pastry bag and pipe onto the cupcakes in thick swirls, using an open tip. Decorate with a small gingerbread man cookie or a garnish of your choice.

Turn the page for an exclusive look at Jenn McKinlay's next Library Lover's Mystery . . .

FATAL FIRST EDITION

"How's the windy city?" Nancy Peyton asked.

Lindsey Sullivan glanced at the tiny faces of her friends on her phone. She was missing their weekly crafternoon meeting at the Briar Creek Public Library, where she was the director and the group had just video called her to see how her archivist conference was going. They were all crammed together, peering into one phone.

"Windy is a very accurate description," she said. She was sitting in one of the meeting rooms created by sectioning the ballroom of the Chicago hotel where the Annual Archivists Convention was being held.

"Who plans a conference in January in Chicago?" Beth Barker asked. She was the children's librarian and Lindsey could just make out the astronaut costume she was wearing, bubble helmet and all.

Jenn McKinlay

"Archivists who choose to meet in the off-season so they can spend their money on rare books instead of conferences," Lindsey answered. "I assume outer space is the theme for story time this week?"

"You know it," Beth said. "On the story countdown, we've got *Mousetronaut* by Astronaut Mark Kelly, *On the Launch Pad* by Michael Dahl, and *Moon's First Friends* by Susanna Leonard Hill. It's going to be far out."

The crafternooners behind her collectively groaned and Lindsey laughed. Beth had been her roommate in library school and her enthusiasm for children and reading hadn't waned one bit over the years.

"Where's that brother of mine?" Mary Murphy asked. She was squinting into the phone on their end.

"He's braving the mob at the coffee shop in the lobby," Lindsey said. Mike Sullivan, known to everyone in Briar Creek as Sully, was Mary's brother but more importantly, to Lindsey at any rate, he was Lindsey's husband.

"Good man," Violet LaRue observed. She was a retired Broadway actress who now ran the local community theater and had been a crafternooner with her best friend Nancy Peyton since Lindsey had started the program several years before.

"Did I hear Violet talking about me?" Sully appeared, carrying two cups of coffee as he took the seat beside Lindsey.

Lindsey turned the phone so that their friends could see him. They all cried, "Hi, Sully!" and he toasted them with his coffee cup.

"What's the craft today?" Lindsey asked. She didn't want to be rude, but, not being the crafty sort, this was the only part of the program that she didn't love, so she wasn't that upset about missing it.

"We're working on wire coiled bookmarks," Paula Turner said. She held up a sample of her work in progress. It was the silhouette of a cat with a spiral for its belly. She deftly placed it in on a page in the book of the week, which was *A Gentleman in Moscow* by Amor Towles, and closed the book. It looked like the cat was sitting on the top of the pages. It also looked complicated.

"That's amazing!" Lindsey wondered if her lack of enthusiasm was obvious.

"Right, I'll make one for you," Paula said. "I can try and make it look like your cat, Zelda."

Lindsey grinned. It was clear she hadn't fooled Paula a bit.

"Not to give you a case of FOMO, but you're missing Violet's pulled pork sliders," Mary said. She held one up to the camera. It looked delicious on its fluffy bun, dripping with barbecue sauce and packed with shredded pork and coleslaw. Lindsey felt her stomach growl.

"Don't be a tease, Sis," Sully said. He grinned and added, "We're going to Monteverde for dinner tonight."

"Now who's the tease?" Mary chided him. "You know it's cruel to taunt a woman who owns a restaurant with the news that you are dining at one of the finest Italian restaurants in Chicago."

"Sorry not sorry," Sully said. Mary shook her head at him.

A man stepped onto the stage at the front of the room and Lindsey said, "We'd better go. The program is about to start. We return on the train tomorrow, so we'll be home the day after!"

The crafternooners waved and said good-bye. Lindsey ended the call.

"Homesick?" Sully asked as he handed Lindsey her coffee.

"No . . . Maybe just a little," she said.

"You're turning into a regular Creeker," he said. He looked pleased as he draped his arm around the back of her chair.

Creekers were what they called lifelong residents of their hometown, Briar Creek. Sully and his sister, Mary, had been born and raised on the Thumb Islands, an archipelago just offshore from the Connecticut village. Lindsey had lived there for only a few years, but the quaint community had definitely become home.

Lindsey's friend Beth had become the children's librarian in Briar Creek right after they graduated and had encouraged Lindsey to apply for the director's position when Lindsey had lost her archivist job at the university in New Haven due to downsizing. It had taken some time and a lot of patience to get the small community to accept her. Marrying Sully, a native, had certainly helped.

"That might be one of the nicest things you've ever said to me," she whispered to him.

He smiled at her and she marveled for the thousandth time that this man, with his reddish-brown wavy hair and bright blue eyes, was her husband. They weren't a natural fit. He was a boat captain, who ran tour boats and a water taxi around the Thumb Islands in the bay, while she was petrified of water over her head, especially if she couldn't see the bottom. He was in his glory being outside all day battling the elements, whereas, other than walking their dog, Heathcliff, or bicycling to work and home, Lindsey preferred to be inside with a book. Still, somehow they just clicked and Lindsey couldn't imagine spending her life with anyone else.

"Good afternoon, everyone." The man on the stage spoke into the mic.

Lindsey recognized him right away. He was Henry Standish, the director of the archivists conference. Because her initial interest in a library career had been in preservation, Lindsey had known of him while in graduate school, as Henry had been the curator of a very exclusive private collection on the Upper East Side of Manhattan.

Shockingly, a few years prior, he'd been let go amid rumors of fraud. It had been quite the scandal in academic circles, but nothing was ever proven. The taint of the accusation remained however, ending his curator career. However, Henry had somehow landed the coveted position of conference director, and had been in charge of the annual meeting ever since.

Lindsey hadn't attended the conference in ages, but having just acquired a rare collection of first editions when a former resident of Briar Creek donated them to the public library, she had felt the need to get back in the game. Sully had been more than happy to join her and had spent most of his time looking up his old Navy buddies in the Chicago area while she sat in on panel discussions about preserving the past.

"I am thrilled to present one of the best book restoration specialists in the country," Henry continued. "She's certified in book arts, conservation, and authentication. She's internationally acclaimed and has won the Grand Prize in the Lawton-McNamara contest. Also, she's come all the way from San Francisco to speak with us, so please give a warm welcome to Brooklyn Wainwright." Henry held out his arm, gesturing to the left side of the stage. The packed room applauded as a pretty blonde on the tall side of medium climbed up the short staircase, leaving a ruggedly handsome, dark-haired man in a bespoke sport coat standing at the base of the steps.

Brooklyn waved as she crossed to the podium, carrying what appeared to be an archival box. She shook Henry's hand and moved to stand in front of the microphone.

"Hi," she greeted the room. The microphone screeched; she winced and moved back. She cast an exasperated glance over her shoulder at the handsome man, who lifted one eyebrow at her and smiled. When she turned back to the room she, too, was smiling. "Now that I've got your attention, let's talk book restoration."

Lindsey settled back in her seat. This had been in her top three talks to attend. Brooklyn Wainwright was not only an expert respected in the field, but she'd been tied to several high-profile murder investigations, which made Lindsey feel that Brooklyn was a kindred spirit, since Lindsey's own life in recent years had also been rife with dead bodies, which was not something a book restorer or a librarian typically dealt with.

Brooklyn was wearing white cotton gloves and holding up a book she had recently restored as an example of how she had returned it to its former glory. It was riveting, at least to Lindsey. Whoever was behind Lindsey was not nearly as interested. First, they rammed the back of her chair. She shifted in her seat and refocused her attention on the stage. Then the person muttered and banged into Lindsey's chair again. She cast a glance at

Sully and he began to turn around, looking as if he was going to say something.

Lindsey put her hand on his arm. He glanced at her and she shook her head. She didn't want to risk causing a scene during the talk. He sighed and turned back to the stage. Whoever was behind Lindsey knocked her chair one more time and then she heard them stand up and leave. They actually left! Brooklyn was just getting to the best part, about how she put the books back together once she'd restored them. Well, it was that person's loss.

The lecture ended to enthusiastic applause and Brooklyn stepped back from the podium. She put the book back in its archival box and stripped off her gloves. The man who'd been standing by the stage watching her joined her and took the box out of her hands.

Lindsey turned to Sully. "Wasn't that fascinating?"

He raised his eyebrows and said, "I had no idea that a book from eighteen-forty would be easier to mend than a book from nineteen-forty because the quality of the paper was so much better before they started using wood pulp. She's an interesting speaker."

"I think so, too," Lindsey said. "I'd love to meet her, but I don't want to bother her."

Lindsey reached down to grab her shoulder bag from where she'd tucked it under her seat and found the handles of a canvas conference tote bag instead. Her bag! She leaned forward and peered between her legs, pushing aside the long hank of curly blond hair that blocked her line of sight. Relieved, she spotted her shoulder bag under the conference tote given to everyone in attendance. She frowned. She was certain she'd left her tote bag in her hotel room. Who did this one belong to?

She grabbed both bags and sat up. She opened her shoulder bag to check that all of her personal belongings were inside. They were. *Phew.* Then she examined the tote bag. It was beige canvas with the conference logo of an open book printed on the front in a bold shade of blue. The zippered front pocket was empty, but there was an item in the body of the bag. Lindsey glanced behind her to see if whoever was sitting behind her had accidentally pushed their bag under her chair.

The seat was empty; in fact, the entire row was empty. She wondered if the person who had knocked into her seat had dropped their bag. She glanced around the room to see if anyone appeared to be distressed. The remaining people in the room were chatting and laughing. *Hmm.* She unzipped the tote and looked inside to see if she could find something to identify the owner.

The only item was a book. Not an extraordinary find, given that she was at an archivists conference that dealt primarily with books and other primary source materials. Lindsey took it out of the bag and examined it. It was a copy of Patricia Highsmith's *Strangers on a Train*. The dust jacket looked vintage, with dark colors and haunting portraits of an anguished-looking man and woman. The paper felt fragile, so she opened the book carefully.

"Did you buy a book?" Sully asked.

"No," Lindsey said. "I found it under my seat."

Sully glanced at the chairs surrounding them and then at the people lingering in the room just as Lindsey had.

Lindsey glanced at the title page. It took her a moment to decipher the handwriting. Then she gasped. "I think this is inscribed by Patricia Highsmith to Alfred Hitchcock."

"Really?" Sully leaned closer to see. He studied the inscription and said, "I think you're right."

Lindsey glanced back at the spidery writing. The inscription read: *For Hitch, It was a pleasure. Warmly, Pat.*

"If it's a genuine inscription, this book has to be worth a fortune," Lindsey said. She closed the book and put it back in the bag. "I'm going to ask the speaker what she thinks."

She glanced up at the stage, where Brooklyn Wainwright was talking with Henry Standish while her handsome companion, who had joined her onstage, looked on.

"Good idea. Maybe someone brought it to show her," Sully said.

They rose from their seats and made their way to the stage. The room had thinned out as the panel attendees scattered, hurrying to the next talk on their schedules.

Lindsey tried not to be nervous as she approached the famed book restorer. She'd read articles about Brooklyn Wainwright and watched online videos where she discussed her various projects. She was everything Lindsey had hoped to be when she'd been in library school studying to be an archivist.

"Excuse me, Ms. Wainwright," she said.

Brooklyn turned away from Standish and gave Lindsey her full attention. "Hi, how can I help you?"

"I'm sorry to bother you, but I have a book here that I was hoping you'd take a look at?" Lindsey used upspeak, turning it into a question so that she didn't sound demanding. She held out the bag and the man beside Brooklyn took it before Brooklyn could.

"Really, Derek?" Brooklyn asked the man, but he ignored her and opened the bag, peeking inside.

"Yes, really, darling," he said. Lindsey noted his British accent and immediately warmed to him as he reminded her of their friend Robbie Vine, also a Brit, back home in Briar Creek. "If I've learned one thing whilst being married to you, it's that books can kill."

Sully turned to Lindsey with his eyebrows raised. "He's not wrong."

Lindsey glanced at Brooklyn and in that moment she knew she was right and they really were kindred spirits. Not just in their love of old books but also in the men they'd married.

"It's clear." Derek handed the bag to Brooklyn.

"Thank you," she said. She took the book out of the bag holding it gently, just as Lindsey had.

She examined every bit of it, cloth cover, edges, and spine, and when she opened it and read the inscription, she gasped. "This could be worth a fortune. It's a first edition with what appears to be the original dust jacket and it's in amazing shape. It'd go easily for several thousand, but the inscription, if authenticated, makes it an extremely rare collectible for both fans of Highsmith and Hitchcock. The bidding war at an auction for this book could be off the chart."

Henry Standish, who'd been speaking with one of the conference volunteers, identifiable by the lanyard and badge that he wore, joined them. "Thank you again, Brooklyn, always a pleasure. Our next speaker is here, however, so . . ."

He made a shooing motion with his hands. Well, that was abrupt.

Brooklyn and Derek exchanged an amused glance. She put the book back in the bag and handed it to Lindsey.

"It appears to be in excellent condition. You have quite a treasure there."

"It's not mine," Lindsey said. "I found it under my seat." Henry glanced between them, clearly impatient for them to depart. Lindsey held the tote bag out to him. "Do you have a lost-and-found for the conference?"

"Yes, of course. You can check with the registration staff," he said. "I'm sure they have one set up right there by the main doors."

He began to walk, ushering them like a flock of ducks across a busy road.

"I've only taken a quick glance at the book and I'd need more time to be certain, but I think that book is very valuable, as in tens of thousands of dollars," Brooklyn said. "Potentially even more than that."

Henry stopped ushering. "Excuse me?"

Brooklyn nodded. "First edition, excellent condition, and inscribed by the author to a famous movie director? We're talking big money."

"And probably a murder," Derek muttered under his breath. "In fact, I think we need to go so you don't get involved in yet another life-threatening situation."

"Me?" Brooklyn put her hand on her chest, the picture of innocence.

"Sound advice," Sully said. He and Derek exchanged a look of complete understanding. "We should go, too."

"But the book," Lindsey and Brooklyn protested together.

"Will be just fine in my keeping," Henry said. He took the book bag and waved it in the air. "Penny!"

"Yes, Mr. Standish?" A young woman with dark brown hair pinned into a donut-shaped bun at the nape of her neck and thick-framed black glasses hurried across the stage towards them. She was wearing a headset, carrying a clipboard, and judging by the dark circles under her eyes, hadn't slept in days.

"Take this!" Henry thrust the bag at her. Both Lindsey and Brooklyn cried out, protesting the rough treatment. Henry glanced at them and then back at Penny and said, "And be careful with it. It's very valuable."

"Yes, sir," Penny said. She took the bag. "Um . . . What is it?"

"A book, obviously," Henry snapped. "It was left in here during the last program. I haven't got time to deal with lost-and-found items, so you'll have to find whoever lost it and return it to them."

"Of course, Mr. Standish," Penny said. Her eyes were wide behind her glasses, as if she had no idea how she was going to accomplish such a thing.

"I could take . . ." Lindsey and Brooklyn said at the same time, while both Sully and Derek shook their heads.

"No need," Henry said. "I've got this. Don't fret, ladies, I am a professional archivist, after all."

Brooklyn frowned and Lindsey knew she was doing the same. The entire situation felt very unsatisfactory.

"Henry!" An older woman strode across the stage towards them. "I need water with a slice of lemon in it, no ice, and a mic check. I'm on in five!"

"Yes, Adriana, right away. You heard her." Henry nudged Penny with an elbow and she hurried forward with the book clutched beneath her clipboard. "Step lively, Penny, and try not to bungle things this time."

A flurry of people appeared wielding makeup brushes and hair spray; apparently Adriana came with an entourage, separating Lindsey and Sully from Brooklyn and Derek. Lindsey waved and Brooklyn smiled and waved back before she was swallowed up by the next speaker's squad.

"It's too bad there's another speaker scheduled in this room. I would have liked to talk to Brooklyn some more," Lindsey said.

"She and her companion Derek definitely felt like our people; maybe we'll see them again," Sully said. "Come on. According to your schedule, we're to be in conference room H for a discussion on Web Archiving."

"Right," Lindsey said. "I don't want to miss that. So much stuff published online is ephemeral in nature; how do we determine what to save and what to delete?"

"It's a quandary," he said, sipping his coffee. Lindsey gave him the side-eye. Was he making fun of her? He turned and met her gaze and then blinked, the picture of innocence. She had endured a three-day-long boat show for him last summer, which had left her mind-numbingly bored. She couldn't fault him if he felt the same about this.

"Off topic, and maybe I misheard, but did Derek say something about murder?"

"He did. I heard him, too," Sully said. "I get the feeling he's seen a thing or two."

"You don't think he actually meant someone would murder a person over that first edition Highsmith, do you?"

Sully thought about it for a second. "Nah. I mean it's cool and all, but it's not like it's an illuminated manuscript from the late fifteenth century. Comparatively, who would murder someone over a mystery book from the nineteen-fifties?"

"Oh, you just referenced the program we attended this morning," Lindsey said. She clasped her hands over her chest. "So you really don't mind when I drag you to these things and then go on and on about the history of books?"

"Of course not," Sully said. "You light up when you talk about your musty old books. How could I not listen?"

Lindsey sighed. And that right there was why she'd married him.

"Sully put his arm around her shoulders as they made their way through the crowd to the next talk. "Don't worry about the book. I'm sure the director will find its rightful owner."

"You're right," she said. "The librarian in me just has to let it go."

As they made their way down the hallway to the next discussion, she noticed that everyone they passed was carrying a conference tote bag. The book she'd found could belong to anyone. How would Penny ever find them? And how could a person just lose a book like that? It boggled.

Ready to find
your next great read?

Let us help.

Visit prh.com/nextread

Penguin
Random
House